Warrior ᐯ

Protection, Inc., # 4

By Zoe Chant

2

Author's Note

This book stands alone. However, it's part of a series about Protection, Inc., an all-shifter private security agency. If you'd like to read the series in order, the first book is *Bodyguard Bear*, the second is *Defender Dragon*, and the third is *Protector Panther*.

Table of Contents

Chapter One

Raluca

Raluca fled across the sky on dragonwings, frequently glancing back. It had been an entire day since someone had tried to murder her, but she wasn't taking any chances. She'd given up everything she had in the hope of finally getting to have a life, and she was not going to let some unknown assassin take that from her before she got the chance to experience it.

Her silver wings stretched out wide to catch the sea breeze. Above, the sky was blue as turquoise; below, the ocean was a darker blue, like sapphires.

She possessed both gems in her hoard, along with many others; after she'd renounced her title as crown princess of Viorel, leaped off the palace balcony, and become a dragon in mid-air, she'd flown to her room, transformed into a woman, snatched up the brocade pack that held her hoard, and shifted and flown away again before an alarm could be raised.

Raluca had taken nothing but her hoard and the clothes she'd been wearing, but that had been sufficient. After reluctantly deciding that she could bear to part with a valuable diamond that had been a gift from her evil Uncle Constantine, she'd sold it and had been living off the proceeds ever since. It had been a good choice; that diamond had so many bad associations that she didn't miss it, even though it had sparkled beautifully in the sunlight.

Her uncle had controlled her for her entire life. He'd attempted to force her into a marriage with a man she didn't love to ensure a treaty between their nations that would line his own pockets. He'd even tried to murder her fiancé's true mate! Raluca was well rid of Uncle Constantine and everything that had come from him.

Her thoughts drifted back to that crucial moment when she had declared her independence and fled. She'd felt so free as she'd leapt off the balcony, become a dragon, and soared away. Her entire life had been ruled by her duties as a princess, with Uncle Constantine monitoring and controlling her every action. Now she could do whatever she wanted.

It had taken her less than a week to realize that she had no idea what she wanted.

She'd first met her fiancé, Prince Lucas, when they were both eighteen, awkward teenagers forced into an arranged engagement that neither had the strength of will to refuse. When they'd met again, five years later, both had changed physically. Lucas was taller and broader across the shoulders: a handsome young man, not a boy. Raluca's daily lessons in posture and dance had finally paid off, transforming her from a clumsy girl uncomfortable in her own skin to an elegant dragon princess who controlled every movement of her body with exquisite grace.

But Lucas had changed inside, too. He'd gone to America and become a bodyguard — such a strange job for a prince — and found the courage to defy his family. When he met his mate, the American backpacker with the charming name of Journey, he'd stood up for her, foiled Uncle Constantine's attempt to murder her, and finally given up his kingdom for her. Now Raluca's uncle was in a dungeon for the rest of his life, Lucas was presumably living happily in America with Journey, and Raluca…

Raluca's breath gusted out of her in a dragon-sized sigh, blowing a hole in a cloud. She'd drifted from Venice to Vienna, staying in the best hotels and seeing the famous sights, but none of it had made her happy. She'd thought she'd feel free, but she felt more trapped than ever. With the entire world at her feet, she'd felt lonely and empty.

Until someone broke into her hotel room and tried to stab her to death as she slept.

Some tiny noise must have startled her, for instinct prompted her to roll off the bed before she was even fully awake. She'd fallen to the floor with a thud, opened her eyes, and stared up in shock at a glittering blade poised above her heart. Then the masked assassin holding the knife tried to plunge it home.

But Raluca's dragon speed outmatched the assassin's training. She threw herself to the side. The dagger smashed into the marble floor. Before the man could try again, Raluca transformed. Her unfurling wings flung the black-clad assassin across the room. The flask he'd been holding in his other hand burst against the wall, releasing the distinctive sharp odor of dragonsbane, the poison that prevented dragons from shifting.

The assassin scrambled to his feet and fled out the door. And Raluca, with a distinct feeling of déjà vu, grabbed her hoard pack in her talons and launched off the hotel balcony.

For the first time since her leap from the palace balcony, she felt alive again. The threat to her life jolted her back into the realization of how much she valued it. She might not know *how* she wanted to live, but she definitely *wanted* to live.

Also, she wasn't stupid. That attack hadn't been random— the dragonsbane proved that the assassin knew she was a dragon, and presumably also knew exactly who she was— and Raluca had a good idea of why someone might want her dead. She'd renounced her title, but she had the right to change her mind and reclaim it. As long as she lived, she potentially stood between the throne of Viorel and everyone who was now in line to inherit it.

Unfortunately, that didn't narrow down the suspects as much as one might hope. Raluca had the only clear claim to the throne. With her out of the picture, that left about twenty cousins and other relatives who, last she'd heard, had been fighting over the crown by any means necessary, from duels to debates to very expensive lawsuits. And that wasn't even counting Uncle Constantine, who might have bribed someone from within his cell with the promise of infinite riches once Raluca was dead and he was free.

No matter who was trying to kill her, they'd tracked her down once and could do it again. And they wouldn't give up after one missed chance.

As a dragon, Raluca could defeat a human. But if she was splashed with dragonsbane, she wouldn't be able to transform, and the next assassin would undoubtedly use the dragonsbane first and the knife second. As a human, she had no idea how to fight. Dragon princesses learned feminine arts like embroidery and gem-carving, not swordfighting or boxing. She needed a bodyguard.

Luckily, she used to be engaged to one.

Raluca didn't know Lucas's home address — they hadn't been in contact since the balcony, and she'd checked into hotels under an assumed name — but his workplace, Protection, Inc., had a website with a business address. And Raluca had looked it up often enough since she'd fled to have it memorized, thinking wistfully of meeting up with the one who would understand why she'd given up her royal title.

She flew over the beaches of Santa Martina, her dragon magic hiding her from sight, and into the city. It wasn't easy finding an address from above, and she had to circle repeatedly before she finally figured out which of the several towering office buildings was the one she was looking for.

Raluca landed on the roof of Protection, Inc. She glanced around to make sure no one was watching, then let her magical invisibility slip away. She thought of human things — the slide of silk between her thighs, the clack of high heels across a marble floor, and the lonely ache in her heart — and became a woman.

To her chagrin, she found herself standing barefoot in a nightgown, wearing no makeup and with her hair rumpled from sleep, clutching a heavy pack. She must look like a hobo! It was hardly the impression she wanted to make, especially if anyone but Lucas, who was as close to a friend as she'd ever had, was at Protection, Inc.

It could be worse, Raluca thought. *If I was any other type of shifter, I'd be naked.*

Only dragons could transform and take their clothing and their hoards with them. The reason for that was obvious; Raluca would have fought to the death rather than abandon her hoard. All the same, her lack of nudity was cold comfort. It wasn't even her best nightgown, but a simple fall of pewter silk she'd picked up in Vienna, unadorned and cut low in the chest. Every time she bent over, it threatened to expose her nipples.

Raluca opened her pack, wishing a golden hairbrush and mirror would magically appear. Unfortunately, she knew every item in her hoard by heart, and she had no such things. But she certainly wasn't going to walk into Protection, Inc. half-naked and unadorned. She might have renounced her title, but she wasn't going to disgrace herself.

She combed her hair as best as she could with her fingers and rubbed her eyes, making sure no stray sleep crumbs clung to her lashes. For jewelry, she made do with a pair of pearl hair clips, a delicate silver necklace, a gold and pearl bracelet, and a mere three rings: a band of sapphires, a gold and pearl ring that matched the bracelet, and a ruby ring that had been a favorite since she'd been a little girl.

The touch of gold and gems to her skin gave her confidence and courage. Drawing upon the strength and pride of dragonkind, Raluca strapped on her pack, tugged the nightgown up, lifted her chin, straightened her back, and marched downstairs to knock on the door of Protection, Inc.

A man opened it. He was so huge that he nearly filled the doorway, made of pure muscle without an ounce of fat. His brown hair brushed the top of the doorframe, and his hazel eyes blinked at her in surprise.

"Whoa," said the man in a deep, rumbling voice. "Uh… May I help you?"

Inwardly, Raluca gritted her teeth; outwardly, she drew herself up to her full height. Her nightgown instantly slithered down. She snatched at it and clutched it in her fist, destroying whatever dignity she'd briefly achieved.

"I am looking for Lucas," she said, carefully modulating her voice.

The big man was still staring at her. He probably thought she was a robber bedecked in her ill-gotten finery. "Lucas isn't here. Are you…" He stared some more, his gaze moving from her bare feet to her fistful of silk to her necklace. "…a relative? Or a friend?"

Raluca and Lucas were, in fact, very distantly related, though one had to go back seven generations to find the connection. But she didn't think this strange, large American would care about that.

"I am a friend," Raluca said. "Please give me his home address."

"I'm afraid I can't do that," the man replied. She was both annoyed and impressed at the polite firmness of his tone; Uncle Constantine couldn't have taught him better. "I'm Hal Brennan, and I run Protection, Inc. And you are…?"

He extended his hand just as she swept into a curtsey. Both of them hastily moved to correct their error. Raluca straightened up with a jerk and stuck out her hand, but she was stiff as a robot she'd once seen in a movie. Hal hesitated, then ducked his head and shoulders in a bow that vividly conveyed how embarrassed and awkward he felt to be bowing at all.

In the silence that followed, Raluca looked for a balcony from which to fling herself. Unfortunately, there was none.

Hal's booming laugh shook the walls. "Well, that was a disaster. Let's try again. This time, let's forget about impressing each other. I'm Hal, Lucas's boss. I'm a bear shifter —"

Shocked, Raluca interrupted, "You'd tell me that? You don't even know who I am!"

Hal gestured at her right arm. She'd forgotten that the nightgown, which had straps rather than sleeves, exposed her glittering silver dragonmarks. "Lucas told me what those meant. So I know you're a dragon shifter. Hey, are you his ex-fiancée?"

"We did not complete our engagement ceremony," Raluca began. Then, catching some of Hal's informality, she said, "That is to say, yes. I am Raluca, the princess — former princess — he was to marry."

Hal's grin broadened. "Pleased to meet you! Lucas told us all about you. I wish I could've seen you jump off the balcony. That must've been a sight to see. Why don't you come inside?"

Raluca followed Hal into the lobby. She was immediately struck by one of the framed photos on the wall. It showed the palace of Brandusa at sunset, with a golden dragon soaring overhead. She stepped forward to get a closer look.

"Yeah, that's Lucas," Hal said. "I hope you didn't come to America just to see him. He's on an assignment in another country, deep undercover, and he'll be gone for at least another week. In the meantime, is there anything I can help you with? Maybe find you a hotel?"

If it hadn't been for her years of training, Raluca would have blushed. Forcing back the hot blood that threatened to color her face, she said, "Yes. A hotel recommendation would be greatly appreciated. But also… I need a bodyguard."

"Oh!" Hal's rugged features instantly shifted from amusement to wariness. His body language changed as well, subtly settling into a deceptive relaxation that Raluca knew meant he was ready to fight for his life. She had seen it before, watching the dragon princes train. "Hmm. Well, you're safe for now. No one can break into Protection, Inc. But you can't stay here forever. Could someone have followed you here?"

"Not directly," Raluca said. "I looked behind me as I flew. But I was tracked down once already. And given that Lucas and I parted on good terms, this is a logical place to look for me."

Hal seemed to appreciate her reasoning. "Yeah, you're probably right. Why don't you have a seat? I'll make you some coffee and you can tell me all about it."

Raluca seated herself in an armchair. It gave way pleasantly beneath her, neither too soft nor too hard. The entire office was more comfortable than it looked, warmed to a pleasant temperature rather than air-conditioned to chilliness.

While Hal went into another room, she examined the other photographs on the walls, all of beasts in their natural habitats. (The natural habitat of a dragon, of course, was a palace.) Lucas was the dragon, and Hal had said he was a bear shifter. One photo was of a bear at a river. Perhaps that was Hal in his shifted form. Probably all the bodyguards were shifters, and all the animals in the pictures were them.

Raluca examined them one by one. A tiger stalking through a lush green jungle. A pride of lions lounging on a savannah. A snow leopard leaping across an icy abyss. A panther lying in wait for its prey. A gray wolf with fierce green eyes, leader of a pack. Which would she want to protect her? They all looked equally strong; any of them would be more than a match for a human, or several humans.

Her gaze drifted down the line, then stopped at the wolf. There was something fascinating about him. At first glance, those eyes, deep as emeralds, were filled with ferocity. But as she looked longer, she thought she saw something else beneath the anger, something that echoed in her own heart.

Loneliness, hissed her dragon. *Pain.*

Why would he be lonely? Raluca silently asked. *He has a pack.*

Her dragon answered with a shrug, a rustle of wings. *I do not know the* why. *I only see what I see.*

Hal returned with a china cup of cappuccino, which he cradled with surprising delicacy in his enormous hands.

"Are those your bodyguards?" Raluca asked, indicating the photos.

Hal nodded, handing her the cup. "Lucas didn't tell you much, did he?"

Raluca's gaze lowered to the coffee. It not only had foam, but a sprinkling of brown powder atop. She wondered if the office had servants, or if Hal had actually made the coffee himself. Perhaps he had, with the aid of a machine. She had seen such things in Europe.

"Our arrangement was a matter of honor, not love," Raluca said. "Lucas told me as much as he felt comfortable revealing in the short time we had together."

She was mildly irritated at the way Hal smiled every time she spoke. His expression was one of amused familiarity, as if she was some relative whom he met only at holidays but whose quirks he found charming rather than annoying. He should not find her familiar. They had only just met.

"You sound just like Lucas when he first came to America," said Hal. "It's really too bad he's not here. Why don't you start at the beginning, and tell me exactly what's going on and why you need a bodyguard? Don't leave anything out — there's details that may not seem important to you, but could mean a lot to me."

Hal sat down behind a desk, and took out a notebook and a pen.

Raluca took a delicate sip of her cappuccino. The powder was chocolate. In her own country of Viorel, it would have been nutmeg. She forced her mind away from how lost and alone and alien she felt, and began, "At the age of eighteen, Lucas and I were promised in marriage…"

She had been trained to recount a tale clearly and with detail; Hal made few interruptions, but took many notes. When she explained her theory that someone wanted her gone to clear their path to the throne, he nodded and said, "That makes sense."

An odd warmth stole into her heart at his simple words. She was used to being respected, of course. But it was for her position and family and wealth, not for her intelligence. She had learned to read people — Uncle Constantine had made her watch him hold diplomatic meetings with politicians or interrogate prisoners, and then quizzed her about them — and so she could see that Hal was used to having to steer clients to the point, and appreciated that he didn't have to do so with her.

"So I need a bodyguard," Raluca concluded. "I do not know how to fight, and I cannot publicly become a dragon. I would die before revealing the existence of shifters to the world. Someone must protect me who can do so in their human form."

Hal nodded; this too made sense to him. "Of course. And I assume you'd like to know who's behind the plot?"

"I would," Raluca said. "So I need someone who is strong, courageous, *and* intelligent."

Hal smiled and leaned back in his own armchair. "That goes without saying. I only hire the sharpest knives in the drawer. But what sort of things do you want to do while they're guarding you? I'd assign a different person depending on whether you want to go to hot new nightclubs, or Santa Martina's fanciest parties." He chuckled, more to himself than to her, as he said, "Or frat keggers and fight clubs and flea markets."

Raluca hadn't had any particular plans other than "find Lucas" and then "get a bodyguard." But Hal's offhand joke struck a chord with her. Why *not* see how the other half lived? She'd had enough fancy parties to last her a lifetime. But she'd never been to a nightclub. She didn't even know what a frat kegger or fight club or flea market was, other than a place or activity Hal wouldn't expect to see her at. Presumably they were rough and low class.

"I want to go to hot new nightclubs," Raluca said. "And also fight clubs and flea markets and — er —" The last term was so unfamiliar to her that it slipped her mind. "That other thing. I want to do everything a princess of Viorel never gets a chance to do. Peasant things. Dangerous things. American things."

Then honesty forced her add, "And also fancy parties. I do enjoy them. I would be very sad to leave America without attending a single ball."

"I think we can get you into at least one." Hal smiled at her. He seemed to sincerely like her, which was pleasant but strange. Most people neither liked nor disliked her; she was the princess, to be regarded with awe and respect and deference. Liking didn't enter into the picture.

"You're in luck," Hal went on. "Almost everyone but Lucas is available right now. Don't get the wrong impression; everyone's extremely competent, and anyone here can protect you. But if it's possible, I try to pick the ideal bodyguard for the job. Would you rather have a man or woman, or does it not matter? Do you want someone who'll look intimidating, or would you rather have someone who people won't even know is your bodyguard?"

Raluca hadn't thought of anything beyond needing *someone* to protect her, since Lucas wasn't there. She had no idea who the other bodyguards were. And though she knew Lucas must trust Hal, or he wouldn't be working for him, she'd been trained her entire life not to reveal anything more than was absolutely necessary.

Cautiously, she said, "Why don't you tell me a little about who you have, and then I'll decide."

To her relief, Hal seemed to find that a reasonable request. "Sure. I'll show you photos, too, so you can get a sense of who might blend in where."

Hal took a file from his desk drawer and opened it. The first photo was of Lucas, looking every inch a dragon prince in a three-piece suit. Hal flipped it over without comment.

The next was of an elegant blonde woman. If Lucas looked like a prince, that woman looked like a young queen. Raluca started to reach out for her, but Hal slid the photo aside.

"Fiona's on an assignment now," he said. "Too bad, I think you'd get along. Maybe you can at least meet her later."

The next picture was of a Latina woman, curvy and small, smiling confidently at the camera. Hal turned that one over as well. "Catalina's a new hire; she's still in training. But you can have your pick of the rest of the team."

"Are you including yourself?" Raluca wouldn't mind having Hal as a bodyguard. He seemed both competent and friendly, and his size alone should intimidate all but the bravest assassins.

"No, sorry," Hal said. "I have my hands full managing the team. I don't usually take solo assignments. But Shane's available. Here."

Hal showed Raluca a photograph of a tall man with black hair and eyes blue as ice. "Shane is a panther shifter, and he has other powers too. He can terrify people by looking into their eyes, and he can also make people not notice him at all. Since it's not clear who's after you or why, someone who can disappear at will might be the best choice. Shane can not only protect you, he can investigate and infiltrate for you."

Shane wasn't smiling for the camera, and something about him unnerved Raluca. She couldn't imagine enjoying a nightclub — or anything else — with that dark presence at her side.

Politely, she said, "I'd like to see everyone before I choose."

14

As if Hal had read her mind, he said, "If you'd prefer someone more easygoing, I have two bodyguards who fit that bill."

He spread out two photos. One was of a strikingly handsome Latino man, strong-looking but with a relaxed posture and pleasant expression. The other was of a curvy black woman with lots of braids and a merry smile. She didn't match Raluca's idea of a bodyguard. But both of them did look a lot more friendly than Shane.

"Rafa used to be a Navy SEAL, with me," Hal said. "He's a lion shifter. He can be intimidating if he needs to be, but he won't scare people accidentally. The only problem with him is that if you're hoping to meet men, they may not approach you if they see him with you."

Raluca considered the photo again. "I see what you mean. What about the woman? I assume she's stronger than she looks."

"Absolutely," Hal assured her. "Destiny is a tiger shifter and an Army veteran. She has shifter strength, she's a crack shot, she's very level-headed, and she's equally comfortable on the streets and in high society. Since you don't know who's after you and you want to find out, you're probably better off with a bodyguard who doesn't look like one. Destiny can protect you, but as long as you don't hold hands or anything, anyone who sees you together will assume you're just friends."

Hal gave a firm nod, pushing Destiny's photo closer to Raluca. "Destiny's perfect for you. And you'll get along, I promise."

Destiny did sound good, and Raluca liked the idea of a female bodyguard. She'd had so few opportunities to make friends with other women — or with anyone, for that matter. And while Destiny was casually dressed in the photo, Raluca could also imagine her in an evening gown, perhaps with her hair done up in a more formal style.

Raluca picked up the photo. She was about to say, *"I'll take her,"* when she caught sight of the picture beneath Destiny's.

Curious, Raluca glanced at that one. It showed a young man staring challengingly into the camera, as if he was trying to intimidate the photographer into looking away. His hair was black, his eyes were an unusually intense shade of emerald green, and his muscular arms, which were folded across his chest, were covered in tattoos.

Dragon shifters never tattooed themselves; they were born with dragonmarks, glittering birthmarks the color of their dragon, unique to each individual. Tattooing was a taboo, considered inferior to a dragon shifter's natural marks. Raluca, used to the beauty and elegance of dragonmarks, had always thought that tattoos were tacky at best.

But this man's tattoos were different. Raluca picked up the photograph to get a closer look. Tree branches stretched along his arms, some gnarled and ancient, some young and smooth, with each crack in the bark and vein in the leaves depicted with exquisite detail and realistic shading. A slim vine, green as spring itself, twined around one finger.

The tattoos were cut off by his shirt sleeves, but they obviously extended beyond them. Raluca wondered how much of his body was tattooed. If his arms had branches, would his chest show the trunks? What would the muscles of his chest look like under that exquisite tattoo? Would his nipples be covered in leaves, or left bare? Would wind seem to move in the trees as he breathed in and out…?

A noise made her jerk her gaze upward.

Hal had cleared his throat. "Like I said. Destiny's the one you want. I'll call her right now."

"What about this man?" Raluca held up the photograph.

"Nick?" Hal shook his head. "Not the right guy for this job. I wasn't even going to show him to you."

"Is he not available?"

"Oh, he's available." Hal seemed to be trying not to laugh, as if he had heard the punchline to a joke that Raluca was too ignorant to understand. It annoyed her.

Icily, she inquired, "Is he incompetent? Unintelligent? Weak?"

"No, of course not. He's just — look, you mentioned fancy parties. I assume you mean princess-level fancy parties. That's not Nick's style." Hal chuckled, again seeming amused at some private joke. "He'd be great at the fight clubs, though."

Her dragon hissed within her. *Choose Nick.*

Raluca's dragon was normally very quiet. She'd already spoken more in the last hour than she often did in an entire week. That caught Raluca's attention as much as her words.

Hal reached for the photo.

Instinctively, Raluca jerked it away from him, clutching it to her bosom. "In formal attire, he would wear long sleeves. Most of his tattoos would be covered. If necessary, he could wear gloves to conceal the rest."

It would be a shame to cover up those beautiful tattoos, but those strong hands would also look good in black silk gloves. His big knuckles would make a tempting contrast, a suggestion of roughness beneath the elegance. She could almost imagine the smooth touch of his silk-covered hand on her bare arm as he escorted her to the dance floor. After the dance, when they were alone, she could remove the gloves for him. With her teeth, perhaps. Very delicately, pulling gently, her lips brushing across his muscular wrist and the back of his hand in a trailing kiss, taking her time, making him shudder with pent-up desire...

Hal cleared his throat again. Raluca dropped back to reality with a jolt. What was wrong with her? It was completely unlike her to drift into a sexual fantasy in the middle of a business conversation — especially a fantasy of something so completely inappropriate. She was hiring a guard, not a lover. And if she did take a lover, it would certainly not be a tattoo-covered bodyguard. It would someone suited to her station. If not royalty, at least a man from a high-born family. Or perhaps a billionaire.

Though if she did hire this man — Nick — people might *mistake* him for her lover, as Hal had warned could happen if she was seen with Rafa. The rumor might get back to Viorel. Everyone who had ever known her would be absolutely horrified. Appalled. Disgusted. Furious.

Especially Uncle Constantine. He'd be so enraged to imagine her with this rough, tough, tattooed commoner, he might actually have a stroke.

Raluca smiled. "I choose Nick."

Hal was shaking his head. "You really don't know what you're getting yourself in for..."

Exasperated, Raluca said, "If you have an objection, please state it clearly."

"You know what, it'll be easier to show than tell," Hal said. "I'll introduce you two. If you still want him once you've met him, it's fine with me. If not, Destiny's your woman. Actually, this is great timing. He should be —"

The sound of footsteps broke through Hal's voice. One set sounded much like Hal's, evenly paced and belonging to a big, heavy man. The other set was lighter, but fast and hard, slamming into the floor like they had a grudge against it. Along with the footsteps came a man's voice, loud and angry enough to be heard through the door.

"No, I don't want to take a deep fucking breath," the man said. "He fucking flipped me off and I didn't fucking kill him, and when I was fucking alpha I would've fucking had to whether I wanted to or not, so that's all the fucking self-control anyone fucking needs."

Raluca's eyes widened in amazement. She was too shocked to even be offended. She knew the word, of course. No one would say it in front of a princess, but she'd been incognito ever since the first balcony leap, so she'd occasionally overheard it from passersby. But whoever this foul-mouthed person was, he'd just said that word more times in a few seconds than she'd heard it in her entire previous life.

The heavy footsteps seemed to go in a different direction, getting softer and fading away. But the other set got louder, coming closer.

The door was flung open, and a man stormed in. He went straight to Hal, turning his back on her without even looking at her first. How rude!

It is a very nice back, her dragon remarked.

Who cares? Raluca retorted silently. *He's a mannerless lout. I'm certain he was the one who was using…* She couldn't bring herself to repeat it, even in thought. *…that word.*

But she couldn't help agreeing with her dragon. The view from behind was excellent. The rude man was black-haired, tall, and broad-shouldered, wearing a black leather jacket which concealed his literal back. His back*side,* however, was showcased by a pair of tight black jeans. Raluca was not in the habit of staring at men's behinds, but since it was turned to her anyway, she had to look at it. Like his legs, it was firm and muscular, nicely curved, making her want to touch it.

In theory. If it belonged to a different man. One with manners, money, a high-class family, and —

The man with the good body and bad manners jerked his thumb over his shoulder, toward the door. "Hal, if you catch Rafa at the gym, you tell your fucking buddy to mind his own fucking business."

Hal's deep laugh rumbled through the air.

"What's so fucking funny?" the man demanded.

"You are," Hal said. "And next time, keep in mind that clients sometimes walk in without an appointment, so don't start swearing until you see who's in the lobby. I'm talking to a prospective client *and* a friend of Lucas's. Meet Raluca."

"The fucking foreign princess!?" The man swung around.

Their eyes met.

It was the man from the photograph. Nick, the one with the exquisite tattoos. She could see them now that his hands were in view, the ivy leaves and curling vine even more beautiful in real life. Her gaze lifted from them to the hard masculine planes of his face, his stubborn-looking chin, the rough-looking stubble around lips that might be soft if you touched them with your own, and his tousled black hair with a stray lock falling over his forehead.

But more than anything else, his eyes captured her attention. They were even more startlingly green in person than in the photograph, bright as emeralds and deep as the ocean. On the surface, they were angry, narrowed with what she interpreted as a habitual intensity and willingness to fight to defend himself or others. But like the eyes of the wolf that she guessed was his shift form, they seemed to hold some terrible sorrow beneath the surface, a loneliness that made Raluca want to reach out and draw him close to her, holding him like a treasure. If she did — if he allowed her to — perhaps she'd ease not only his pain, but her own...

Mine, hissed her dragon.

What do you mean? Raluca asked silently. But she had a horrible feeling that she already knew.

He's the one, her dragon replied. *Our mate.*

"No!" Raluca said aloud.

Nick was shaking his head and backing away, as if he too had heard some inner voice and didn't like what it had to say. "No fucking way!"

Raluca straightened her spine. "I am a princess — a former princess —I am a lady, and I don't like that word. Please do not use it in my presence again."

"No one fucking tells me how to talk!" Nick instantly retorted.

Hal banged a huge fist down on the desk, making the papers jump. "Nick, she is a *client!* Raluca, shall I call Destiny now?"

A long silence fell. Nick and Raluca stared at each other.

Mine, repeated her dragon with deep satisfaction. Then she corrected herself, *Ours. Our greatest treasure. At last we've found him.*

Raluca was so torn between horror and shock — and an unwanted rush of desire so intense that it left her wet between the legs — that she could reply to neither her dragon nor Hal. She'd abandoned *her entire life* to escape an unwanted marriage. She was not going to throw herself away on some cursing commoner who didn't even like her!

Nick's eyes raked over her body, hot and angry… and hungry. She could almost feel him taking in every inch of her, as if he was caressing her body with his gaze alone. Her nipples hardened, pulling at the sheer fabric of her nightgown. Raluca dropped the photo like a burning coal and folded her arms over her breasts.

But she wasn't the only one to physically react to the other's presence. A bulge appeared between Nick's legs. With equal haste, he yanked down his leather jacket, concealing the evidence of his arousal. But Raluca knew it was still there. Maybe even growing, if that was possible, pushing hard at his tight jeans. She hoped it was uncomfortable.

She wanted it buried deep inside her.

No, I don't! Raluca hastily told herself. *So he's attractive. In a shallow, physical way. So what? He's rude and crude and he's incredibly turned on by me — I mean, he sees me as nothing but a sexual object. He's wildly inappropriate, and he's* not *what I want.*

Nick's hands clenched into fists. His jaw tensed as if he was gritting his teeth. He took a step backward, every muscle as taut as if he was straining against chains that pulled him toward her.

Hal, bent over to collect his papers, missed the entire silent exchange. When he looked up, both Raluca and Nick straightened and turned their gazes to him. He took a cell phone out of his pocket. "Nick, take off. Raluca, I'm calling Destiny to give her the job."

Raluca opened her mouth to agree. But instead, what emerged was a vehement, "No!"

"No!" Nick burst out, his denial simultaneous with hers. "If she's a client, she needs protection. Nobody fucking protects my — that woman — but me!"

"I already told you I don't like that word," Raluca snapped.

Nick folded his arms across his chest. "Well, you better get used to it, because that's how I talk and I am sticking to you like fu — like glue."

Since Nick had at least made an attempt, Raluca tried to moderate her tone. Nobody liked being scolded. "Also, I will not only be going to nightclubs. If you speak like that at a diplomatic function, it will draw unwanted attention."

"I have to protect you at diplomatic functions?" Nick sounded horrified. "Hal never gives me those sorts of jobs."

Hal looked at Nick, then at Raluca. The amusement he'd shown when she'd first inquired about Nick returned to his face. "There's a first time for everything. Raluca, if Nick's willing and you want him, he's yours."

Once again, the words that came out of her mouth were the opposite of what she'd intended to say. "Yes. He's mine."

"Yeah, of course I fucking want to protect her," Nick said immediately, then looked perplexed, as if he too had spoken against his own will. "Well — I guess Rafa or Shane can coach me on the diplomat stuff."

"Then we're all squared away." Hal stood up. "I have to get back to work. Raluca, please tell him everything you told me. You can leave your hoard in one of our lockers. In Lucas's, if you like. Protection, Inc. is as secure as it gets. Nick, she needs a place to stay and something to wear. The pack's her hoard — she doesn't have any luggage. Take her to the locker room and get her one of Fiona's workout outfits, so she doesn't have to walk around in her nightgown. And then I'd start by taking her clothes shopping."

Chapter Two

Nick

Mine, growled Nick's wolf again. And once again, he spoke with a possessive tone that Nick had never heard before.

Nick was never at a loss for words. But he found himself standing in baffled, angry, and incredibly turned-on silence as Hal scooped up a stack of papers, walked out of the lobby, and closed the door with a very final-sounding click.

You are out of your fucking mind, Nick told his wolf. *That woman is a fucking* princess. *You couldn't pick a worse match if you tried. And also, did it escape your notice that she fucking hates me?*

Nick was used to fighting with his wolf. Ever since he'd left his gang and joined the good guys, half his energy had been spent on restraining that snarling voice within him that urged him to kill, to abandon himself to sheer animal rage, to act on instinct and not hold back.

But this time, Nick's wolf spoke with uncharacteristic smugness. *She's your mate. She's crazy about you. She wants to throw you up against the wall and fuck you here and now.*

Nick shook his head. *Buddy, you are out of your goddamn mind. That woman can't even stand to hear the* word *fuck. If she's ever had sex with anyone, which I really doubt, it was with a prince on some giant fancy bed, and they did it in the dark. With their eyes shut. And she just lay there. Bored.*

Maybe, his wolf allowed. *But she wouldn't be bored if it was you.*

Nick's memory flashed back to the sight of Raluca's nipples hardening, pushing that silky fabric into sharp points. Oh, sure, it was only because she was under-dressed and cold — he'd overheard enough conversations about weather-related nipple hard-ons between Fiona and Destiny to know how that worked — but it had still been almost unbearably sexy to see.

Raluca was still standing with her arms folded over her breasts, hiding them, but she couldn't erase his memory. That sheer fabric had outlined every delicious curve. They were small but luscious, like a pair of ripe peaches; he'd be able to close his hands over them and touch every last bit of her skin. Their shape was burned into his mind, all the way down to the size of her nipples. The only thing he didn't know was their color. Would they be the same ivory as her face, or even paler? Would her nipples be rose-pink, or peach-colored, or brown? And would the intricate swirls of her glittering silver dragonmarks extend past her shoulder and over her chest, to curl around her nipples like silver chains...?

His cock swelled even more at that image. He squirmed uncomfortably, trying to get a little more room in his jeans. They were stretched so tight, they felt like they might tear. And he was so hard and cramped that it actually hurt. He had to stop thinking about that woman.

It would be easier once she got out of that fucking bra-less nightgown.

"Come on," Nick said. "I'll take you to the locker room."

Raluca walked beside him, stepping delicately as a ballerina, her bare feet soundless. Her ridiculously fancy backpack, however, clinked with every step. If it contained her hoard, it was full of gold and gems. In other words, metal and rocks. It must weigh sixty pounds at the absolute minimum. He thought of offering to carry it, but she walked easily, her slim frame upright and her shoulders showing no sign of strain.

She looked so delicate, like a piece of china that would shatter at his rough touch, but it was an illusion: she had shifter strength. If she ever cut loose, which obviously she never did, but *if,* she might ride a man so hard, she'd break the bed.

Fucking stop it, Nick told himself. He already had the world's worst case of blue balls. The last thing he needed was the image of Raluca straddling him.

The image stayed with him, getting more vivid by the second. Her head thrown back in ecstasy, her long silver hair brushing against his thighs, his cock buried in her wet heat.

Nick clenched his jaw and shoved that vision out of his head, but it was too late. His whole body felt on fire, his balls actually hurt, and he was in serious danger of coming in his jeans without even being touched. Hal and Lucas and Shane were all fucking assholes, going on and on (or, in Shane's case, saying it once but memorably) about how finding your mate was the best thing that could ever happen to you. What the fuck had they been on? It was fucking torture.

Trying not to move too much, he opened Fiona's locker and shoved an armful of clothing at her. "Here. Wear this. You're about the same size. Yell when you're done."

Nick ducked into the bathroom, where he gave serious consideration to jerking off while she changed. He'd only have a minute or so. On the other hand, the way he felt, he'd probably explode in ten seconds and have fifty to spare to clean up. And then he wouldn't be so distracted.

"Why the fuck does she have to be so hot?" he muttered.

Because she's our mate, growled his wolf. Smugly, he added, *She's the hottest woman in the entire world. And she's ours.*

Shut up about that mate crap, Nick said silently. *I fucking hate rich people, and she's a fucking princess carrying around a backpack full of gold. She's been handed everything her whole life, without ever having to work or fight for anything. She thinks people like me are the mud under her ruby slippers, and she's sure as hell not about to get her hands dirty.*

"I'm ready," Raluca called, in her voice like a crystal bell.

Nick pulled his jacket farther down, wishing he'd gotten to business the second the door had closed behind him. Now he'd have to wait for his hard-on to go away on its own. He hadn't had anything like this happen since he was a teenager.

It's just because she's female and practically naked, he told himself. *She won't look half so sexy in workout clothes.*

Nick opened the bathroom door. Raluca had stashed her hoard pack in Lucas's locker. She stood in front of it in her habitual perfect posture, spine absolutely straight without appearing stiff.

She was *incredibly* sexy in workout clothes. Raluca was slightly taller and fuller-figured than Fiona, so the black fatigues that were loose on Fiona were form-fitting on Raluca, showing off the slim grace of her body. The color contrast, which was also noticeable with Fiona's pale skin and blonde hair, was even more striking with Raluca's ivory skin and silver hair.

The princess had switched out some of her jewelry, keeping the silver necklace that drew his eyes to the elegant column of her throat, but changing the rest. Now her hair was secured with a new pair of clips, butterflies with silver bodies and wings of black and pink jewels sliced paper-thin, so the light actually shone through them. Her rings were silver, two plain with delicate engravings, one a net of silver mesh enclosing seed pearls, and one set with a large black stone with a rainbow sheen. A black opal? Was there such a thing?

Nick cleared his throat. "You need a bulletproof vest. Here. Put it on over your shirt, and then button the jacket over it."

He held out the vest and jacket. She took them, frowning at the vest's bulk and heaviness. "I cannot wear this over a ball gown."

"No," Nick said. "But wear it when you can."

She put it on, but seemed puzzled by the straps. Most clients were. Nick was used to showing them how to wear the vest. He'd had female clients before, and had helped them with the vest with the professionalism Hal was always nagging him about. He wasn't a hound dog like Rafa. Some clients had been pretty, sure, but Nick didn't flirt on the job. He was there to protect them, and that was all.

"I'll help you," Nick said, and stepped forward.

The radiant warmth of her body enveloped him. He and Lucas had sparred together and been jammed together in the back seats of cars on stake-outs often enough for Nick to notice that dragons ran hot. But what was only a familiar nuisance with Lucas, who always seemed to get stuck in close quarters with Nick on the hottest days of summer, was a whole different story with Raluca.

Though there was half a foot of air and a whole lot of clothes between them, she gave off so much heat that it felt as if their bodies were pressed together. He could practically feel the softness of her skin against his, as if they stood naked together, like they really were about to fuck up against the wall.

Why did you have to put that fucking image into my head? Nick demanded of his wolf. *It's not helping.*

Raluca jerked backward when he reached out for the vest. Of course she didn't want his low-class hands on her.

"I'm not going to fucking feel you up," Nick snapped.

"I thought nothing of the sort." Raluca drew herself up, her chin lifting arrogantly. "I did not imagine that Hal would hire a common criminal."

You walked right into that one, Nick thought.

Raluca drove him crazy, and not in a good way — well, not *only* in a good way — anyway, he couldn't resist the straight line she'd just fed him.

"You're wrong about that, baby," Nick said. "I have a record a mile long. I'm just not the sort of common criminal who'd touch a woman who didn't want me, that's all."

"Don't call me —" Raluca began, then broke off. Her extraordinary silver eyes widened in a double-take that made him want to laugh. "Excuse me?"

"You heard me the first time." Nick hadn't planned to tell her anything about himself, let alone his criminal record, but her reaction was funny enough that he was glad that he had. Let the snob princess know exactly who was guarding her. "Now, do you want to stand there and try to figure out the straps while I watch and you feel stupid, or do you want me to show you how to put it on? They're tricky if you've never worn a bullet-proof vest before."

"Or you could wait in the bathroom, so I don't have to watch you watching me," Raluca said ominously.

"Nope." Nick folded his arms. "I need to know it's on right. Either I watch you put it on, or I put it on for you. Your choice. Princess."

She glared at him, then gingerly lifted first one strap, then another. He didn't try to hide his amusement as he watched her discover exactly how non-intuitive it was. Finally, she gave a carefully unconcerned shrug. "You do it. Just this once. I'm a quick learner."

"I bet you are."

She ignored the double entendre, but watched him carefully as he buckled on the vest. He could feel her burning with curiosity about him, just like her goddamn hot skin burned into his without even touching it. Nick wanted her so much, it made his balls hurt. When he accidentally brushed a fingertip against her hand, they both jumped. He barely managed to step back before her thigh would have collided with his aching hard-on.

He backed away. "Okay. You got it. Now let's go shopping."

Raluca's elegant eyebrows rose as she buttoned Fiona's black jacket over the vest. "I cannot help my attire. But aren't you going to change? Or at least bring a change of clothing with you?"

"What's wrong with what I'm wearing?" Nick demanded.

"I wish to purchase both formal and casual clothing," Raluca said. "You will look out of place in a formal boutique."

"So?"

"My jewelry makes up for my clothing. Salespeople will assume I was on some casual errand, then entered on a whim or temptation. They will see that I belong, in any case. You, however, will not seem to belong."

A familiar anger flared up in Nick. She was right, and he knew exactly how the snob salespeople would stare at him. "They can suck it."

Raluca looked exasperated. As if she was explaining the alphabet to a slow child, she said, "You will feel uncomfortable."

"No, *they'll* feel uncomfortable," Nick said. "Fuck them."

A tiny noise like fine porcelain grinding together filled the air: the princess was gritting her teeth. "Will you please stop saying that word?"

"Does it make you 'feel uncomfortable?'" Nick inquired, imitating her tone.

He expected her to lose her temper and snap at him. Instead, she looked him in the eye until *he* felt uncomfortable. More, he felt ashamed. Sure, she was a stuck-up, prim princess. But she'd also had someone try to kill her the night before, and had then gotten stuck with an ex-gangster as a bodyguard. An ex-gangster who was being an asshole to a woman who was out of her depth and running for her life. Nick was used to danger, but Raluca wasn't. This was all new to her. And not in a good way.

"Yes," Raluca said simply. "It does."

"Sorry," Nick muttered. "I'll try to keep a lid on it."

"Thank you." Her tone was unapologetic, but sincere. Once again, he felt like the world's biggest dick. "Now, please take me to one high-end boutique and one shop for clothing suitable for the sort of nightclub that you would attend."

Nick blinked. He did go to nightclubs occasionally, but his dates chose them, not him. And "high-end boutique" was beyond him. "Hang on. I gotta make a call for that one."

He sat down on the bench and called Destiny.

"Hey, Nick," Destiny responded immediately. There was an odd echo on the line. "What'cha want?"

"A rec for a high-end boutique. And wherever you buy whatever you wear to go clubbing."

Her laugh echoed as well, as did her reply, pitched to imitate a kid on a schoolyard. "Oooh, Nicky's found himself a girlfriend!"

"Fuck, no," Nick snapped. He didn't have to turn around to see Raluca's disapproval — he could feel it burning into his back. "It's for a *client*."

"Ah-ha." That echoed most of all. The penny dropped as the door opened and Destiny strode in, her phone pressed to her ear. With a grin, she spoke into the phone even as she winked at Nick. "How high are we talking about?"

"Haute couture." Raluca stepped out from behind Nick. "Hello. I am Raluca, Lucas's former fiancée."

Destiny stared at Raluca, then at Nick. Then back at Raluca. Destiny was rarely at a loss for words, but it looked like the unexpected appearance of Princess Balcony Leap had shocked her speechless.

"You must be Destiny," Raluca said, when it became clear that Destiny wasn't going to say anything without further prompting. "I am very pleased to meet you."

Raluca held out her hand in a slightly awkward gesture, as if she wasn't sure if Destiny would shake or kiss it. Destiny grabbed it and gave it a vigorous pump. Nick knew the strength of his teammate's deceptively small hands, so he watched for Raluca's reaction. The dragon princess's eyes widened in a flicker of surprise, then narrowed. Muscles bulged in Destiny's forearm; Raluca's slim arm tensed.

Nick stifled a chuckle. He'd seen Destiny do that before, but only to men who doubted her physical abilities. It was odd that she'd do it to a woman who wasn't even her client. As the silent battle continued, Nick's amusement faded into an annoyed protectiveness. It was unfair of Destiny to use her strength on a delicate, fragile princess. And why was she even doing it? Raluca had done nothing to provoke it.

Just as Nick opened his mouth to tell Destiny to knock it off, the women released hands, Destiny with a laugh and Raluca with a formal nod. From the new respect that showed on their expressions, Nick guessed that the battle had ended in a tie. He was surprised. He'd assumed Destiny would win — she was not only a shifter, but a veteran and a highly trained bodyguard — but then again, Raluca was a dragon and had shifter strength, though she'd undoubtedly never worked out a day in her life, let alone ever done any actual work.

"Nice to meet you," Destiny said with a grin. "Lucas told us *all* about you. I wish I could've seen the header you took off the palace balcony! That must have taken so much courage."

"I can fly," Raluca pointed out.

Destiny shook her head, sending her braids bouncing. "I didn't mean the jump. I meant standing up to your family. Leaving the only way of life you've ever known couldn't have been easy."

"It was not."

The women looked each other over again, this time slowly and thoroughly. They were opposites all the way down to their clothes, with pale, slim Raluca in black fatigues and dark, curvy Destiny in a white tank top and flared tennis skirt.

Nick hadn't realized how tall Raluca was until he saw her standing beside Destiny. She'd looked tiny beside Hal, but he towered over everyone. Now Nick realized that Raluca was almost his own height. No wonder he'd had that thought of standing-up sex when he'd helped her with her body armor. They were exactly the right height for it. He wouldn't even have to lift her. She could just stand on her tip-toes. Or on his feet.

Nick swallowed, trying to choke down the rush of desire that had washed over him at *that* image. He needed to focus on his job, not on sexual fantasies. Once Raluca was absolutely safe and no longer needed his protection, he'd have the jerk-off session of the century.

Destiny frowned. "Hey, are you Nick's client, or are you still unassigned? I'm free."

"She's *mine,*" Nick said immediately. He heard the possessive snarl in his own voice, saw Destiny staring at him like he was a lunatic, and added, "Hal already assigned her to me."

"Whoa, really?" Destiny laughed. Nick glared; Destiny laughed harder. "Guess he wasn't kidding about forcing you to get comfortable with high society."

Nick couldn't help glancing at Raluca, just as she glanced at him. Both instantly covered their reactions, Nick with a "you got me" eye-roll and Raluca with a haughty stare.

"Hal suggested you, Destiny," Raluca put in smoothly. "I would have agreed, but a female escort would be unusual at a formal ball. For my purposes, it seemed better to hire a man."

"Makes sense," Destiny said. To Nick's relief, it didn't seem to occur to his teammate to doubt that explanation. As far as he was concerned, no one ever needed to know exactly why he'd volunteered. "But why do you need protection?"

Raluca briefly summarized her situation and needs. When she was done, Destiny borrowed Nick's phone and typed in a list of places, helpfully labeling them "haute couture" (whatever that meant; fancy, Nick supposed), "clothes for nightclubs," "nightclubs," and "hotel."

"Let me know when you go clubbing," Destiny suggested to Raluca. "Or any time you'd like to have a girls' night out. I know Nick's your bodyguard, but we can trade for a night. And you said you wanted to see how the other half lives. Sometimes that's different for men and women. There's a couple places I could take you with my girlfriends where Nick couldn't get in the door. At least, not unless he stripped and let us all stuff dollar bills into his jockstrap."

Hot blood rose to Nick's face as Raluca let out a chiming laugh. "That sounds charming. I would be delighted to meet your friends, Destiny."

Before Destiny could say anything more about jockstraps, Nick cleared his throat. "Okay, great. Thanks, Destiny. Raluca, let's get going. I want to get you set up with everything you need before I take you to your hotel for the night."

He hustled Raluca out. Though he knew Protection, Inc. was safe, his bodyguard instincts were in full swing the moment he left the locker room, scanning for danger and always keeping himself between her and anything potentially threatening. When they reached the underground parking garage, he halted her to inspect it, sniffing the air for enemies, before he was satisfied that it was safe to lead her to his car. Even so, he walked between her and the other cars, his gaze wary, until he unlocked his Dodge Viper and held the door open for her.

She settled into it, making an odd gesture that puzzled him until he realized that she was reaching to sweep in skirts that she wasn't actually wearing. Raluca caught his gaze as he slid into the driver's seat and jerked her hand back, looking embarrassed. "I am not accustomed to trousers."

"I can tell." Nick took the sports car from zero to sixty, darting out of the garage and merging into traffic. He drove aggressively, daring the other cars to get out of his way, leaving a trail of angry gestures and honks behind him. This seemed to irritate Raluca; he could practically feel her biting her tongue.

Finally, she said, "I take it you are not concerned about discretion."

"Nope." Nick swerved into the left-hand turn lane, forcing some rich asshole in a BMW to stomp on the brakes or collide, then zipped on to the freeway. Traffic was flowing nicely; the Viper skimmed in and out of lanes like the lean, mean driving machine that it was. No one even tried to follow them.

"You want discreet, you get Shane," Nick said as he left a nice Ferrari eating their dust. "But discreet isn't the only way to go. Look around: is anyone following us? If they were, they'd have a hell of a time keeping up. And I'd notice."

He hadn't expected Raluca to understand, or to admit it if she did. But as he spoke, she turned her head to examine the traffic streaming behind them. "Indeed. They would be most conspicuous."

"Plus, it's more fun this way." Nick stepped on the gas. "You're a dragon. You like speed, right?"

Raluca gave a tilt of her head, which he read as agreement with reservations. "I enjoy the wind."

Nick hit a button, lowering her window. "It's not flying, but..."

The cool air whipped back her silver hair. Raluca smiled. "Close enough."

He brought the Viper to a fast but smooth stop in front of Girasol, the nearest place on the list Destiny had given him. He'd never heard of it before, but that didn't surprise him; it was the one labeled 'haute couture.' It was in one of the ritziest neighborhoods of Santa Martina. Nick hadn't been there in years.

He handed his keys over to the valet and fell into step protectively beside Raluca as they approached Girasol, holding up a cautious hand to scan the interior before he let her inside. It held few hiding places beyond the doors; a small number of jaw-droppingly fancy dresses were scattered on mannequins, but most of the place was empty space and white marble.

Every single person, from other customers to the sales clerks to the fucking valet, was better-dressed than Nick was. His shoes clomped on the floor, which was polished to such a brilliant sheen that he actually left scuffs on it. Nick wasn't a huge guy like Hal, but he felt like a bull in a china shop. Or like a wolf in a designer clothing store.

While Raluca too was underdressed, the salespeople universally looked from her posture to her jewelry and approached her with deep and sincere respect. Nick could see that they weren't worried that she couldn't afford their undoubtedly terrifying prices, or that she'd come to browse rather than buy. He'd learned a thing or two in his years as a bodyguard, and one was how to read faces. They'd taken one look at her, and correctly identified her as their customer of the year.

He could also tell that they'd taken one look at him, seen that he didn't belong, and were trying to figure out his exact relationship to Raluca. Inappropriately dressed bodyguard? Vaguely thuggish distant relative acting as a chaperone? Bad news boyfriend?

Raluca had been right. Nick did look out of place, and he did feel uncomfortable. Not only that, but he was making the salespeople uncomfortable too. They didn't know how they were supposed to treat him or how much power he had or how much of an asshole he might be, and that probably had them worried that he might complain about them. They were employed at a shop for snobs but they were still working people, like him, and he was making their jobs harder. It was clearly his day to accidentally be a dick.

As opposed to being one on purpose every day, his wolf said helpfully.

Shut the fuck up, Nick snarled back. *If I'm a dick, it's because someone was asking for it.*

"Please, have a seat," said a saleswoman, indicating a set of plush chairs. She addressed Raluca, but gave Nick an uncertain glance, obviously unsure of whether he should be included. "Would you like a latte while we review your needs? Or a cocktail, perhaps?"

So that was how the other half lived. Go clothes shopping, get a free cocktail. No wonder rich people looked so goddamn smug all the time.

"A cocktail, please," said Raluca. "Refreshing. Cool. Not too sweet."

Raluca was clearly enjoying herself, in her element for the first time since they'd met. She gracefully settled into the offered chair, then glanced quizzically up at Nick.

"Ignore me," Nick said to the room at large, trying to keep the annoyance out of his voice. "I'm her bodyguard. I can't drink or sit on the job."

Everyone, including Raluca, looked relieved to have that made clear. The salespeople promptly ignored him and focused their laser-like attention on Raluca.

"I found myself in Santa Martina unexpectedly," Raluca said. Nick couldn't help admiring the smoothness with which she both explained her lack of clothing and preemptively squelched any awkward questions about it. "I am in need of at least one outfit for every occasion. Including one couture ball gown."

"Ah!" The salespeople's eyes widened with delight. Nick figured they had to be working on commission. Raluca had probably made sure everyone's rent was getting paid for the next few months, not to mention a couple trips to Disneyland.

He kept a lookout for assassins, of course, but his finely tuned werewolf senses would tip him off long before Raluca would be in any actual danger. So he was free to breathe in the scent of her iced cocktail— vodka, cucumber, mint, and something floral— and watch as she extended a graceful foot to have a selection of shoes placed on it.

Nick had never had any particular thing about feet, but watching the saleswomen put shoes on Raluca was making him reconsider. Her ankles were slim and flexible. The high arch of her foot curved like the doorway to some ancient palace. Her skin was perfect, her soles unmarred by calluses.

Everything about her was perfect — her grace as she stood to walk around in a pair of black stiletto heels, the turn of her head as she inspected a slithery silk dress, even the bob of her throat as she sipped her drink.

Raluca set the glass down on a tray. "I would like to try on some clothes."

"I have to check the dressing room," Nick said immediately.

The salespeople looked slightly offended, but Raluca said, "Of course." To them, she added, "I cannot give details, but you will see why I need him when you help me change."

She meant the bulletproof vest. But something tugged at Nick's chest when he heard "I need him" come from her lips, in her chiming tones. It made him wish she meant more than that he was just a human bulletproof vest, an annoying but necessary protection. He wished she meant she'd needed *him,* Nick, as a person.

As a mate, his wolf growled.

Shut up, Nick snarled.

He checked the dressing room for traps or bugs, gave the saleswoman a quick once-over to make sure she wasn't carrying anything lethal, and then reluctantly stepped out. The saleswoman pushed in a rack full of dresses and shoes, jackets and skirts, blouses and bras. And then she and Raluca shut the door in his face.

Nick stood outside for a very long time, trying not to think of Raluca naked in there, with nothing separating them but a door.

Ours, growled his wolf. *Our dragon princess.*

Fucking drop it, Nick silently retorted. *She's not into us. This is just a job.*

Ours. His wolf's snarl was inside his head, but it seemed to reverberate through his entire body. His nerves hummed like the engine of his Dodge Viper.

"Nick?" Raluca opened the door a crack. All he could see of her was a bit of her face and one storm-gray eye.

Nick jumped. "Yeah?"

"I would like a man's opinion."

Raluca opened the door a little wider. A saleswoman emerged with a full rack of clothes; another saleswoman rushed inside with a tray of cocktails, then ducked out again without it.

Once the flurry of movement subsided, Nick caught sight of slightly more of Raluca: part of her firm jaw, half a set of luscious lips, a cheekbone that might have been carved from marble, and one arched eyebrow. And that was it. She was standing back from the door, the rest of her obscured by another rack of clothes. He couldn't even tell if she was wearing any —

A slim ivory hand beckoned him inside. He stepped into the dressing room. Once he was inside, Raluca emerged from behind the rack.

To his disappointment, she was fully dressed. Sort of. She wore a black silk sheath dress, backless and low-cut. Simple, but hella sexy.

Other than that, the room looked much as it had when he'd first checked it: a velvet loveseat the color of red wine, a rack of clothes, a table that now had the bullet-proof vest and Fiona's black fatigues folded atop it, one wall that was a floor to ceiling mirror, and a tray table that now held an array of cocktails. Nick leaned over to sniff at the drinks.

"What are you *doing?*" Raluca demanded. She sounded as if she'd caught him jerking off. In church.

"Checking for poison, of course," Nick replied. "Or drugs. What did you think I was doing?"

"I do not know. It seemed odd, that is all. You did not smell my first drink."

"Of course I did. You just didn't notice. You were too busy getting your feet fondled."

Raluca glared at him. "You mean, 'trying on shoes.' You make it sound as if I was committing some obscene act!"

"Same to you," Nick replied promptly.

"I —" Raluca seemed about to snap at him, then cut herself off with visible effort. "I suppose I did. My apologies."

Once again, Nick felt adrift. She *had* accused him, but when he'd accused her back, she'd accepted the blame rather than escalating the argument. He undoubtedly *had* looked weird. And there was no reason for her to be used to the idea that someone might try to poison her. Forcing her to apologize for something that wasn't her fault was a dick move.

Again.

"It's not your fault," Nick said. "You hired me to protect you, so I'm protecting you. If you already knew all this stuff yourself, you wouldn't need a bodyguard."

"No, I still would," Raluca admitted. "Even if I could scent poison, I cannot fight. I suppose the drinks are safe?"

Nick nodded. "They're fine. Help yourself."

Raluca glanced at the tray, then at Nick. "Detecting poison — is that a werewolf ability? Or something anyone can learn?"

"Both, I guess. I have sharp senses, even for a wolf. But they're not magic or anything. I'm not *totally* sure the drinks aren't poisoned."

Raluca, who had started to reach for the tray, jerked her hand back. "What?!"

Nick shrugged, trying to keep his amusement off his face. Raluca was so easy to tease, he couldn't resist it. "Some poisons and drugs don't have scents. I can tell you that no one spiked your drink with cyanide, or anything else with a distinctive smell. Or dragonsbane, of course."

Raluca gave a lofty shrug. "Even I can recognize the odor of that. But how do you know of it?"

"Lucas told us about it: how it stops dragons from shifting and hurts them if they're splashed with it. How it's poisonous if you drink it. He brought some to the office so we could all learn what it smells like. The antidote, too: heartsease. We all carry little vials of it with us, now."

Raluca had been watching him intently. Her silver eyes narrowed. "You sound angry."

"I saw Lucas after he'd been poisoned with dragonsbane. He didn't say much about it — he doesn't talk about anything he thinks might make him look weak — but he'd obviously been to fucking hell and back." Then Nick remembered that Raluca had been there when Lucas had been poisoned, in his home country of Brandusa. "But you know that. You were there when it happened."

Raluca shook her head, sending her hair swinging like a sheet of liquid silver. "No. Oh, I could see that he was ill. And he did say that he'd been forced to swallow dragonsbane. But I thought he meant one drop, not half a bottle. And he said he'd already taken the antidote. I had no idea of how serious it was, or I would not have left him. By the time I found out, he had long since recovered."

"Yeah, that's Lucas," Nick said. "Guess he thought it was unmanly or something to say he'd been poisoned and he might be dying."

"Lucas is proud," Raluca replied. "Dragon princes are taught to be so. Even so, I cannot imagine what it must have been like. I have only been touched by dragonsbane once in my life. Even a dragon princess must experience that pain, so if we ever are attacked with it, the shock will not be such that we will be unable to defend ourselves. My uncle Constantine poured a single drop on to my hand, and made me sit with it for an hour before allowing me to wash it off and take heartsease. The pain was like nothing I have ever felt, before or since. And to be forced to *swallow* it —!"

Raluca shivered. Nick moved closer, instinctively protective even against an imagined threat. "Baby, that will never happen to you. Never. That's what I'm here for, okay? Nothing's gonna get past me to hurt you."

"I believe you," Raluca whispered.

Her tremors subsided, but an angry heat burned within Nick at her story. She was so delicate, so helpless. It had been cruel to hurt her, even if had been meant as life-saving training. Constantine's motives had probably been mixed at best.

Lucas had told Nick how Constantine had tried to force Raluca and Lucas to marry so he'd have power over them both, and then tried to assassinate Lucas and his mate Journey. Sure, Constantine was in a dungeon in Brandusa now, but it wouldn't surprise Nick one bit if he was somehow orchestrating the attempts on Raluca's life from behind the scenes.

Raluca drew in a deep breath, straightening her spine and stepping away from Nick. The moment of vulnerability vanished as if it had never been, leaving nothing behind but the hard princess shell.

"Enough of such unpleasant topics," Raluca said. "I am certain that they will never come to pass. Nick, I have selected most of my wardrobe in consultation with the saleswomen, but I wished to get a man's perspective on a few dresses, if you will. Then we will be done here."

"Sure." Nick took the opportunity to check Raluca out thoroughly while pretending he was just inspecting her outfit. "The dress is hot. Uh. I mean pretty. I like it."

Raluca's eyes rolled so hard, he was surprised they didn't go bouncing across the room. "This is a slip, Nick. An undergarment. I have not yet put on the dress."

"Oh."

Since Nick obviously couldn't say anything right, he decided to shut the fuck up. He watched in silence as Raluca wriggled into a floor-length dress, then posed for him.

The skirts flowed around her hips and legs like water, floating and rippling in every shade of blue, as if she had risen dripping from the ocean. While the skirts were feather-light and loose, the blouse was skin-tight and covered in sparkling jewels shading from sky-blue to sapphire to a blue so deep it was nearly black.

The dress was backless, allowing him to see more of her glittering dragonmarks. They wound sinuously around her left shoulder and upper arm like chains of silver, trailing along her side and across her chest. The low-cut front showed more of Raluca's cleavage, but Nick still couldn't tell exactly how far the dragonmarks went. A winding line of silver curved above one breast and then disappeared under her blouse. He wondered if it looped around her nipple…

"Well?"

Nick swallowed, hastily jerking his gaze upward. "Gorgeous. You look fu — you look great. Beautiful dress. Perfect."

Raluca's lips quirked in an amused smile he was getting to know all too well. "I was going to ask if you'd help me zip it up."

She indicated a zip on one side, nearly invisible against the jewels.

"Right." Nick took the tab and tried to pull it upward.

The seam gaped open; he had to use his other hand to hold it together, sliding his fingers upward as he went. It was impossible to close it without touching Raluca's hot skin. Why did she have to pick a dress so tight that she couldn't zip it up herself? It was killing him to feel her skin, so silken-soft, and not caress her or pull her into his arms or spin her around and kiss her.

He'd lay money that she usually wore perfume, probably the sort that came in a crystal bottle and cost about $10 per drop if you divided the amount of liquid by the price. But she must have washed it off before she'd gone to bed the night before, because all he could smell was her natural scent. It was a little bit like Lucas's, with overtones of hot metal — a dragon's scent — but sweeter. Like roses in a steel vase in the sun.

Nick breathed it in deep as he inched the zipper up, making sure not to snag it in her hair. But her hair was everywhere, flowing over his hands like silk, like the skirts flowed over her hips. It was cool against the heat of her skin, smooth as satin but oddly heavy. It felt like real silver beaten impossibly thin, each strand strong and slightly weightier than it looked.

The tab caught on some snag. Nick had to step in closer to disengage it. He was trying not to stare, not to put his hands anywhere inappropriate, not to fucking breathe—

He forced his gaze away from her. Or at least, he tried. But when he looked straight ahead, he saw them both in the mirror. He stood behind her, with his big hands on her body, one palm flat on her waist and one at the top of her bodice. Her hair moved in the air conditioned currents, drifting across his broad shoulders and settling over his forearms, as if she was binding him in silver chains.

He looked like he was holding her, like they were dancing together. But his jeans and boots and black leather jacket and tats were all wrong for the person who should be holding her — *he* was all wrong for her. She was every inch a princess in her jewels and silk and gauze. The only thing they had in common was the designs on their skin. But she'd been born with her royal dragonmarks, while his tattoos were the brand of his gangster past.

Raluca didn't turn to look back over her shoulder. Instead, she caught and held his gaze in the mirror. Still looking straight ahead, she reached down. He watched in the mirror as her hand closed around the stem of a cocktail glass and lifted it. But to his surprise, her hand reached the level of her mouth, then moved backward. Raluca lifted the glass to *his* lips.

"For your help," she said. "It must have been very dull to stand guard while I enjoyed my shopping. So take a moment for your own enjoyment. I presume that you drink?"

"Not on the job." His voice came out hoarse. The drink and her hand were right beneath his nose. The sharp alcohol odor of the cocktail and the steel-and-roses scent of Raluca herself nearly overwhelmed him, the contrast as intense as that of the heat of her body and the cold of the drink.

"Really?" Raluca didn't set down the glass. It stayed right where it was, taunting and tempting him — not with the cocktail, the drink itself was nothing, but with the idea of accepting it from her. Of drinking from her hand.

She couldn't possibly know what that meant to a werewolf... Could she?

"Would one sip of alcohol affect your reflexes to the extent that you'd be unable to protect me?" Her tone was lightly teasing.

She didn't know. He could hear it in her voice. Nick wasn't sure whether to be disappointed or relieved. She was just fucking with him. She probably thought it was harmless, playful revenge for every rude and teasing thing he'd said that day. But she'd accidentally struck a nerve, and he couldn't match her lightness in his reply.

"No, of course not. I'm a fucking werewolf —" The word slipped out despite his resolve to not use it around her. "Fuck! I mean, sorry!"

Raluca's eyes glinted in amusement. Apparently watching him get flustered was worth hearing him swear. "You were saying?"

Nick plowed on, trying to regain his composure. "Anyway, no, it won't. I'd have to drink a bottle of Jack for it to affect me at all. Two bottles before it would really fuck with — mess up my reflexes. Wolves have a high tolerance."

"Company rules, then?"

He knew she was leading him on purely to make him lose his cool, to get her own back, and because she apparently found him just as irresistibly teaseable as he found her. He *knew* it. But that didn't make it any less tempting. Nick had to go slower and slower with the zipper, keeping tight control over his hands, or they'd start shaking and she'd feel it.

"Do I look like I care about fucking rules?" His voice came out rougher than ever. He sounded like he was squaring off with some punks in an alley, forcing them to retreat with the power of his voice alone.

He expected Raluca to glare or scold him or kick him out of the dressing room. Instead, she just kept on looking at him. He'd never seen anything like the silver of her eyes, bright and hot as molten metal. He could've sworn they hadn't looked anywhere near as metallic when they'd come in. If they had, he'd have gotten her a pair of shades. Even the most oblivious passerby would notice that those weren't human eyes.

"Then drink," Raluca whispered. "Or else take off your jacket. It's hot in here— you're burning up."

"I'm not hot," Nick said. "That's you."

Her lips curved into a smile. Had he seen her smile before? If he had, it sure hadn't been one like this, provocative and sensual and daring.

She's just fucking with me, Nick told himself. *Any second now, she'll tempt me into making some kind of move on her. And then she'll go full-on princess and tell me to get my filthy hands off her, and I'll have to slink away with my tail between my legs.*

She will not, growled his wolf. *She is teasing, but she means it, too.*

Nick ignored his fucking crazy wolf. He had to stay cool. Professional. Keep —

Raluca moved the glass until its rim touched his lips, then tipped it backward. Icy liquid washed against his mouth. He had to either drink or let it spill down the front of his shirt.

Or step back and make her *look stupid, pouring a cocktail on the dressing room floor,* Nick thought.

He had a split second to decide. The last was so obviously the best option — harmless, but giving her a taste of her own medicine — that he had every intention of doing it.

Instead, Nick opened his mouth and drank from her hands.

She doesn't know what she's doing, he reminded himself.

But it didn't matter. The part of him that was pure wolf, uncivilized and untamed, knew what it meant. He'd just signaled his intent to give himself to her and hold nothing back, offering her a power over him that had nothing to do with dominance or submission, and everything to do with love.

I drink from your hands. His wolf's voice was low and deep, shaking Nick to the core as he silently spoke the ritual words. *I give you my heart.*

Nick drained the tiny glass in a single swallow. When he spoke, it was in his wolf's snarl. "You don't know what you've done."

"Yes, I do." Raluca turned at last, making his hands slide over her body as she moved to face him. Her voice was changed too when she spoke again, not the light ring of crystal but the deeper resonance of a tolling bell. "I'm doing what *I* want to do. Finally."

They collided as much as embraced. For a split second he still thought he could step away, but then her mouth found his, or his found hers, and then no fucking power on earth could make him stop. Her lips were soft and hungry, seeking rather than yielding. And hot, so hot. Her mouth was like a furnace, her tongue a caress of fire. He could still taste the cocktail she'd given him, bourbon and bitters, and the fainter vodka-cucumber-mint-elderflower of the one she'd had earlier. Her scent rose up until he thought he could taste that too, flame and metal and roses, sweet and spicy, hot and strong.

The glass dropped from her hands. He didn't hear it break, so maybe it hit the carpeted floor and rolled away. But he couldn't spare a moment to look for it, not with her cool hair falling all over him and her hot hands cupping his face as she kissed him with a wildness he'd have never imagined. He caught a glimpse of her in the mirror, all silver hair and ivory skin and skirts like ocean foam. Then her hands reached up, and her hot fingers ran through his hair, and he bent to her touch.

They fell together against the wall, lips locked on each other, bodies pressed together. He was desperate to get out of his clothes, to take off hers, but unable to pull away from her touch for long enough to do anything. His hands roamed all over her body, stroking the skin of her back and arms and face, everywhere that was already bare. She could touch nothing but his hands and face and hair, but she pushed herself against him, and her heat seared through her clothes and his.

He was shaking with desire, his head spinning. He'd never felt anything like this before. She too was trembling in his arms. He couldn't tell where she ended and he began. If she was hot, he was on fucking fire.

In a brief flash of sanity, Nick knew that he had to protect her and he couldn't do that if he was distracted by kissing her, let alone fucking her. But he couldn't make himself stop. So he moved to put his back against the door, which was locked anyway, so anyone who tried to get in would have to go through him first.

Raluca moved with him, those hot little hands of hers dropping down to reach under his jacket. He involuntarily thrust into that heat. She caught him and *squeezed,* sending a bolt of lightning up his spine, and he groaned into her mouth.

Nick had never felt so out of control in his life. He might do anything at all. Nothing seemed impossible. He still could hardly believe that the fucking princess was kissing *him.*

Kissing, fuck — she was giving him a fucking hand job, right through his jeans. One hand stroked his cock, making him groan again, while her other stole lower down, cupping and caressing his balls through the tight denim. Where had she learned to do that?

And how was she managing to look so cool while she was doing such dirty, dirty things below his belt? Nick caught a glimpse of himself in the mirror. His face was flushed, his eyes blazing green, his black hair tousled and damp with sweat. Not cool at all.

His head spun with the conflicting desires to let her go on touching him forever or until he came, and to break that impossible reserve of hers.

Or maybe he could do both.

He reached down and lifted her skirts, piling them over one arm. There were layers and layers of them, gauzy and light. They seemed to go on forever, making him feel like a fumbling idiot. But it was nearly impossible to do anything while she was working away at him with her hot little hands, sliding them slowly down his cock and balls, then stroking his inner thighs.

Nick finally got his hand under her skirts, brushing the heated skin of her bare thigh. She gave a little start, and he felt her inhale against his mouth. That was more like it. He drew back to nip at her soft lips as he stroked upward, taking his time, until he felt the lace and silk of her panties.

I'll give you a taste of your own medicine, he thought dizzily.

Nick cupped her mound, silk and all. She gasped again, then nipped back. If it hurt, he couldn't tell. And if this was medicine, it could raise the dead.

He stroked her through the thin silk, feeling her moist heat. He could feel the soft hair over her mound, and the folds of her inner lips. Her hands stilled, clutching at his thighs rather than stroking them. But he didn't mind. He *was* breaking her cool, and he loved it.

Nick could feel it happening with every one of his heightened senses: her already-damp panties getting outright wet, her juices slicking his fingers, her scent becoming both more heated and more animal, her womanly musk overwhelming her delicate roses. Her breath caught in her throat, turning from her deep and measured rhythm to quick, shallow gasps. She broke off their kiss to gulp for air. He grinned, pushing aside her panties and pressing his fingers in deeper, feeling her heartbeat accelerate. Raluca was shaking in his arms, her ivory skin flushing at last to a delicate pink. She broke out in a light sweat that made her skin seem to glow.

"I —" Raluca gasped. "I can't — I've never — Oh!"

Nick had a pretty good idea of what she'd never done: had sex in an inappropriate place, with the most inappropriate man imaginable. But she was doing it now, all right, and she sure didn't sound like she wanted to stop.

He found the nub of her clit and rubbed it, letting her gasps and shudders tell him how hard or soft, fast or slow to go. He wrapped the arm that held the skirts around her waist, in case she was one of those women who seemed to melt when she came.

He had two fingers pushed inside her, stroking her walls as he caressed her clit with his thumb. Raluca thrust against him, rubbing herself against his hand with an abandon he'd never imagined when he'd first seen her, gasping rhythmically. Her eyelids fluttered, sometimes brushing against his skin in a butterfly kiss. Her eyes were molten silver.

"Come on," Nick said. He meant to whisper, but it came out in a low growl. "Come for me, baby."

She cried out and came against his hand, her hot walls pulsing, her swollen clit throbbing. Her hands clenched on his thighs, bruising him with her shifter strength, but he didn't give a fuck. Princess Raluca was coming in his arms, shaking and gasping and spilling her hot juices until they ran over his hand and down her thighs.

And then, just as he'd guessed, she melted into him, all her muscles relaxing at once. Her head fell against his shoulder, and her cool hair slid all over him. A few locks even slithered inside his shirt, where they lay silky over his skin. He held her tight, his beautiful, delicate, daring princess, and never wanted to let her go.

But soon enough, she was stirring. Raluca lifted her head and opened her eyes, and Nick got to see the soft glow of contentment brighten to molten desire.

"You," Raluca said, her cut crystal voice once again deepening as she spoke. "I have done nothing for you."

She glanced from her still-upraised skirts to the bulge in his jeans, then put her hot little hand over it. Nick's whole body jerked like he'd stuck his finger in an electric socket. He couldn't think straight — he could barely think at all — with her hand on him, but he forced himself to focus. He had to protect her, in every way, not just from assassins.

"Are you on birth control?" Nick had to force the words out. He was panting for breath, his heart pounding like a jackhammer. Her lightest touch drove him half out of his mind.

Raluca stiffened in his arms. For a woman who had just thoroughly enjoyed a hand job in the dressing room of the ritziest clothing shop in Santa Martina, she looked bizarrely offended. "Certainly not! I am a dragon princess — former princess — but still!"

Nick had no idea whether it was dragons or princesses or specifically dragon princesses who didn't believe in birth control, let alone why, but he wasn't going to stop to discuss it. He didn't have any condoms, but he didn't care. He had to know what those hot fingers would feel like on his bare skin.

"Use your hands," he gasped.

She settled down again, a teasing smile hovering at her lips. "As you wish."

With excruciating, taunting slowness, Raluca unbuttoned his jeans, making sure she brushed against him, but no more than that, with every movement. Then she began undoing the zipper the exact same way.

"God!" Nick finally exclaimed. "Just pull it!"

"It's very tight," Raluca said, not going one bit faster. "If I yank on it, I might break it off. Dragon strength, you know."

She tugged it the tiniest increment downward. Her other hand strayed to his balls, toying with them, running a heated finger around them in light circles.

"I don't fucking care," Nick said. "Break it, rip it off, what the fuck ever."

Another tenth-of-an-inch down. She glanced up at him through her silver eyelashes. "Are you begging? That might get better results than swearing."

"Yes, I'm fucking begging!" Nick burst out. "Come on, Raluca, get the fuck on with it, before I come in my fucking pants!" As an afterthought, he added, "Please!"

"Since you phrase it so elegantly," she teased.

But to his immense relief, she did pull down the zipper. He shoved his own jeans and boxers down past his hips, unable to wait for her. His cock pressed against his belly, thick and swollen with blood, throbbing for release.

Hold back, Nick told himself. *Don't come the second she touches you. Take your time to enjoy it, because there's no fucking way she'll ever do this again...*

Raluca's hand closed over him. He had a second to see those delicate fingers adorned with jewels, slim hand, fine ivory skin, and small oval nails painted silver, wrapped around his cock — a glimpse that he knew would sear itself forever into his memory — before sensation took over, and he could see nothing at all.

Her fingers were fire itself, if its burn gave pleasure rather than pain. She squeezed hard as she drew her fist upward, and maybe it did hurt *too,* Nick was too far gone to tell. All he knew was that he'd never felt anything like her touch. It set him on fire, body and soul. He wanted it to go on forever, but he couldn't hold out against that intensity. Everything in him was building toward his climax, pushing him with irresistible force.

"Taste me," Raluca murmured.

With her free hand, she lifted his, still wet with her juices, and pushed one of his fingertips into his mouth. He tasted the tang of metal and the sweetness of a woman on his own rough finger, just as she slid her hand all the way along the length of his cock.

Nick came so hard, he thought for a second that he was going to black out. It was a release like he'd never felt before, shaking him body and soul. Raluca's hot fingers slid back down as he spurted again and again, spilling himself into her hand.

When it finally ended, he found that he too had relaxed so completely that he'd have slid to the floor if someone hadn't held him up. He'd collapsed against Raluca's chest, his face buried in her smooth, cool, heavy hair. She was holding him up with one arm.

Dragon strength, he thought dizzily. *Some delicate princess...*

The scent of sex and of *her* hung around them. He straightened and took his own weight, glancing down. She followed his gaze. The glow of contentment faded a little from her face as she looked at her damp thighs, at the skirts Nick was still holding up, and at the white ribbons of his come on her hand.

"Do you have a handkerchief?" she asked. "I left mine in Vienna."

"Sorry, baby." Nick barely stopped himself from admitting that he'd never owned one.

Then he spotted the napkins on the cocktail tray. With his free hand, he picked one up. She pulled off her panties and tossed them into a tiny trash bin. He wiped her hand dry, then took another napkin to more gently clean the rest of her. Finally, he wiped his own hands off.

Raluca surveyed their hasty clean-up, then dipped the remaining napkins in one of the cocktails and did what Nick had to admit was a more thorough job on both of them. Then they tossed the napkins in the trash to follow the panties and hopefully hide them. Or not. It wasn't like either of them was likely to come back.

Raluca finished by emptying the remains of the cocktail into the bin. The sharpness of alcohol killed the scent of sex for anyone but a shifter. But Nick could sure as hell still smell it. He hastily put down Raluca's skirts, then pulled up his boxers and jeans, zipped up, and dropped down his jacket. Just in time, too. He was starting to get hard again.

"I hope this room was soundproof," Raluca said.

"Did you talk to the saleswoman while you were in here?" Nick asked.

"I did. We had quite a long discussion about what dress and shoes I should wear out of here."

"Then we're fine," Nick said. "I was right outside the door, with werewolf senses, and I couldn't hear you."

Raluca gave a sigh of relief. But Nick, replaying the conversation in his mind, frowned. "Wait, did you say you were going to wear something from here? Now?"

"Yes." Raluca lifted a clothes hanger from the rack, then indicated a pair of shoes.

The outfit she'd selected looked like a little black dress at first glance, but when Nick looked closer, he saw that it was covered in intricate black embroidery. The shoes had heels so high that Raluca would seem taller than him, and were polished black except for startling, bright red toes.

Put together, the outfit probably cost more than Nick had earned in his entire life to date. It would be stunning on Raluca. For a moment he was stuck on the image of her in that little black dress. Between the high heels and short skirt, her legs would seem to go on forever. And it would be so easy to reach up that skirt…

Then he forced himself to shake his head. "Nope. You have to change back into Fiona's workout gear. Her shoes, too."

"Why?"

"Because we have at least one more shopping stop, you can't wear a bulletproof jacket over that dress, and you can't run in heels."

"But you said it was impossible for me to wear a jacket at all times," she protested. "What is the point of buying clothing I can't wear?"

"You can wear it," Nick said. "Just not right now. Like, the nightclub — Destiny or I will check it first, and it'll have guards at the door. Or the parties. We're talking about fancy shit with royalty and diplomats and politicians, right? So they'll have their own security. But Destiny's favorite shop for buying dance clothes won't have any security but me. Just have the dresses and shoes packed, okay?"

"*Packed?*" Raluca sounded as shocked and appalled as when he'd mentioned birth control. "No, they'll be delivered to the hotel."

"The fuck they will!" Horrified, Nick said, "Did you tell the saleswoman which hotel you're going to stay at?"

"Yes, of course…" Raluca's voice trailed off as Nick saw her realize her mistake. "Oh, but surely an employee of Santa Martina's best haute couture shop would not betray me. And I used a false identity."

"What the fuck does working at a fancy shop have to do with being trustworthy?" Nick demanded, though he knew the answer: if you're a rich snob, then you figured even anyone working for a rich snob had to be okay. "And even if she is, once you told her, you also told everyone she talked to, their delivery guy, and anyone who can hack into the store's computer. As for the fake ID, you're only the most recognizable person in the universe."

Nick's heart accelerated as he spoke; assassins could already be on their way. "Fuck! What were you thinking?"

Raluca's eyes narrowed and cooled until they looked like slivers of gray ice. Haughtily, she said, "Unlike you, I am not trained in professional security. Nor am I accustomed to running for my life. Nor am I telepathic. If you wish me to do or not do something, you must inform me of it."

Her tone got up his nose, but she had a point. He couldn't assume that she knew *anything* security-related. "Fine. From now on, don't tell anyone who's not on my team where you're staying or where you're going. I'll find you a new hotel. The clothes can be delivered to… Wait, why are the clothes even being delivered? I have room in my trunk."

Raluca stared at him like he was out of his mind. "They are on hangers. They must be transported either on a clothing rack, or in packed flat in tissue paper. You couldn't fit a single dress into your trunk either way." Grudgingly, she added, "We could take the shoes in boxes."

"Oh, yeah, shoes in boxes, that'll fix everything." He let out a groan, then conceded, "Fine. I'll hit up someone on the team to rent a van, pick them up, and bring them to the hotel. What a fucking pain in the ass."

Icily, Raluca replied, "I am so sorry to make you *work* at your *job*."

An uncomfortable silence fell. Nick was sure she was regretting the hell out of the sex. Worse, so was he. Her crack about his job had hit home.

She was so naïve that she didn't even know not to give her address to some random salesperson, and he'd been so overcome with desire that he'd completely dropped his guard. When she'd grabbed his cock in her bare hand, he wouldn't have noticed a hundred ninjas dropping from the ceiling. If anyone had attacked her while they were having sex, they'd probably both have been killed.

The recollection of Raluca coming against his hand flashed through his mind and body, making him instantly rock-hard again. If he'd only had a condom in his wallet, maybe he could have felt her come with him inside her, too.

But now he never would. He didn't know who he was more pissed at, himself or the fate that had brought them together once and once only, just to taunt him with what he could never have again.

"We can never have sex again," Nick said.

Chapter Three

Raluca

Raluca had already decided that if Nick didn't say they could never have sex again, she would have to. All the same, hearing it from him hurt like a drop — no, like a bucket — of dragonsbane in the face.

For only the second time in her life, she'd followed her heart rather than her head, doing something wild and outrageous and absolutely unbefitting a dragon princess, because it was what she'd wanted to do. And for the second time, it had been a complete disaster.

Nick — supposedly her mate, the person who ought to love her unconditionally and forever — hated her. They'd had incredible, earth-shattering sex exactly once, and only minutes later he was scornfully pointing out her utter foolishness and ignorance, then vowing to never touch her again.

Or maybe it was only incredible and earth-shattering for me, Raluca thought gloomily. *He couldn't have faked his actual climax, but maybe for him, it was only an average sexual encounter. Or even below average.*

After all, there had been no penetration, and she knew how important that was to men. In her admittedly limited previous sexual experience, men stuck it in as soon as they got their clothes off and didn't bother with anything else.

She drew upon all her years of training to sound and look unconcerned and unbothered as she said, "I was about to say the same thing."

Something flickered in his emerald eyes that reminded her of the eyes of the wolf in the photo at Protection, Inc. Could he too have regrets? Then it vanished, leaving only the anger he seemed to carry with him like a sword. His tense shoulders lowered like he was forcing them down.

"Right," Nick said. "It was a mistake, that's all. It's my job to protect you. And from now on, that's all I'm going to do."

Another awkward silence fell. This time they spoke simultaneously.

"I should prefer that you not mention —" Raluca began.

"If you tell my teammates, they'll never let it go, so —" Nick started.

They both broke off, then Raluca gave a cool nod. Keeping her voice even, she said, "We are on the same page. Excellent. As far as we are both concerned, for both others and ourselves, this never happened. We shall not mention it, and we shall not repeat it. Now please leave the dressing room. I need to change."

Nick walked out without a word. The door closed behind him with a very final-sounding click.

Cursing herself for her foolishness, Raluca put on the shirt and pants and shoes that didn't quite fit, and the heavy, awkward jacket that never let her forget that someone was trying to kill her. Then she made herself emerge to face Nick.

To her relief, he seemed to have already spoken to the salespeople. One hurried to fetch the clothes on the rack, and another loaded the shoe boxes into the trunk of Nick's car.

He beckoned her into the passenger seat, waited with visible impatience for her to put on her seatbelt, then stomped on the accelerator. The car darted into heavy traffic, but he avoided a collision while leaving a trail of honks and angry yells behind them. Raluca resigned herself to his driving. He was the bodyguard, and she had never learned how to drive at all. She'd always had a chauffeur when she'd been a princess, and later she'd used taxis.

Nick brought the car to a smooth if somewhat sudden stop in front of a distinctly less fancy shop.

"Destiny's nightclub place," he explained.

"Thank you." She reached for the car door, but he was already out of the car and opening it before her fingers could close around the handle. Then he gave a quick glance around that included inside the shop, then held that door open for her too.

He moved quickly and with grace, she couldn't help noticing. Like his wolf, perhaps. Beautiful...

Competent, she corrected herself. *As Hal promised.*

Raluca looked around the shop with interest once she was inside. She had observed such places before, but never gone inside. It had clothes that she'd seen but never worn, some on mannequins but most crowded onto racks: leather corsets, skirts that glittered with sequins rather than jewels, tank tops with designs that were printed instead of embroidered. Not quite a peasant shop, but certainly not a billionaire's shop, either.

She waited, but no one moved to greet her. The salespeople were eyeing her and Nick with suspicion, not pleasure. Raluca looked at how the employees were clothed, then at herself and Nick, and guessed that he was still under-dressed, while her jewels made her over-dressed. And also, that perhaps she was meant to select her own clothing rather than have it brought to her.

Raluca wasn't going to be intimidated by a bunch of commoners, but neither did she intend to linger long where she wasn't wanted. Holding her back straight and her chin high, she quickly gathered clothes, thinking of what might taunt Nick with the body he'd sworn to never touch again.

Soon she had more than she could easily carry, but no one offered to help. In fact, they seemed to be pretending not to see her, while watching Nick as if he might steal something. She opened her mouth to reprove them just as Nick made a grab for her armful of clothes.

"Here, I'll take those," he said.

Raluca felt in every inch of her body what would happen if she let Nick into the dressing room with her and then closed the door. He might dislike her, but their chemistry was undeniable. She could feel it even now. But she couldn't give in to it. If there was anything more foolish than having sex in a dressing room with a tattooed criminal werewolf who didn't even like her, it was doing it twice.

She jerked away. "You are *not* accompanying me while I change."

"Fine." Raising his voice, he demanded of the room at large, "Are you all on a fucking lunch break? Get the lady some help!"

A salesperson came over. He wasn't especially friendly, but he did help Raluca take her selections into the changing room. She closed the door on them both, discarded the clothes that didn't fit, and from the remainders, selected an outfit that would horrify Uncle Constantine, shock everyone who had ever known her as a princess, and, she hoped, make Nick regret his entire existence.

Holding everything so Nick couldn't see it, Raluca marched to the counter, paid for her selections, and carried them away in the bags she was given.

"No hangers?" Nick inquired.

"Not necessary." After a moment, Raluca admitted, "I hope. I have not worn clothes like this before."

As they climbed into the car, her stomach rumbled audibly, reminding her that she hadn't eaten all day. She first hoped Nick hadn't heard, then remembered his werewolf senses.

"Please take me to my hotel," she said, hoping to pre-empt any rude comment. And also that he'd made a new reservation at some point while she'd been in a dressing room.

"Sure," Nick said easily. "But let's have dinner first."

Without giving her the chance to object, he skidded through traffic, whipped down several narrow alleys, and finally pulled up at a bizarre building. Once again, he was out of his door and holding hers open for her before she could say anything, leaving her with no graceful alternative but to get out.

She stepped out of the car and stared incredulously upward. "What is that?"

Nick stated the obvious. "It's a building with a giant fake hotdog wrapped in giant fake bacon on the roof."

"And why does the building have a giant fake hotdog wrapped in giant fake bacon on the roof?"

"Because this is Big Bacon." Grinning, Nick beckoned her to the order window, which overlooked the sidewalk. "You said you wanted to do American things. Big Bacon is as American as it gets."

Raluca was certain that he was getting revenge for every cold look she'd given him. On the other hand, the one thing she'd heard about America was that it was big and full of big things. If anyone had told her about Big Bacon, she'd have thought they were teasing her. But there it was, with its looming giant fake hotdog.

Raluca was faced with a choice: go along and pretend this was all normal, or outright order Nick to take her to the hotel. Part of her wanted to push him around for a change. But she *had* said that she wanted to do American things. And despite her annoyance with him, his boyish grin was hard to resist.

In fact, she realized, right now and while they'd been having sex had been the only times when the anger and tension had completely gone from his face. She liked the way he looked now, teasing but not malicious. Playful.

I'll go along with it, she decided. She couldn't bring herself to wipe that smile off his face. *Let's see how far* he'll go.

After all, he'd have to eat at Big Bacon too.

Nick ordered for them both. It seemed that Big Bacon only served one item, and it was to be eaten standing right on the sidewalk. He watched her closely as the man in the window shoved their order at them. If anything, his grin was even wider.

Raluca couldn't help but blink at the gigantic, bacon-wrapped sausage piled with condiments in colors not found in nature. Then, looking straight at Nick, she crammed the largest bite she could fit into her mouth.

His astonished stare made it all worthwhile.

You didn't think I'd really eat it, did you? Raluca thought.

Swallowing, she announced, "Delicious."

Nick blinked. "Really?"

"We have such things in Viorel." Raluca determinedly ate another bite, then stared at Nick until he did too. "The concept of meat wrapped in meat is not unique to America, you know."

"Well..." Nick laughed suddenly. If his smile changed his face, his laugh transformed it. Raluca wondered if she was catching a glimpse of the boy he had once been, before... Surely *something* had to have happened to him, to make him so angry. "Yeah, you got me, princess. Meat wrapped in meat. Fucking universal."

"I'm not a princess any more. And please don't say that word." Then, seeing his smile begin to fade, she quickly added, "I once traded my lunch with that of my maid. She had a sausage wrapped in ham and baked into a bun. It's peasant's food, not the sort of thing ever served at the royal table. I was curious."

"How was it?" Nick asked.

Honestly, Raluca said, "Far better than Big Bacon."

"Yeah." Nick tossed the remains of his meal in a trashcan. "You don't have to finish it. Big Bacon is more of a landmark than..."

Delicious, Raluca thought, gratefully discarding the rest of hers. It tasted primarily of chemicals. In fact, she was not entirely convinced that it was not made of plastic wrapped in plastic.

"...fine dining," Nick finished. "I'll take you to the hotel. You must be beat."

By the time she'd figured out that he meant "tired," it was too late to agree. Once he'd mentioned it, the exhaustion of the entire day came crashing down on her. She fell into something of a doze as he drove her to the hotel, took a duffel bag out of the trunk and got a bellboy to collect the shoe boxes and her bags, checked them both in, and then escorted her to the hotel shop and bought all the necessities that a guest might have forgotten to pack — toothpaste, a nightgown, a hairbrush.

"Thank you. I was so weary, I would have forgotten," Raluca said.

"No problem."

Nick escorted her to her two-bedroom, two bathroom suite. He put the bag down on one bed as she glanced around the rooms. It was an average five-star hotel, nothing special— Raluca had stayed at converted castles and palaces— but for a modern hotel, it was quite adequate.

"My hoard —" Raluca began.

"We can fetch it tomorrow." Nick didn't move away to go to his own room, but stood over her as she sank down to the bed.

Stood *guard* over her, she realized. He didn't make a show of it, but by now she had noticed that he always placed himself between her and any possible danger, with her unguarded side by something relatively safe — a wall, perhaps, or a room he'd already checked. His intense green eyes never stopped taking in everything around them, watching for danger.

"I'm fine," she said. "You can go to your own room. I'll lock the door."

He shook his head. "No, don't lock it. If I have to get in fast, I don't want to waste seconds breaking down the door. Don't worry, if it's not an emergency I'll knock first."

"But..." Then she realized: the other room of the suite was for him. Of course he wouldn't leave her alone; of course he'd taken the room with the door to the corridor, where danger might come from. Her door led only to his room. "I know you will knock."

He shot her a look. Raluca gritted her teeth: he'd obviously figured out her mistake. She seemed forever doomed to have him catch her being naïve.

"Good night," she said firmly.

56

"Night. Call me if you need anything." Nick closed the door between their rooms.

Raluca quickly made her bedtime toilette, by now used to doing such things by herself rather than with the help of her maids, then went to bed. She was so tired, she expected to fall asleep instantly.

Instead, she tossed and turned, preoccupied with thoughts of the man in the room next door. The door that wasn't even locked. Had he gotten undressed? At some point while she was naked, had he been naked too? Or was he still sitting up, guarding her?

She cursed herself for not stripping him naked while she'd had the chance. He'd have let her. He'd clearly have done anything at all. And now she'd forever lost her chance to see his hard nude body, let alone to have it pressed against hers.

Raluca squirmed, wet and throbbing between the thighs. But she didn't dare touch herself. Nick might hear the sounds of her private pleasure with his finely tuned werewolf senses. She glared in the dark, toward the general direction of his room. If *he* was pleasuring himself, she'd never know. Her dragon abilities did not include enhanced hearing or smell, and Nick wore no jewelry. If he wore precious metal, she might be able to sense its movement, though she wasn't sure if she could do so from a room away.

We must gift him with silver, her dragon said unexpectedly. *An earring or necklace for everyday, perhaps. And when we are alone, we could wind a long silver chain around his naked body.*

The picture her dragon sent her made Raluca blush hotly, and sent even more heat lower down.

We're not gifting Nick with anything, she snapped silently. *He wouldn't take a… a bacon-wrapped hotdog from me!*

Undeterred, her dragon replied, *You must find out what jewelry men wear in America.*

None, Raluca retorted. Then, remembering Hal, she said, *Just wedding rings.*

Her dragon gave a snort. *All humans adorn themselves.*

Shaking her head, Raluca turned over and tried to banish thoughts of Nick, of naked Nick, of naked Nick wrapped in silver chains, of Nick laughing as she rose to his challenge of Big Bacon. It was a long time before she fell asleep.

***

The next morning, Raluca awoke to bars of sunlight across her face. She had slept late. When she went to the shower, she found that the borrowed clothes and nightgown she'd worn yesterday had been laundered and were folded on the table, along with the bulletproof vest and several other sets of clothing and shoes, none of which she'd bought the day before.

A piece of paper lay atop them. In slashing capitals that she knew had to be Nick's writing before she even got to the signature, she read,

HAL FOUND A FORMAL BALL FOR TOMORROW. DINNER AND DANCING. IT'S WHITE TIE, WHATEVER THAT MEANS. DON'T WORRY, RAFA'S GETTING MY OUTFIT. I BET YOU ALREADY HAVE SOMETHING, BUT IF NOT, WE CAN GO BACK TO THE FREE COCKTAIL SHOP.

DESTINY DROPPED BY WITH CLOTHES FOR YOU. WANT TO DO MORE AMERICAN THINGS TODAY? WEAR ONE OF HER OUTFITS OR YOU'LL GET FUNNY LOOKS. OR WE COULD GO TO A MUSEUM OR SOME OTHER CLASSY THING. YOUR CHOICE.

NICK

Raluca showered, then inspected the clothing. Apart from the fatigues and undergarments, Destiny had provided two business suits, one in blue and white, one in gray and red, along with polished black pumps that would go with both, one set of blue jeans with a red and pink floral print blouse, a pink cloth jacket, and strappy red sandals, and one set of black jeans with a white tank top, a black leather jacket with multiple straps and buckles, and black boots with short heels.

She considered them. All were obviously meant to be worn with the jacket zipped over the bulletproof vest. Raluca had no desire to ever wear Fiona's fatigues again. They would forever remind her of her stupidity in the dressing room. That left the business suits, which would be reasonable attire for visiting museums or other elegant attractions, or one of the jeans-based outfits. The black leather one would not have been out of place at Big Bacon.

The buckles and chains on the jacket were merely polished metal, not real silver, but they couldn't help catching Raluca's eye.

She liked the boots, too, which went over the jeans and halfway up her thighs, and were also adorned with sparkling buckles and zips. They were obviously the "American things" outfit — a feminine version of Nick's clothes, in fact.

Raluca considered the possibilities, then shrugged and put on the jeans. She *had* wanted to give American commoner things a try. If she hated them as much as she'd hated Big Bacon, at least she'd know rather than wondering forever. And she had the fancy party the next day.

That being said, she ordered room service breakfast. She couldn't face Big Bacon or its breakfast equivalent (Big Bagel?) first thing in the morning.

When someone knocked on her door, Raluca called, "Come in!"

Nick kicked open the door between their rooms, holding a tray in both hands. His own door, which opened to the corridor, was closed, and no hotel employees were in sight.

Raluca, noting the scuff his boot had made on the door between their rooms, pointed out, "You could have just asked me to open the door for you."

"Didn't think princesses opened doors for people."

"I'm not a princess, and if the alternative is kicking them open, I certainly do."

Nick stood still, staring at her. Ah. The black leather. He had undoubtedly expected her to wear one of the business suits. She smiled inwardly, keeping her expression bland until she saw him suddenly realize that he was frozen with a tray in his hands. He hurriedly came forward and set the breakfast tray on the table.

Raluca indicated the other chair. Uncertain if Nick had already eaten, she'd ordered enough for two. "Breakfast?"

"I already ate."

"Big Bacon?" Raluca inquired.

"Nah. They don't deliver."

Uncertain whether he was teasing her or not, she said, "You could have coffee… Do you drink coffee?"

"My life's blood." Nick picked up the china coffee pot, his boyish grin flashing. He poured for her first, then for himself.

Raluca added plenty of milk and half a spoon of sugar to her coffee. Nick took his coffee black, with two heaping spoons of sugar. Sugar and caffeine, no milk. If he was an ordinary man, she'd think he wanted a jolt of energy, a jittery edginess vibrating through his nerves. Though he'd said that because he was a werewolf, it took a lot of alcohol to affect him, so maybe caffeine and sugar worked the same way.

She opened her mouth to ask, then closed it, uncertain if that was a nosy question. She wished she knew *anything* about werewolves. Maybe if she knew more about his shifter type, she'd understand more about him. He was such a fascinating mystery.

Raluca thought about him as she ate and he drank, clearly pacing himself to match her. She had the distinct impression that if she hadn't been there, he'd have finished his coffee in two gulps. He clearly knew the basics of manners, though it was obvious that he'd never been taught formal etiquette.

Still, the rudeness was at least partly deliberate. He *did* know how to behave properly, more or less. The f-word, on the other hand, was clearly something that had been ingrained into his speech for a very long time, given how it slipped out even when he was trying not to say it. And even his basic manners slipped when he wasn't paying attention. That was the mark either of someone who'd been taught as an adult rather than a child, or of someone who had lived a very long time without even the most basic of niceties.

He'd said he was a common criminal and had a record, and that had sounded completely honest. She wondered what he'd done, why he'd stopped, and how he'd come to work for Hal. But there was no polite way to bring up the first two. The third, though, was ordinary conversation. Every guide book on America had said that so long as you didn't ask how much money a person made, inquiries about employment were normal topics of conversation among strangers, as neutral and common as remarks about the weather.

"Being a bodyguard must be such an interesting job," she began.

"It's got its moments." Nick topped off her coffee and poured himself another cup, then absently began pouring sugar straight from the pot into his cup, rather than using the spoon. There he went again, his manners slipping when he got distracted. Raluca hoped it was because he was engaged in the conversation, not because she'd annoyed him.

"What made you choose it as a profession?" she asked.

Raluca instantly knew that she'd made a mistake. Nick froze. Infinite heartbreak flickered in his emerald eyes before it was replaced with anger, then guilt. Sugar cascaded into his cup in a white waterfall, pouring and pouring until his coffee trembled at the rim of the mug, about to overflow.

Then his expression went blank, a calculated look that she knew all too well. He put down the sugar pot and lifted his coffee to his lips with impressive steadiness. The cup was filled to the brim, but not a drop spilled. He drank, made a face, and set it down.

With a less-than-convincing shrug, he said, "Pay's good. I get to drive fast and fight, and it's all legal. There's not many jobs like that. If I was in the military, I'd have to follow orders. If I was a cop, I'd have to do my own paperwork. Bouncers make lousy money. Being a bodyguard's a good fit for me."

I'm sure that's all true, Raluca thought. *But I don't think that's why you just poured the entire pot of sugar into your coffee.*

"You done?" Nick asked.

Raluca stood up. "I am."

"So what's your pick? Museums and art galleries? Or real America?"

"Real America," Raluca replied. She'd already decided on that, but now she wondered if there might be a more subtle way of finding out more about Nick. She added, "*Your* America. You know, places that people like you go."

Once again, she immediately knew that she'd said the wrong thing. Anger flashed in his eyes, and she knew she was in for it as he said, "*My* America. Okay, princess. You got it."

Now what? Raluca thought glumly, realizing that whatever plans he'd had in mind had just been switched with the intention of annoying her.

What had she said to upset him? She replayed her words, but could find nothing offensive in them. The guidebooks said that Americans, like natives of any country, enjoyed advising foreigners on the best that their land had to offer, and were particularly fond of being asked about places off the beaten path.

Why was Nick so touchy? She didn't even feel comfortable asking him what she'd said to offend him, in case *that* offended him. She wished she hadn't agreed to go anywhere with him. But it would be undignified to suddenly change her mind.

Raluca followed him out of the hotel and to his Viper. Her heels clattered pleasingly against the floor, and the jeans and tank top were unexpectedly comfortable. She reminded herself to thank Destiny the next time she saw her.

This time Raluca remembered not to sweep away non-existent skirts as she got in. "Where are we going?"

"On a road trip." Now Nick sounded more teasing than angry, to Raluca's relief. "It doesn't get any more American than that."

He rolled down the windows and peeled out of the parking garage and into the streets, threading his way through Santa Martina. Raluca looked curiously around the city. It was different from the European cities she was used to. Less elegant, but it did have a certain quality she liked.

As Nick passed a group of skateboarders practicing jumps in front of a graffiti mural of a beautiful black woman with an explosion of rainbow-colored hair, she thought, *Lively. Vibrant. Unexpected.*

She wouldn't have minded seeing more sights like that. But Nick soon left the city and began speeding down a highway that led into the countryside. Raluca watched the scenery, but soon became bored: it was nothing but field after field, with the occasional herd of cows. She could have seen as much in the countryside of Viorel, though the fields would have been smaller, the sky less vast.

They drove and drove, until Nick suddenly pointed at a billboard. He was going so fast, Raluca barely had time to read, WORLD'S BIGGEST CHAIR: NEXT EXIT before they were skidding off the highway, down the exit, and pulling up in front of another sign announcing, WORLD'S BIGGEST CHAIR.

Nick bounced out of the car and opened her door.

"What is this?" Raluca asked, before remembering the folly of asking Nick rhetorical questions.

Sure enough, he replied, "It's the world's biggest chair."

He paid the admission fee as Raluca wondered if this was some bizarre prank. Then again, Big Bacon was real...

A moment later, they stood in an open lot, looking up at a gigantic armchair the size of a house.

"Well?" inquired Nick. His green eyes gleamed teasingly. "What do you think?"

Raluca was determined not to rise to the bait. If he had decided to pay her back for an infraction that she didn't even understand, she wasn't going to give him the satisfaction of seeing her annoyance. "It's certainly quite large."

She waited, but there appeared to be no more to the attraction than its size.

"Okay," Nick said. To her satisfaction, he seemed disappointed in her lack of visible reaction. "Onward!"

They returned to the highway and passed more and more fields. Raluca drew upon her training at enduring boring diplomatic meetings until Nick pointed again. This billboard read, WORLD'S BIGGEST LOBSTER: NEXT EXIT.

That actually intrigued Raluca… until they paid their admission and found, not an aquarium housing an immense live lobster, but a gigantic fake lobster, painted bright red and long as a city block.

"World's biggest lobster!" Nick announced.

"I see," said Raluca.

They looked at it for a few minutes, then returned to the highway. As Nick began driving again, Raluca waited till he was distracted by passing a car, then stole a look at him. To her satisfaction, he seemed frustrated, no doubt by her lack of reaction; to her secret alarm, he also seemed determined. She wondered how many WORLD'S BIGGEST things were within driving distance of Santa Martina.

She sat silently, calmly watching the monotonous fields and sneaking glances at Nick whenever he wasn't looking at her. He became more and more visibly impatient as time went on, shifting in his seat and tapping his fingers against the wheel, but was apparently unwilling to start a conversation. Raluca was also unwilling, given that everything she said only seemed to annoy him.

Then she caught his lips twitching in a way that she'd come to recognize as *Let's irritate Raluca.*

He turned on the radio. Reception was bad in the country; the first few stations were nothing but sizzles and hisses. He stayed briefly on a preacher bellowing about fire and brimstone in between long bursts of static, skipped through several music stations that sounded at least potentially enjoyable, one Spanish and one classical, and then found one playing a type of music that Raluca had not heard before.

With a distinctly evil grin, he dropped his hand. Clearly this was something she was meant to hate. At first Raluca couldn't tell why. The instrumentation had a heavy emphasis on twanging guitars, but was otherwise unobjectionable. Then she began to listen to the lyrics.

My wife done run off with my best bud
Now I'm in a bar drinking my fifth Bud
Wonderin' how my life got to be such a dud

Raluca shrugged inwardly. Many popular songs had unimpressive lyrics. Nick would have to do better than repetitive rhymes if he wanted to get under her skin.

When the song lamenting the loss of the singer's wife to another man ended, another song began. This one, also set in a bar, lamented the loss of the singer's job. The third song didn't begin in a bar, but the singer ended up in one after his dog died. The fourth was also set in a bar, this time because the singer's beloved truck had been destroyed in a crash.

Raluca re-thought her stance on the music. The glum subject matter, the monotony in which the only difference between songs was what the singer had lost that had driven him or her to drink, and the incessant twanging was beginning to get on her nerves.

Lost everything I loved on an ice patch on an old dirt road
My wife Sally-Jo, the lovingest woman God ever bestowed
Ol' Red, the best sniffer of a hound dog I ever knowed
The truck that helped me carry my heavy load
Got fired and can't pay all the money I owed
So here I am in this bar, drinking like a thirsty old toad

"What is this?" Raluca burst out.

"Good old American country music," Nick replied. He was visibly struggling to keep a straight face. If the joke had been shared with her rather than at her expense, she would have laughed aloud. "Gotta have real American music on a real American road trip."

"Viorel is in Europe, not another planet," Raluca retorted. "I have heard American music before. I know that it is not all like this!"

"You probably heard the songs that got popular in Europe because they weren't that American," Nick said. "But hey, it's your road trip. If you're sick of American things already, I'll look for la-di-dah opera from a hundred years ago. In French."

Raluca gritted her teeth, refusing to back down so easily. "Find me a station playing American music without twanging and trucks."

"No twanging, no trucks." Nick's eyes glittered in a way that would have been charming if he wasn't so obviously set on finding something else that she'd hate. "Got it."

He again began turning the dial, skimming past stations that sounded potentially listenable until he found one with a booming beat that instantly made her ears ache. Raluca wasn't even sure she would call what she heard music; it was spoken, not sung, though it did have a rhythm.

Fuck that ho! Yeah, find that pussy and fuck that ho!
Nothing fucking better on a fucking cold day
Than a fucking hot pussy on a fucking hot ho!
A chorus joined in, chanting, *Fuck that ho! Fuck that ho!*
It continued in the background as the speaker went on,
I'll fuck you up if you get in my way
Fuck you! Today's my fucking lucky day
And I'm fucking finding that fucking hot ho!
The chorus switched to *Fuck! Fuck! Fuck that ho!*

Raluca hit the off button so hard that her finger slammed it several inches into the music player. Sparks flew. She got a small but painful electric shock. But it was well worth it; the song, if you could even call it that, stopped.

"Hey!" Nick stared at her, his green eyes sparking brighter than the broken wires. "You wrecked my radio!"

Coolly, Raluca replied, "Send me the bill."

Nick looked again at the hole she'd left, then at her hands. "You smashed it with *one finger*. Fuck, you're strong."

For a mad instant, she thought she heard reluctant admiration in his voice. Then she decided that she'd imagined it. He couldn't be impressed that she'd destroyed one of his possessions. And he hated her. Everything about this trip was specifically designed to annoy her.

"I'm a shifter," Raluca replied, making sure he heard the subtext of *you idiot.* "And as you are well aware, I do not like that word. That other word too."

"What other word?" Nick asked with exaggerated innocence that made her want to shake him.

"The one in that... I am not sure I would even call it a song..."

"That was rap," Nick said. "Real American music. So yeah, it's a song. An *American* song. But which word did you mean? I already know how you feel about 'fuck,' so was it 'pussy' or 'ho?'"

Raluca had meant the first, as she'd never even heard the other before and didn't know what it meant, though she could guess by context. But it was obviously a swear word, so she replied firmly, "Both of them."

"Check," Nick replied. "No fuck, no pussy, no ho."

The surge of rage that burned through Raluca actually made her vision cloud with red. She was seriously tempted to throw him out of the car without stopping first. He had werewolf healing; he'd survive.

She shoved her hands under her thighs and sat on them, then stared out the window. Cows. More cows. Fields. More fields. The pastoral scene should have calmed her, but it instead made her more angry. With the window down, the odor of manure was strong.

This will not go unavenged, she thought. *Tomorrow is the formal ball. Let's see how you feel getting dragged into* my *territory.*

An hour of fields and cows later, Raluca had to work hard to keep her annoyance off her face when Nick called her attention to a billboard reading, WORLD'S BIGGEST BALL OF TWINE: NEXT EXIT.

A few minutes later, they stood looking up at a ball of string the size of a house.

"Well?" asked Nick.

"Will our next stop be to see the world's biggest cat that coughed up this hairball?" Raluca inquired.

Startled, Nick laughed, then hastily turned it into an unconvincing throat-clearing. "I was thinking of the UFO Watch Tower, actually."

Raluca was hot and tired and hungry, angry and frustrated and disappointed. The completely pointless giant hairball, showed to her for no reason other than to annoy her, by her supposed destined mate who couldn't stand her, seemed to sum up her entire existence.

"No." Raluca felt her dragon rise to the surface, and knew her eyes were glowing silver.

Nick's eyes too changed, letting her see his wolf. But his eyes deepened in color rather than glowing, until they were the exact shade of her favorite jewel in her hoard, a priceless emerald found in the deepest jungles of India. His instinctive alpha dominance was responding to her challenge, though she hadn't meant it as one.

She readied herself for a fight — not a physical one, but a battle of wills.

He cannot fight, her dragon said unexpectedly. *He is honor-bound to protect you. And so long as he is your bodyguard, he is also bound to obey you, so long as it does not conflict with your safety. Do not humiliate him by forcing him to back down.*

Angry as she was, Raluca recognized the truth of what her dragon had said. She felt the heat and silver glow fade from her eyes as she said, "I am weary. I would like to rest. I have seen enough sights for one day. Please take me back to the hotel."

Nick's wolf faded as well. His green eyes were still bright, but the deadly alpha ferocity left them. He even sounded slightly guilty as he said, "Sure. No problem."

They drove back in silence. Raluca thankfully entered her air-conditioned hotel, closed the door between her and Nick, removed her boots, and flopped down on the bed. Her closet door was open, showing her that her haute couture clothes had been delivered as promised. But not even the thought of the ball could console her.

She longed for her hoard to comfort her, but it was at Protection, Inc. She wished she had a book rather than television, which she'd never particularly cared for. But to get either, she'd need to collect them with Nick, and she didn't want to see him. The combination of his obvious dislike of her with the physical attraction that she couldn't repress was sheer torture.

Raluca ordered room service, took the tray from Nick without speaking to him, and closed the door. She ate with little appetite, then slept badly, dreaming that she had inexplicably flown to America on an airplane rather than on her own wings, had checked her hoard into luggage, and the airline had lost it. She spent the entire night vainly searching for it, with Nick appearing periodically to shout "Fuck!" and then disappear without helping her.

***

She awoke at dawn, tired and annoyed. Without bothering to shower or get out of her nightgown, she opened the door to Nick's suite, hoping to catch him in some embarrassing state of undress.

To her disappointment, he was fully clothed and watching her door.

Werewolf hearing, she thought. He'd heard her coming. Oh, well, at least she knew he was competent. He might hate her, but she was in no danger so long as he protected her.

"I intend to stay in today," she announced. "I wish to be fully rested for the ball."

"That's fine," Nick said.

"All I require from you is your protection while I buy some items from the shops downstairs," she added.

"Sure."

"I presume I do not need to wear a bulletproof jacket within the hotel or to the ball?"

"No." He sounded tired. She looked at him more closely. He had dark smudges beneath his eyes, easily visible against his pale skin. Perhaps he hadn't slept well either.

If they could have only curled up together, no doubt they'd have slept marvelously. Or gotten no sleep at all, which would have been even better.

Raluca stamped on that thought. Also on the thought that followed, which was to feel sorry for Nick. One bad night's sleep was nowhere near enough punishment for the appalling music and the World's Biggest Hairball.

She retired to her room, where she showered and put on the blue jeans and floral blouse Destiny had provided, had breakfast without inviting Nick to join her, and then went with him to explore the hotel stores.

Like many five-star hotels, it contained several shops, all with good and varied selections of their products. She first bought some books, noting that while most of his attention was on guarding her, he periodically glanced at the thriller section while she selected some critically acclaimed fiction. He didn't buy anything himself, but he didn't seem to mind watching her browse.

The makeup store, however, visibly bored him. So she took far more time than she needed to select the perfect shades of lipstick, foundation, powder, eyeliner, and mascara, waiting between each just long enough for him to think she was finished before turning to the next aisle.

When she was done, she returned to their rooms. Standing in the doorway between them, she said, "We must leave early. I need to drive to Protection, Inc. so I can get some jewelry from my hoard."

This is your chance, her dragon hissed. *Ask him what jewelry men wear.*

Raluca inwardly shook her head at her dragon's ridiculous conviction that some day she would adorn Nick, but it was true that she might never get a better lead-in for the question. "Do American men wear jewelry?"

"Uh… I think Rafa said he'd get me cufflinks," Nick said. "My suit's at Protection, Inc. too. So yeah, we'll leave early. I'll brief you while we're there."

"Please do," said Raluca. "I have an excellent memory, so if I say anything foolish or dangerous or naïve, it will be because *you* failed to warn me not to."

Before Nick could reply, she stepped back and shut the door in his face.

It was a gratifying moment. But it was the only one for the rest of the day. Her dragon was dissatisfied with the response to the jewelry question, and kept breaking into Raluca's attempts to read and relax with remarks on the insufficiency of cufflinks as a mating gift.

We're not mates, Raluca protested, but her dragon ignored her and continued to brood over American men's lack of good taste. Eventually she began making hopeful suggestions that Raluca could break with American fashion, give Nick a proper dragon's gift, and perhaps start a nationwide trend.

Anything he wears might inspire others to vain attempts to look as handsome, her dragon suggested.

Raluca was already having difficulty concentrating, and her dragon wasn't helping. Nor was the periodic swearing she heard from the next room. Nick appeared to be getting a lesson on etiquette over the phone, and sounded outraged at the entire concept.

My dragon has gone mad, my supposed mate hates me, unknown assassins are trying to kill me, and I never even saw Lucas, whom I came here to find, she thought.

The hotel balcony called to her. She longed to leap off it and fly away. But she would then have to extract her hoard from Protection, Inc., and that would require explaining herself to Hal. She disliked the idea of admitting that she had made a mistake — many mistakes — every possible mistake. Choosing Nick. Coming to America. Perhaps even renouncing her title and leaving Viorel.

She could return to Viorel and reclaim her position, Raluca supposed. But she suspected that doing so would not solve the problem of the assassins. Someone had decided that they wanted the throne or to be the power behind the throne, and they were willing to kill her to get it. Once that decision had been made, it didn't matter whether she was officially a princess or not. She was nothing but a piece on a chessboard, a pawn who must be destroyed before she could become a queen.

She stepped on to the balcony and stood looking out at the busy streets. The sun was setting, lighting the sky in a blaze of red and orange. It reminded her of dragonfire.

Raluca made her decision. She would attend the ball, if for no other reason than to annoy Nick by making him dress formally, speak politely, and eat elegantly, just as he'd annoyed her by making her eat at Big Bacon, listen to terrible music, and pay to look at World's Biggest Wastes Of Time.

And then she would take her hoard and fly back to Europe. Or Asia, perhaps. She'd change her name again, and take her chances with the assassins. If they killed her, so be it. Her mate didn't love her, anonymity was no better than the chains of royalty, and travel had brought her no joy. At least she would fly free again before she died.

Raluca turned her back on the balcony, changed into her blue couture gown and glumly zipped it up herself, and added the gloves, shoes, and clutch purse that would make it white tie. She went to the bathroom and did her own makeup. She'd have to leave her hair for when she had ornaments. Then she knocked on Nick's door.

He opened it. And stared. Raluca enjoyed watching lust blaze in his eyes, followed by his jaw clenching as he tried to force it down. He wanted her body as much as he disliked her personally.

Good, she thought. *Let him suffer. I shouldn't be the only one.*

He looked the same as ever, dressed in his usual clothes — black jeans, black leather jacket, black leather boots — but the sight of him, his green eyes, his tousled hair, his broad shoulders, the vine twining around his finger — affected her as much as it had the first time. As much as it always did. He was all wrong for her, and yet she wanted him so much that just looking at him made her nipples harden within their silken cups.

And she didn't only want him sexually. She wanted to hear his laugh, see his smile, and comfort the hurt within him that she sensed without knowing what it was. The few occasions when they'd managed to have a conversation without arguing had been so fun. She wanted his body, yes, but she wanted more than that. She wanted to be friends with him. She wanted him to like her. To love —

But he doesn't, she reminded herself. *And those other things I imagine that I want from him are the mere byproducts of our unfortunate mutual sexual desire. It is a matter of chemistry, nothing more.*

Her dragon hissed, *It is much more.*

Nick sucked in a gulp of air. His gaze, which had briefly drifted — was he speaking with his wolf? — focused again. "Right. Let's go."

Raluca once again seated herself in Nick's car. She started to close the door, but a leather-clad arm shot out and held it open.

"Your dress," Nick reminded her.

"Oh!" Raluca had been about to slam a car door on the trailing skirts of her couture ball gown. She lifted them inside. Nick closed the door for her. "Thank you."

"No problem." He pulled back his arm, leaving the faintest scent of leather in the air before it was blown away by the wind.

When he parked at Protection, Inc., Raluca accompanied him in with some trepidation. She liked Hal, but their introduction had been so embarrassing and awkward. She'd liked Destiny too, but only after the bodyguard had concluded her challenge of strength and decided to be friendly. Raluca wondered if that was some strange American ritual, and if she would again be subjected to a bone-crushing handshake should the other female member of Protection, Inc. appear. Then, too, there was Shane, with his icy blue stare. Raluca wasn't sure she wanted to meet him at all.

But the only person at Protection, Inc. was a handsome Latino man lounging on the sofa with his feet dangling over the arm rests, his muscular body sprawled at ease. He wore a simple white T-shirt and blue jeans, but he wore them well. His black hair, which was longer and smoother than Nick's, tumbled back in a chin-length mane. Raluca was irresistibly reminded of a lion soaking up the savannah sun, even before she remembered that Rafa was, in fact, a lion shifter.

Rafa's big brown eyes opened wider at the sight of her, and then a charming smile lit up his face. He rose from the sofa with easy grace. "What a pleasure to meet you, Raluca. You look ravishing."

He held out his hand in a familiar and elegant gesture. Automatically, she offered him her own. He took it, bent, and brushed his lips against the back of her hand.

"The fuck you think you're doing?!" Nick burst out.

Rafa unhurriedly released her hand. "I'm demonstrating proper etiquette for a white tie ball. Like the one you're going to in an hour. Remember?"

"Yeah, I fucking remember!" Nick snapped. "But we're not at the fucking ball yet, so you can shake hands like a fucking normal person!"

Raluca should have been offended by the cascade of f-words. Not to mention that Rafa had done nothing improper, and in fact had pleasantly reminded her of home. But an odd warmth rose in her at the sight of Nick seething over another man kissing her. If he was jealous, did that mean that some part of him cared about her?

Of course he cares, hissed her dragon.

Raluca shook her head, dismissing her dragon. If Nick was possessive, it only meant that he saw her as a possession: a thing to be used and discarded, not a person he cared for. But she could use his jealousy as another opportunity to get some revenge for the hairball.

"I am pleased to meet you, Rafa," she said, making sure to sound flirtatious. "Since we seem to have offended Nick with a formal greeting, shall we make up for it by shaking hands?"

A spark of mischief gleamed in Rafa's eyes. "Well, Nick did ask us to. Can't refuse a teammate's request."

Rafa took her hand and clasped it just long enough for it to seem like an intimacy rather than mere politeness before he shook it. "There. Now we've been introduced in the styles of your country and mine. I do hope you'll stay until Lucas comes back— I'm sure he'd be disappointed if you left before his return. And he told us so much about you, I'd be very sorry to miss making your acquaintance."

"Rafa, are you fucking done yet?" Nick demanded. "You've got a fucking job to do."

"Nick needs help getting dressed," Rafa explained to Raluca, making it sound like he was teaching his toddler son to tie his shoes.

Nick flushed red, with embarrassment or fury or both. "Because that fucking white tie outfit has something like nineteen fucking parts that all have to be fucking perfect."

"Exactly. Let's start getting them on," Rafa said smoothly.

He led them to the locker room, where Raluca retrieved her hoard pack from Lucas's locker. Its contents sang to her soul, lightening her heart. Nick might not enjoy the evening — in fact, Raluca was quite certain that he would not — but *she* would. And at the end, she'd abandon him and fly away, taking her hoard with her. This whole American trip had obviously been a bad idea, but at least she'd end it on a high note.

Vengeance, gold, and the open sky, she thought. *The three treasures of the dragon. Tonight, I'll have them all.*

Her dragon stirred within her. *That is* not *the saying. It is* honor, *gold, and the open sky.*

Raluca shrugged. *Close enough.*

She took her time arranging her hair and selecting her jewelry, knowing by the muffled sounds of swearing that Nick was indeed not having an easy time with the complex and precise components of a man's formal white tie attire. When she finished, she sat running her fingers through her gold and gems, imagining how ridiculous he'd look and feel, just like she had standing in front of gigantic fake lobsters and fake bacon. It would serve him right.

Finally, the swearing stopped.

"Raluca?" Nick called. "Are you ready?"

"I have been so for the last half-hour," she called, then opened the door and stepped out.

Nick did not look ridiculous.

He looked stunning.

The black tailcoat and pants and white shirt fit perfectly, showing off his broad shoulders, muscular chest, and narrow hips. His physical proportions, which had previously been partly hidden under his ever-present leather jacket, were perfect. He was a vision in black and white, with his clothes echoing and enhancing his pale skin and midnight hair. The one touch of color — his emerald eyes — took her breath away. Everything about him was pure classic perfection.

Fascinated, she took in the little details: the cufflinks of mother-of-pearl, the polished black shoes, the pearl studs on his shirt, the white kidskin gloves that concealed his tattoos, the pressed white linen handkerchief folded in his pocket with a half-inch showing, the white carnation on his lapel. He had shaved very closely, leaving his skin looking smooth as silk; usually he had stubble on his chin, but not tonight.

Rafa, grinning in the background, looked rightly proud of himself. "All right. I'll leave you two crazy kids to it."

With a wink, he stepped out and closed the door behind him.

Nick was hot in leather and jeans. He was hot, period; that was the problem. So he wasn't *more* sexy in formal attire, just differently so. But it was such a surprise that Raluca couldn't take her eyes off him. She'd been so certain that he'd look awkward and uncomfortable. Instead, he stood tall and cool as the hero of a black and white movie from a more sophisticated time. He looked elegant and suave, which were not adjectives she'd ever thought to apply to him.

If he wore a concealed weapon, she couldn't see or sense it. But he couldn't conceal his edge of danger. It showed in how he moved, and in the intensity of his eyes.

Not a black and white hero, Raluca thought. *He's licensed to kill.*

She pushed that thought out of her mind. Certainly, he *looked* good in formal attire. But someone else had selected it and made sure everything was worn correctly. Once Rafa was no longer present to coach him, could Nick manage formal dining, dancing, etiquette, and most of all, speech?

Raluca doubted it very much.

He'd dragged her to a block-long fake lobster, so it felt very appropriate that her vengeance would involve an oyster fork.

Chapter Four

Nick

With Rafa gone and Raluca standing so close he could feel the heat coming off her skin, Nick was burning up inside. It was exactly like he'd been locked in that fucking dressing room with Raluca, as if the fire in her dragon's body had been passed on to him. But that had been pure sexual heat, while the burn he felt now was also fueled by the blazing rage that had engulfed him when she'd sneered that she wanted to see how *his people* — blue-collar, gangsters, riff-raff, trash — lived.

She said none of those words, his wolf growled. *And she did not sneer.*

His wolf had said that before. But Nick had been too pissed off to pay attention. But now he tried to recall her exact words and tone. What *had* she said?

And whatever she'd actually said… What had she *meant?*

Ask her! His wolf sounded ready to rip Nick's throat out.

But the words — any words — stuck in his throat. Raluca was always beautiful, even when she was cranky and sweaty or just woken up. But now, in that dress that made her look like a mermaid, with her hair pouring down her back like a silver waterfall and her glittering dragonmarks swirling around her exposed skin, he couldn't do anything but stand and stare.

She wore elbow-length silk gloves the color of the ocean in summer, clinging tightly to her slim arms and those long fingers that looked so delicate but could punch holes in steel. Her hair clip was a rose of reddish gold with silver leaves. A choker of diamonds encircled the ivory stem of her throat, with a single strand of them dangling down to end in a perfect star sapphire just above her cleavage. Tiny silver bells with golden clappers hung from each ear, giving out a chime when she moved. The sound was so soft that only a werewolf or a man standing close enough to kiss her could hear it.

He didn't know what she'd done with all the makeup she'd bought. Her eyebrows and eyelashes were still the same dark silver, her face still ivory, her lips still rose-pink. Maybe she looked extra-perfect, he couldn't tell: she always looked perfect to him.

She wore high-heeled silver sandals with intricate straps, bringing her to exactly his height. He wouldn't even have to bend over to kiss her.

Raluca was so fucking gorgeous, and he wanted her so much. And she could barely stand to be in the same room with him.

That is not so, his wolf said. *You are mates. You drank from her hands.*

Silently, Nick replied, *That cuts no ice with the fucking dragon princess, buddy. She fucking hates me. Want to bet whether she lasts the entire ball before she calls Hal and asks to be transferred to Destiny?*

Raluca cleared her throat, a polite but firm sound that she'd probably spent years perfecting. God knew what she thought he'd been doing. Staring at her breasts, probably.

"Brief me," Raluca said. "I will remember everything."

Nick choked back his feelings and tried to stay as cool as her. He gave her their fake names and cover stories, plus the hotel she was supposedly staying at and her fake itinerary.

Raluca was Katarina Petrescu, a wealthy tourist from Viorel, and Nick was Adam Peterson, an American relative — a distant one, to account for their total lack of family resemblance, but related enough to explain why they weren't a couple, if anyone asked. He'd figured there was no way she'd go for fake dating, and Nick didn't want to either. If he had to touch her romantically but in pretense, he'd lose his mind.

She repeated it back to him flawlessly, often word-for-word, her tone lightly mocking as if she thought she'd shock him with her total recall. He wasn't shocked. She might be naïve, but she was the opposite of stupid.

"Great," Nick said when she was done. He wanted to praise her more — most clients needed multiple repetitions and role-play before they got it right — but anything else, and she'd probably think he was condescending. If there was one thing he'd proved over and over, it was that he couldn't do anything right as far as the princess was concerned.

They drove through the city in silence, Nick with half his mind on the road and security, and half mentally rehearsing everything Rafa had taught him.

Champagne glass farthest from you and centered above the other glasses, red wine glass below it and on the left, sherry next to red wine on the right, white wine below red wine on the left, and water below sherry on the right.

Or had he mixed up red and white wine? Or red wine and sherry? And what did it matter when a fucking butler was pouring and he could see and smell what everything was?

"Because if you drink the wrong drink with the wrong course, you'll blow your cover. And if you actually *know what you're doing, you'll* look *like you'll know what you're doing,"* Rafa had said, sounding annoyed.

Which was fair. That was the most basic principle of undercover work. Nick shouldn't even swear in his own mind, if he wanted to avoid swearing when he was at the ball.

Next thing Nick knew, he was pulling up at the fanciest house he'd ever seen, a gigantic white thing with about a billion windows and *pillars.*

"The fuck?" he muttered.

"If you use that word here, you will seem out of place and attract unwanted attention," Raluca remarked, a second after he'd mentally cursed himself out.

He handed over his keys to the valet, who wore a suit fancier than anything Nick owned. Unless you counted the suit Rafa had gotten for him, but Nick was hardly going to take it home and wear it again. It could live in Protection, Inc., with the other weird costumes the team had amassed for specific jobs.

Another valet opened the car door for Raluca before Nick could, then just stood there while she just sat there. Belatedly, Nick hurried around and offered her his hand, assisting her out of the car. Even through gloves, a jacket sleeve, and a shirt sleeve, her fingers burned like fire.

The valet took off without giving him a receipt. Nick hoped to hell that was normal. And how the hell much was he supposed to tip when he got his car back? Or was he *not* supposed to tip? Rafa hadn't covered that.

He led Raluca into the house. She walked lightly, regally, as if she wore an invisible crown. Nick felt incredibly awkward in his fucking clothes that were so weirdly precise that he was sure he'd violate some fucking rich person's law just by walking. Rafa had actually taken out a ruler to measure how much sleeve should show below his jacket cuffs!

Nick forced himself to focus. He gave the place a visual sweep, looking for anyone or anything suspicious, and saw nothing but an incredible amount of fancy stuff and people dressed just like him and Raluca, plus more people like the valets — butlers and maids, he guessed.

People came up and greeted them. Nick let Raluca do the talking, and just nodded and smiled and checked them for hidden weapons. There was nothing, just as there had been nothing anywhere they'd gone. Nick was beginning to wonder if either Raluca had ditched her assassins in Venice, or if her transformation there had scared off the entire plot against her. Sure, the assassin had carried dragonsbane, but it was one thing to know that dragons existed, and another to be knocked across the room by one.

All the same, Nick had a vial of heartsease in his pocket, along with a gun in a shoulder holster. They'd been easier to conceal under his black leather jacket, not to mention easier to get to in a hurry. But if it came to shooting or poisoning, all the rules were out the window anyway and he could just rip off his fucking stiff clothes.

Raluca coughed delicately, catching his attention. A pair of double doors had been opened, and people were headed toward a huge dining room. Nick took Raluca's elbow, choking down the surge of unwanted desire that coursed through him every fucking time he touched her, and led her to the ridiculously long table beneath a ridiculously huge chandelier.

Hal had done his prep work: there were place cards under their fake names. Nick pulled out Raluca's chair, then pushed it in for her as she gracefully seated herself. Then he started to pull out his own chair, only to have a waiter or butler or someone grab it. Nick forced himself not to jump — that guy had moved fast, and Nick didn't like people doing that close to his client when he was on the job — but the waiter only seemed to want to pull out Nick's chair for him.

Keeping an eye on the waiter's hands, Nick let himself be seated. But he sat too soon, leaving himself too far from the table. Both Raluca and the waiter looked irritated, and even more so when Nick scooted his chair closer in, making an unpleasant scraping noise and probably damaging the million-dollar hardwood floors.

That was when he got his first good, close, non-distracted look at the place setting.

Nick had never seen *Phantom of the Opera*, but he'd heard that the big stunt was a falling chandelier. As he took in the horrifyingly large and complex array of forks and glasses and plates, all of which he needed to use correctly while guarding Raluca and pretending that he was a fucking rich snob, he wished the chandelier would come crashing down then and there.

As the drinks were poured and appetizers were served, Nick unobtrusively sniffed for poison, first for Raluca and then for himself, before giving her the little nod that meant it was safe. She took a delicate sip of her drink and began to converse charmingly with the people across from her.

"No, of course they are not real," she said, with her wind-chime laugh. "They are *temporary* tattoos, painted on by a makeup artist. I was inspired by Alexander McQueen's fashion show in Vienna."

Nick had been focused on smell, not sight, so it was only then that he took in what he'd been served. It looked like a weird, tiny sculpture, but was presumably edible. Green liquid pooled around a piece of carved red jello, a gray blob covered in white foam was plopped atop the jello, and little black balls and even tinier green flecks were sprinkled over the foam.

He had no fucking idea what it was or how to eat it, but since it had mostly smelled like fish, he hoped the jello wasn't cherry-flavored. Or wasn't actually jello. Now that he thought about it, there was no way it could be jello. This was not a jello-type place.

Nick took a moment to recall his lessons before he touched anything.

"Silverware is used from the outside in," Rafa had said. *"The fork or spoon that's farthest from you is the one you use to eat the first course. Forks are on the left, knives and spoons are on the right, just like a normal place setting."*

Nick reached left, picked up the farthest fork, and poked the red stuff. It wobbled, exactly like jello. The foam dripped down, exactly like spit.

Wishing he hadn't thought of that, Nick stabbed the entire thing and shoved it in, intending to swallow it whole. It came apart in his mouth, making that plan impossible. The jello tasted like bell peppers, the sauce was vaguely herbal, the black things popped between his teeth and released a blast of salty fishiness, and the spit — foam — turned out to have concealed a slimy raw oyster.

Nick battled the impulse to spit it out, which was a challenge as every single bit of it had a gross flavor or texture or mental association or all three, chewed, and swallowed. Then he grabbed the nearest glass and took a huge swig of whatever the fuck was in it, which turned out to be red wine.

He looked up to see everyone within a few seats of him staring at him. Raluca included.

A pompous-looking old dude addressed him in a voice that was helpful on the surface and condescending all the way down to the center of the Earth. "Young man, the oyster fork is on the other side."

Nick took another look at his place setting. Sure enough, a lone, weird-looking fork was on the right, farthest away from him. Everyone but him was using it to eat the oyster-jello-spit thing.

"My bad — apologies. The oyster was buried under the sauce, so I thought it was... something else," he finished unconvincingly.

To Nick's surprise, Raluca backed him up. "Quite true. I nearly used the fish fork myself. I adore the chef's sense of mischief, hiding the oyster like a delightful little surprise gift, but it does put one in danger of making a minor *faux pas* with the silverware."

The equally pompous old lady beside the old man gave a sniff. "Perhaps. I certainly saw *my* oyster. That being said, red wine does not go with either fish or oysters. And the caviar made it clear that the *amuse bouche* contained some form of fish or shellfish."

Nick stifled the urge to throw what was left of his red wine in their faces and thought, *What would Rafa say?*

"I was so struck by the elegance of the presentation, I wasn't looking where I was reaching," Nick said.

Who are you and what did you do with Nick? His wolf growled.

That's called being undercover, Nick said silently. *That line fucking killed it and you know it.*

"Humph," the old couple said in a condescending chorus, then fell silent as the dishes were cleared and more drinks were poured.

Nick breathed in: no poison, no dragonsbane. He looked: no suspicious movements or expressions on anyone, guests or waiters. He nodded to Raluca, then decided to watch what she did before he made any moves himself.

The next course was tomato soup. She picked up the spoon farthest from herself, took a spoonful, then set it down and sipped at her white wine.

That seemed easy enough. Nick took a spoonful of soup. It was ice-cold, not hot. The surprise nearly made him choke, especially since the place was so fancy. Even the worst restaurants might serve soup luke-warm, but not *cold.*

He looked at Raluca, but she was eating hers with a totally straight face. But that was her thing: she'd been trained to be excruciatingly polite. Or was hers all right? No one else was reacting. Maybe it was just his that someone had forgotten to heat up.

He let his hand drift near her bowl. Hers was cold, too. It was both of theirs, then.

In an undertone, Nick said, "Raluca, you don't have to eat it."

"It's quite pleasant." Raluca took another spoonful.

She was obviously going to be polite if it fucking killed her. For the first time, Nick had a sense of how hard it might be to be a princess sometimes. Sure, eating cold soup was nothing compared to the shit that poor people went through, but it was no fun, either. And there was no reason she should put up with it.

"If you don't want to send it back yourself, I'll send it back for you," Nick said. "Waiter!"

A waiter was instantly at his side. "Yes, sir?"

"Our soup needs to be heated up," Nick said quietly. If it had been just his, he wouldn't have made a scene, but no way was he going to sit there and let Raluca eat cold soup.

Raluca kicked his ankle under the table. But it was too late. The waiter and every guest within earshot was staring at him like he was the world's biggest idiot. Nick had no idea what he'd done, but it was obviously, incredibly, disastrously wrong.

"This is gazpacho, *sir*," the waiter said snootily, putting a sarcastic emphasis on the "sir." "It is a classic soup of Spanish origin, and is correctly served ice-cold."

A hot tide of blood rose to Nick's face, half embarrassment and half anger — the latter as much at himself as at all the fucking rich snobs all around him. He'd not only made himself look like an idiot, he'd blown his cover and maybe even endangered Raluca. He had to fix this, fast. But he couldn't think of what to say, other than to mumble, "Sorry. Thought it was something else."

The waiter rolled his eyes and departed.

"Young man, how were you invited to this gala?" the old snob across from him inquired.

Raluca's voice was cold as the soup. "He came with me."

The old snob's snobby old wife tittered, holding a handkerchief to her mouth. Then she put it down and leaned in to speak to Raluca, assuming the intimate yet patronizing tone of an asshole relative. "Katarina, dear, a word of advice from someone who remembers what it was like to be your age. Why, I once dated an *accountant!* We all sow our wild oats. But we leave them where they belong — in the dirt."

Raluca's eyes flashed a dangerous shade of silver. If she didn't cool down soon, they'd start glowing.

Alarmed, Nick nudged her under the table and muttered, "Your eyes. Uh, your mascara's smearing."

To his relief, she understood immediately. Raluca took several deep breaths, visibly calming herself. Her eyes returned to their storm-cloud shade.

Then, staring directly at the snobs, she picked up her glass of red wine and held it high to make sure everyone saw it. There was no mistaking what she was doing, or what she meant by it. Red wine went with the meat course, which had not yet been served. White wine went with soup.

Raluca was standing with Nick, etiquette be damned. Nick's jaw dropped. His amazement was echoed in the shocked expressions of the snobs.

"He *is* where he belongs," Raluca said, her chilly voice pitched to carry all the way across the ballroom. "With me."

She raised the glass of the wrong wine to her lips and took a huge gulp.

Then she spat it out all over the table.

For a delighted instant, Nick thought she was doing the princess equivalent of spitting in their faces. Then he caught the acrid scent of dragonsbane.

"Fuck!" Nick yelled.

He had no idea how he'd missed the poison — he'd smelled that wine when it had been poured, he knew he had, and it had been fine — but how it had been tampered with didn't matter now. All that mattered was that Raluca had just put poison in her mouth.

Nick leaped to his feet, knocking over his chair, and grabbed her shoulder. "Don't swallow!"

Raluca's ivory face had gone white with fear. She nodded.

"And don't speak. It'll send whatever's left of that stuff straight down your throat." Nick reached across the table and snatched up the old snob's untouched red wine glass.

"Hey!" the snob exclaimed.

Nick didn't give a fuck. It was less likely to be poisoned than any of his own glasses. He sniffed it. Nothing.

"Rinse your mouth out." Nick pushed it into Raluca's trembling hand.

She lifted it, then hesitated, looking around the room. Everyone was staring at them, exclaiming and asking questions and starting to stand up. She'd spat once on instinct, but it was obviously much harder for her to do so with everyone watching.

Nick spoke with alpha command. "Ignore those fucking rubberneckers. Swallowing's an instinct. If you run to the bathroom, some of that stuff will go down your throat before you get there. Rinse your mouth. NOW."

Raluca's eyes were wide with shock and fear, like full moons. But she filled her mouth, rinsed the wine around, then spat it out onto her plate.

As shocked exclamations rose up all around them, Nick made sure his voice drowned them out. "Again!"

Raluca rinsed and spat again.

"Okay, hang on. I have —" Nick broke off, then deliberately spoke loud enough for the entire room to hear. "Your medicine, you know, the antidote for that stuff you're allergic to."

Nick reached into his pocket. His fingers closed on empty space where the vial of heartsease had been. Someone had picked his pocket. "Fuck!"

"I have more in my purse." Raluca's voice was clear and calm, but Nick, with his training and experience and wolf senses, caught the pain she was hiding.

"I'll get it," a waiter said. "What's your name?"

"Katarina Petrescu."

The waiter bolted for the purse check area, but Nick had a bad feeling about Raluca's supply. He patted his shoulder holster, then his pants pocket. His gun and wallet were still there. Only the heartsease had been taken.

Nick hadn't seen Lucas until weeks after he'd recovered from being poisoned with dragonsbane, but the hell he'd gone through had been visible in the shadows under his eyes and the stiffness of his posture. That went away eventually, but Lucas still got a thousand-yard stare every time he even heard the word "dragonsbane," the same way Shane did with "black ops." Lucas had underplayed it, of course, but when his mate Journey had said he'd nearly died, she'd only been voicing what everyone could see.

If Raluca hadn't swallowed any of the dragonsbane, she wasn't in danger. She'd even be able to shift if she needed to, if she'd rinsed it all off her skin. But the inside of her mouth would burn like fire until she could take the antidote. If she *had* swallowed some...

A stab of pain went right through Nick's chest as he scanned the room, guarding Raluca in case the poisoner had an alternate plan. The waiter was already bolting back with her purse, or Nick would've already grabbed her and run for it.

Raluca snatched her purse, opened it, and looked in. Her expression of shocked dismay said it all.

"It's okay," Nick said, as much to the onlookers as to her. There was no telling how much the assassin knew already, so he planted a mislead. "I've got extra meds in the car. Then we'll drive to the hospital, just to be sure."

He swept her up into his arms. She was lighter than he'd expected of a woman of her height, an armful of delicate gauze and cold gems and burning, living skin. He could feel her heart pounding against his chest. As he turned to run, he saw her thrust something from her purse into the waiter's hand, but had no time to see what it was.

Nick bolted out the door, holding her as close as possible to shield her with his body in case of snipers, shouting, "Medical emergency! I need the Dodge Viper!"

Someone had apparently already alerted the valets, because his car pulled up just as he got outside. Nick lifted Raluca into the passenger seat, took a final hasty check for assassins, then dove into the driver's seat. As he peeled out of there, Raluca again reached into her purse and threw something out the window, to or at the valet.

"What was that?" Nick gasped. He was going pedal to the metal along the narrow road that twisted down the hill, alternating quick glances at Raluca and the rear-view mirror.

"His tip," Raluca said, as if it was self-evident.

Despite their desperate situation, a startled laugh burst from Nick's lips. "*Now?*"

"I doubt we'll be back," Raluca explained.

"Were you tipping the waiter, too?" Nick asked.

"Yes, of course. He certainly earned it."

"Not if he poisoned you," Nick said grimly.

"Oh, surely not…" Raluca's eyes narrowed, then began to burn silver. "No, you're right. It's possible. Maybe he retrieved my purse just to remove the heartsease."

"Could be." Nick swerved the Viper along a roundabout, then on to a busier street. He darted in and out of traffic, making last-minute turns so fast that his tires smoked and screeched. "How're you doing? Can you tell if you swallowed any of that shit?"

Raluca's hesitation told him all he needed to know. Nick bit his lip until he tasted blood, forcing himself to concentrate on the road. As far as he could tell, they weren't being followed. But there might an ambush waiting for them outside Protection, Inc., if Raluca's enemies had figured out that she'd gone there. It was an easy deduction to make, given that she used to be engaged to Lucas.

"Do you know how much?" Nick asked, once he trusted his voice to stay steady.

"Very little, I think," Raluca replied. "Perhaps one drop, perhaps less."

Nick swerved onto the freeway. "How do you know? Tell me exactly what you're feeling. This isn't the time to be fucking proud."

"I know that, Nick!" Raluca snapped. "And I still don't like that word."

Her annoyance reassured him more than anything else would have. Nick happened to know from personal experience that if you're actually dying, you don't have the energy to sweat the small stuff.

"Sorry," he said. "It's just that Lucas would be too proud to say if he was feeling weak or about to pass out. And I need to know."

"My tongue and the inside of my mouth and my throat burn like they're on fire," Raluca said. "But the pain fades as it goes further down, and stops at the top of my sternum. I don't feel ill or weak. I think the dragonsbane in the wine coated my mouth and throat, and didn't go any farther. I don't think I've been poisoned, like Lucas was. If it didn't reach my stomach, it shouldn't be absorbed by my body."

As she spoke, Nick veered from lane to lane, then swung on to another freeway. But while his focus was on his job, his heart lifted with relief that Raluca would be all right. She sounded so sure, she convinced him, too. And he couldn't help being impressed with her precise reporting of injuries that obviously hurt like fuck. They were to her mouth and throat, too. What must it cost her in additional pain and difficulty to articulate so clearly?

"You're brave," Nick said, wishing *he* was more articulate.

"Oh…" Raluca sounded startled. "Thank you."

"Just calling it like I see it. It hurts to talk, right? So don't say anything unless you have to."

She said no more, so he knew he was right. Nick got out his cell phone, called Hal, and gave a quick report. At the end, he said, "Can I get some back-up, in case someone's waiting for me outside headquarters?"

"Yeah," Hal said. "It's already dispatched. You'll have a greeting committee waiting for you, don't worry."

Nick had guessed as much; he'd heard scribbling in the background, and figured that Hal, who never used a computer when a pen would do, was passing notes to someone.

"I'll be there in ten." Nick hung up. "Raluca, push your seat back as far as it goes."

When she did, he said, "Slide down and curl up on the floor. I'm going to drop something on top of you, okay? It's our bulletproof vests. Don't bother trying to get into one, just drape them over you."

He reached around without looking, into the back seat and under the blanket he'd dumped over them for cover, snagged the vests, and laid them on top of her.

"What about you?" Raluca asked.

Nick shrugged. "I can duck."

"Unacceptable."

"What?"

Raluca rose from the floor, a vest in her hands.

"Keep your eyes on the road," she ordered, then undid his seatbelt.

"What?" Nick protested. "Forget about me. Get back down!"

"The more you argue, the longer I will be up here," Raluca said coolly. "Also, it hurts to speak. Please stop making me."

"Fuck, you're stubborn," Nick muttered. He hastily added, "You don't need to say you don't like that word. I KNOW. Just do it fast."

With no alternative, Nick cooperated as Raluca strapped on his vest, lifting first one arm and then the other from the steering wheel so she could get his arms in while he drove one-handed. His heart thudded against his chest. If someone fired on them now, the bullet would go through her and only bruise him. That was the opposite of how it was supposed to be.

Protect your mate above yourself, his wolf howled.

"Get the fuck on with it," Nick demanded. "If that vest isn't on in five more seconds, leave it and get back down."

Raluca shot him an icy stare. "I go nowhere until the straps are correct."

To his immense relief, she jerked the last strap into place, then dropped back to the floor and curled up silently with the other vest draped over her, exactly as he'd ordered.

Nick's nerves sang with adrenaline as he approached the looming tower of Protection, Inc., but there was no ambush. He got into the underground parking lot as easily as if it was a regular day at work.

He parked, opened the door for Raluca, and lifted her out.

Shane materialized from the shadows. Raluca jumped. So did Nick.

Unsmiling, Shane caught Nick's shoulder to steady him. "I have the antidote."

Shane opened a vial of heartsease and handed it to Raluca. She snatched and emptied it in a single gulp.

Almost immediately, her taut muscles relaxed against his, and she heaved a sigh of relief. "Oh, that's better."

Nick too relaxed. He hadn't even realized it, but he'd been so tense with the knowledge of her pain that his whole body ached. His jaw hurt like he'd been clenching it nearly hard enough to break his teeth.

"You can put me down now," Raluca said. "I'm fine."

Nick didn't want to let go of her, but she *had* taken the antidote. And they *were* safe now. Reluctantly, he set her down on her feet.

She gave Shane a graceful nod. "Thank you for the heartsease. And I am pleased to meet you."

"Pleased to meet you, too." Shane's tone was polite, but his ice-blue gaze swept over her without warmth. He had a way of seeming to see right through people that was unsettling even when he wasn't using his power. Raluca drew back slightly.

"Lay the fuck off, Shane," Nick snapped. "She's had a rough night."

Shane turned that same chilly stare on Nick. "I didn't do anything."

"Well — don't," Nick said. But Shane's cold blue gaze made him feel the idiocy of his words. Nick shut the fuck up.

His head felt like someone was driving a pickaxe into it with every beat of his heart. He hadn't fought, but he felt like he had. Probably he'd feel better if he had. Now that he was back and Raluca was fine, or at least not poisoned and in pain, all he could think of was that he'd failed to protect her, failed to find out who was after her, failed to figure out how she'd been poisoned, even failed to notice that someone had picked his pocket.

He wasn't looking forward to making a more detailed report to Hal. But getting deservedly chewed out by his boss was the least of his problems.

I let my mate get hurt. I didn't protect her.

"I fucked up," Nick said to Shane. "I have to… Wait, is anyone else here?"

"Catalina and Ellie and Hal," Shane said.

Shane's voice softened as he said Catalina's name, so subtly that he probably wasn't even aware of it. She was Shane's mate, Ellie's best friend, and would be Nick's teammate once her training was finished and her probationary period was over.

Nick had liked Catalina right away. Like him, she'd grown up poor and had to fight for everything she'd ever gotten. But his chest hurt again when Shane mentioned her. Even that hard man had found his mate. His love for her rang out like a bell whenever he so much as spoke her name, and glowed like a fire between them when they were together. Ellie and Hal were the same way with each other, as were Journey and Lucas.

Only Nick had managed to piss off his mate until she wanted nothing to do with him. "Fuck-up" didn't even begin to cover that. Someone would need to invent a whole new word.

Shane went on, "Ellie's inside, in case Raluca needed medical assistance. Hal and Catalina are outside, so they could ambush the ambush. But they saw you come in safe, so they'll meet you in the office."

Nick tried to pull his thoughts together. "Ellie or Catalina or you should check Raluca while I report to Hal. Just in case." To Raluca, he explained, "They're paramedics. Shane too. I mean, obviously that's not his job, but he's had the training. I'm sure you're fine, but Hal will order it even if I don't, so you might as well get it over with. It'll be quick. And they're nice. No swearing or glaring, I promise."

To Nick's relief, Raluca didn't object. Instead, she said, "Yes, I agree that I should have a medical examination. Just to be sure."

Nick ditched his bulletproof vest in the car, remembering again how she'd risen from the floor to strap it over his chest. She'd risked her life for him, and she didn't even like him. Maybe it was out of shifters' honor. But Nick could still feel the hot touch of her fingers from the few times she'd brushed against him, skin to skin.

As they headed for the elevators, Nick said to Shane, "Raluca needs a place to stay tonight. We can figure out tomorrow if the hotel is still safe, but I don't think we should risk it. I think one of the spare rooms here would be best. Maybe Ellie and Catalina could help her get set up for the night? All her stuff is at the hotel."

Shane gave a brief nod. "Sounds good."

Nick turned to Raluca. "You're completely safe here. This is the most secure building in Santa Martina. And we have rooms with beds, for this sort of thing or in case one of us needs to spend the night. They're kind of basic, but…"

"That is perfectly acceptable," Raluca said as they stepped into the elevator. "I agree, it would be unwise to return to the hotel."

She was being so cooperative that it made him suspicious. Steeling himself for an explosion, he said, "Okay, I'm going to report to Hal. I think it'll take… uh, maybe an hour? We have a lot to go over. Can you stay awake that long? I want to talk to you before you go to bed."

Raluca showed no signs of exploding. "Certainly. I will await your knock."

"Great," Nick said unenthusiastically.

The elevator doors hissed open. Shane stepped out and gestured to Raluca to accompany him. She went with him without a backward glance.

Nick briefly closed his eyes. He wasn't looking forward to reporting the details of his fuckuppery. But he was looking forward to his conversation with Raluca even less.

Alpha wolves don't whine, he told himself. *You ran the gauntlet. This is just talking.*

He hadn't meant to speak to his wolf, but his wolf replied. *If our mate says what you think she's going to say, the gauntlet would be better.*

Stop making it worse, Nick silently replied.

Protection, Inc. wasn't very formal, which was exactly why Nick could stand to work there. More often than not, reports were made over lunch or coffee, or by calling Hal to give him a quick update. But Nick found Hal in his office, sitting behind his desk with his arms folded across his broad chest, radiating *you really fucked up big-time.*

Nick wanted to get the whole thing as over with as fast as he could. But Hal was good with details. Sometimes he could crack a case from a detail that the person who mentioned it hadn't registered as relevant. So Nick told him everything that had happened since they'd last checked in, including the visits to the clothes shops and the "World's Biggest" excursions, in case Raluca had been spotted at one of those.

He left out nothing but the sex thing, the mate thing, and the breaking of his heart thing. But Hal wouldn't notice that he wasn't reporting on the state of his feelings. Nick didn't have feelings about clients beyond "He was cool" or "She was okay except for being a Mets fan."

Hal only interrupted once, to say, "You took the princess to *Big Bacon?* We're supposed to protect our clients from getting killed, not finish the job."

Nick's face burned. "It's not *that* bad."

He plunged back into his account before Hal could bring up however fucking many cases of food poisoning or chemical overdose Big Bacon was probably responsible for. Nick had told the truth when he'd claimed it was a landmark: a landmark of tackiness and horrible food, mysteriously staying in business even though nobody ever visited it more than once. Except for Nick, who had now gone twice.

When he finally stumbled to the end of his report, Hal gave him a look that made him feel like a teenager hauled to the principal's office. "Let me get this straight. You and your client haven't been getting along, you aggravated this by deliberately annoying her, she was poisoned under your guard, and you got your pocket picked without even noticing."

"That's what I fucking said, wasn't it?" Nick snapped.

Hal banged his fist on the desk, making his papers jump. "Why?"

The aggressive gesture roused Nick's alpha dominance. He slammed his own palms down on the desk. "Because I fucked up, okay? Raluca… I don't know, something about her got to me. Distracted me. It won't happen again."

"How do you know?" It was a real question, not a rhetorical one. Hal leaned forward, his brow creased with both annoyance and concern. "I'm serious, Nick. I think I know how the poison got in her wine. There were waiters going back and forth, refreshing everyone's glasses. One of them probably waited till you'd smelled her glass, then dropped the poison in just as you took a bite or drink of something with a strong enough odor to drown out the scent. But —"

"I know, that has to be it, but I was fucking watching for that! Whoever did that was one fast motherfucker. Fuck!" Nick's hands clenched.

"Watch it!"

Nick relaxed his grip just in time, before he cracked Hal's handmade desk. He'd already destroyed one of Hal's precious desks. Hal would kill him if he trashed another.

Hal went on, "Honestly, Nick, it sounds like that assassin was good enough to slip the poison past any of us. Except for Shane, maybe, and that's only if he went unseen instead of pretending to be a guest. But for you to be so distracted that you didn't notice someone picking your pocket…"

"I know," Nick replied. "Far as I know, there's only one guy good enough to do that when I'm not distracted, and it wasn't him. He'd be pretty fucking hard for me to miss."

Hal nodded. "Yeah, you'd have spotted him. And he has no history with Raluca, and the attempt was on her, not you. Still…" Hal's hazel gaze drifted into the distance, then refocused sharply. "It's an interesting thought. I'll look into it. See if I can track him down."

"Don't bother. It wasn't him. He's out of our lives and he can fucking stay there."

Hal made a noncommittal shrug, then gave Nick his *I'm the boss* look. "You didn't answer my question. How can you — and I — be sure that you won't be distracted from keeping Raluca safe again?"

Nick almost choked on his next words, but he had to say it. He had no other choice. "Because…"

***

While Nick was in Hal's office, he'd distantly registered the sounds of elevators, footsteps, and voices outside. He didn't hear Shane's footsteps, but no one ever did. But Catalina, who was capable of moving just as quietly, didn't bother. Her laugh echoed as she left, presumably with Shane.

When Nick finally left the office, feeling like *he'd* swallowed poison, Ellie rose from the chair she'd been curled up in, leaving a paperback book on the arm and a medical kit on the floor. "Are you done?"

"Yeah. How's Raluca?"

"She's fine," Ellie assured him. "She noticed the poison right away, you did absolutely the right things to keep it from getting into her system, and Shane got her the antidote within half an hour. Absolutely no harm done."

"Is she alone?" Nick asked.

Ellie gave him a sharp glance with her blue-green eyes, catching something in his tone. "Yes, in one of the spare bedrooms. We offered to have someone wait with her till you came back, so she'd feel secure, but she said it wasn't necessary. And you'll be here all night to guard her, of course."

"Of course," Nick said after a pause. Well, he would. And he couldn't face the thought of having that conversation with Hal, Raluca, *and* Ellie. Nick would tell Raluca, and Hal would tell everyone else. It was no skin off Hal's back. "You can take Hal home now."

Ellie scooped up her book and kit. Nick turned away from her happiness, glowing as bright now as when Hal had first brought her to Protection, Inc., as she went into the office to meet her mate.

He went downstairs, hearing the distant sounds of Hal and Ellie leaving. By the time he reached the spare rooms, he knew that he and Raluca were alone in the building.

There were two rooms. One door open and no lights on, one door closed with light shining through the crack at the bottom.

Nick drew in a deep breath, straightened his spine, and squared his shoulders. He might have fucked up like no shifter had in the history of ever, but at least he'd stand up and take it like a wolf. Hal was Protection, Inc.'s alpha, but Nick had been an alpha once and he still was one at heart. And that meant protecting your pack. Sacrificing your own needs for your pack. Bleeding for your pack. Dying for your pack. Protection, Inc. was his pack now. And since Raluca was a client, all the duties of an alpha to his pack also applied to her.

Breaking your heart for your pack.

Nick knocked on the door. "It's Nick."

"Come in," Raluca called.

Nick walked into the room, then closed the door behind him. He'd slept in that cramped room quite a few times himself, so he knew it well: the normal-sized bed (the other room had one big enough for Hal), the little chair (because a bigger one wouldn't fit), the bedside table and lamp, the hardwood floor.

When he'd first come to Protection, Inc., those rooms had been bare; the company had only recently moved in, and Hal hadn't decided what to do with the tiny rooms yet. Nick had been one of the reasons they'd ended up putting beds in them.

He knew that room like he knew his gun. But it was surreal to see Raluca sitting on the bed, still in her jeweled mermaid gown. It made the entire room look new and strange. Almost… magical.

A folded pair of pajamas and another set of Fiona's black fatigues lay on one chair, so it wasn't like she had nothing else to wear. She still had all her jewelry on. Her hoard pack lay beside her on the bed. One of her hands rested atop it. All she'd taken off was her silk gloves, probably so Ellie could check her pulse, and her silver stiletto heels. Raluca's hands looked bare with neither gloves nor rings.

Nick had meant to get straight to the point. But the words caught in his throat as he looked at her slim fingers, remembering how she'd eaten half a Big Bacon in one bite and without a flinch because he'd dared her to, how she'd remembered to tip even after she'd been poisoned, and how she'd risked getting shot to strap a bulletproof vest on him.

"Is this how a princess dresses every day?" Nick asked. His voice cracked. He hoped she didn't notice.

If she did, she gave no sign. "This is how a princess dresses for a ball. Except that if I was still a princess, I would wear my crown."

"What happened to it?" Nick asked.

Raluca tilted her head, her eyes going distant with memory. "It is in my hoard pack. I shall not wear it again... Or so I thought."

Nick had been under the impression that she'd given up her title for good. "Are you thinking of going back to being a princess?"

Her rainy-day gaze met his squarely, making him realize how rarely she looked him right in the eyes. Usually she snuck peeks when she thought he wasn't paying attention. "Yes. I am."

He heard the absolute, unadorned honesty in her voice. He was about to ask her why when his wolf snarled a warning. Nick closed his mouth. He knew why. It was because of him. He'd given her the worst possible impression of America and Americans, just because she'd stung his pride, and now it looked like the World's Biggest Ball of Twine was going to have the World's Worst Consequences.

"I think..." Nick tried to choose his words carefully, for once. Sure, he'd offended her on purpose, but he'd also done it by accident. If he pissed her off one more time, she might bolt straight back to Viorel, and probably be assassinated within the week. "I think you should wait till Lucas comes back, and talk to him first. And..."

He almost choked on his next words, but he had to say them. He'd failed her even more than he'd realized when he'd spoken to Hal. It was unfair to her to stick her with a bodyguard she couldn't stand but was too polite to fire. And if she hated him so much that she'd rather rush into danger alone and unguarded than have him around, then he *had* to offer her an alternative.

"I'm sure Lucas will want to protect you himself," Nick said. "But until he gets back, you can have a different bodyguard. I already talked to Hal about it. He'll let you pick, but if you're not sure who you want, I recommend Destiny. She's funny, but she's sensitive, too. She wouldn't piss you off. And she doesn't swear. Or Rafa — he knows all about high society, like you saw, and he's very professional once he's on the job. He wouldn't flirt or tease if you were his client. Or Shane. I know he seems a little scary, but he's a really good guy, he's fantastic at his job, and he has total self-control. You tell him once not to swear, and he'll never swear again."

This is madness! Nick's wolf growled. *I told you once, and I am telling you again, you must not —*

"Why…" Raluca began.

Nick plunged on, desperate to get it over with. "You don't want me. You don't want me so much that you're about to risk your life just to get away from me. Raluca, you don't need to do that. I'm not your fiancé. I'm not even your boyfriend. I'm just a guy you hired for a job. So fire me. Or if you'd rather, I'll resign. And once I'm gone, I'll stay out of your way. I'll stay out of your *sight*. Just say the word, and you'll never have to see me again."

Do not do this! Nick's wolf snarled. *Only you may protect your mate!*

Raluca's lips parted in surprised hurt. "Do you wish me to have another protector?"

"Fuck, no!" Nick blurted out. "But if you'd rather run back to a fucking nest of assassins than have me protecting you, then yeah, you should have someone else."

"That is not…" Raluca began, her gaze sliding away. Then she straightened her spine, just as he had before walking in, and once again met his eyes. "Why do you dislike me so?"

"I don't —" Nick began.

But Raluca spoke over him, her chiming voice drowning his out. "Is it my title? My wealth? My personality? Is it something I said or did? Is it *everything* I have said and done? Why were you offended enough to take vengeance when I asked you to show me the real America? The guidebooks say that is both polite and pleasing. Are they wrong? Why —"

"Whoa, whoa!" Nick held up his hand, overwhelmed by Raluca's unexpected flood of questions. He'd thought she'd tell him who she wanted to take his place, then kick him out the door. "First of all, I don't dislike —"

"Liar," Raluca said coolly. "Look me in the eyes and tell me you did not take me to the world's biggest hairball specifically to annoy me."

"I —"

She is your mate, snarled his wolf. *You cannot lie to your mate!*

Nick's head ached. His wolf's voice had reverberated through his bones. His whole body ached. He was so exhausted, he couldn't seem to think.

If he was going to sit, it should be in the teeny chair, but the
way things were going, it would probably collapse under his weight.
So he sank down on the bed, as far from Raluca as possible. The
pressed cloth of his suit crunched, reminding him that he hadn't
changed either. He felt like an imposter, completely out of his depth.
His wolf and his supposed mate were both furious with him. His
impulse was to swear, to deny, maybe to brush it off with a joke...

...but that was exactly what had gotten him into this fucking
mess to begin with.

Nick looked within himself, and tried to put his feelings into
words. Words that did not include "fuck," "fucking," "fucked,"
"fucker," or anything else in the swearing dictionary.

"I was mad at you," he said carefully. "But that doesn't mean
I dislike you. You can ask anyone here. Everyone single one of them
has pissed — has made me angry. And I've been a dick — I mean a,
um, an annoying person — to all of them. God knows why they put
up with me."

Raluca was listening intently, her eyes molten silver. Her
dragon was very close to the surface. She was feeling something
deeply, but he couldn't tell what it was.

Nick went on, "Where I come from, guys aren't supposed to
show their feelings. That's weak. It's not manly. And it could get
you killed. Well, some are okay. You can be angry and proud and
happy and... uh... oh, yeah, you can be bored. And drunk. Is drunk a
feeling?"

Raluca's lips quivered as if she was trying not to laugh. "It is
a *feeling*. I would not call it an *emotion*."

"Then you get the picture. So I want you to know how hard it
is for me to say that even though my teammates and I have pissed
each other off about a million fucking times, we still..." He forced
himself to spit it out. "We still love each other." Hastily, he added,
"Like brothers and sisters. Or best friends. That sort of love. You
know, uh..."

Raluca actually smiled. "I understand, Nick. You are not
confessing a secret love affair with Rafa."

"No, but I love him like a brother and I trust him with my
life. So I hope you heard me yelling at him the day I met you. Uh,
and over the phone. And earlier tonight. It doesn't mean I hate him.
And me being a fucking asshole to you with the rap and lobster and

stuff, that doesn't mean I hate you. It means *I* have a problem. Me. Not you. And I'm so sorry I took it out on you. If there's anything I can do to make it right, tell me and I'll do it."

"You have apologized," Raluca said. "I accept it. That is all I require in terms of amends."

Nick had hoped she'd accept his apology, but she'd spoken so formally, he wasn't sure if she really forgave him or if she just felt obliged, or if she'd even believed he was sincere.

He tried again. "I'm serious. Destiny says I should take anger management classes, Rafa says I should get the chip on my shoulder surgically removed, Hal says I should take three deep breaths before I open my mouth, Shane doesn't say anything but he *looks* at me like — point is, everyone who knows me thinks I need to chill the fuck out. And it fucking kills me to admit it, but they're right. The chip removal surgery starts now."

"Truly?" Raluca asked.

"Truly," Nick repeated, hoping she'd believe him if he used her words. God knew she didn't like his. He had no idea if it had worked. But since he'd gotten on the honesty kick, he went on, "Remember the world's biggest hairball?"

"It was unforgettable," she replied drily.

"Well, tonight was the world's biggest wake-up call. I didn't protect you, I broke my cover every time I opened my mouth or touched anything —"

Nick broke off. She knew all that. Gloomily, he finished, "And I look like a fucking idiot in this suit."

Chapter Five

Raluca

Nick fell silent, staring down at the floor. He still wore the white kid gloves of a gentleman over the hands of a warrior. Nick was no dragon, but his posture was that of a hero from some tragic tale who sacrificed all that he loved for honor's sake.

Had he sacrificed something that he loved?

Ellie and Catalina had asked Raluca if she'd felt dizzy, lightheaded, or unsteady. She'd told them she did not. But now she did. And she didn't think it was the dragonsbane. Could she truly have misunderstood Nick so badly, or was she misunderstanding him now? And could he have misunderstood her just as drastically?

She opened her mouth to ask, but instead blurted out the most absurd reply possible, to the one trivial thing he'd mentioned amongst all the important ones. "You look great in the suit."

Nick raised his head, his emerald eyes bewildered. "I do?"

Since she'd already said it, she might as well commit herself. After all, he'd been honest with her. "Yes. You look like James Bond."

Nick's expression of doomed determination dissolved into a grin. It wasn't particularly Bond-like, boyish rather than suave, but it made him look a lot more like himself. "Which one?"

Raluca had been thinking of the archetype of the elegant and deadly spy rather than a specific actor. She ran them through her mind's eye, considering each in turn, then said, "Timothy Dalton."

"Not Daniel Craig?"

"Daniel Craig has yellow hair and blue eyes," Raluca pointed out. "And very large ears. You have black hair and green eyes. And your ears are… proportional."

"Proportional ears," Nick said doubtfully. "That's not exactly number one on the 'What Women Find Hot' list. Destiny says Daniel Craig is the sexiest Bond." Then he seemed to reconsider her words. "But Destiny has a thing about blonds. Who's *your* favorite Bond?"

"Is this a trick question?" Raluca inquired. "Since I have already said which one you most resemble…"

"Nope. If I'd meant 'Who do you think is sexiest?' I'd have said so. I meant, which one do you like best as a character?"

"Oh. In that case, Sean Connery is my favorite." Raluca wondered if she'd revealed her naiveté again. Probably Sean Connery was too old-fashioned, even apart from his lack of resemblance to Nick.

"Mine too," Nick said, far too promptly for it to be anything but the truth. "First and best."

"You do not prefer the most modern version?"

Nick shook his head. "Sean Connery is the fucking definition of timelessly cool."

Silence fell. The air between them seemed charged with electricity, as if before a storm. Raluca no longer wanted to embarrass Nick or make him uncomfortable. She wanted to keep talking with him about which Bond was the best and why, even if it meant hearing a million more f-words. She wanted to dance with him in a place where they were both comfortable, if such a thing even existed.

She wanted to strip off his elegant clothes and adorn his bare body in silver. She'd still never seen him naked. She'd never even seen him with his shirt off. How far *did* his tattoos go?

He'd never seen her nude, either. She wondered if he wanted to.

When she looked up at him, she knew that he did. His brilliant green gaze was fixed on her, hot and hungry. Whatever she'd said or done to anger him, he seemed to have forgotten or forgiven it.

"God, you're gorgeous." His voice was husky; he swallowed. "Can I say 'God?' I'm reminding myself every fu — every second not to say that other word."

"It does not bother me." Raluca's reply echoed strangely in her own ears. It was her own voice, but it sounded so unnatural. False, even though her words were true. "And thank you. For the compliment — for the attempt to not say that word — for protecting me — for everything."

He shook his head, the shadow of that bone-deep hurt falling over him. "I didn't protect you."

"Here I sit beside you, alive and breathing," Raluca pointed out. "You protected me in the only way that matters. Nick, you are too hard on yourself."

"But —" Nick began.

"Hush." Raluca laid a finger across his mouth.

He cut off his words with a sharp inhale that she felt as well as heard. His lips were so soft to the touch. So cool, compared to her own heat. Like a perfect spring morning. He sat absolutely still, his emerald eyes growing brighter and brighter. She didn't have werewolf hearing, but she was sure his heart was pounding as hard and fast as hers.

Raluca felt as if she'd drunk several cocktails in quick succession. It was all she could do to keep from closing his mouth with kisses, from tearing off his clothes, from finally touching every part of his body with her own. And she knew he felt the same way. She could *feel* it, like a mist hanging in the air between them.

Surely a brief but sincere apology, an even briefer conversation about James Bond, a stumbling but honest explanation of his behavior, and an attempt on her life in which he failed or succeeded in protecting her, depending on one's point of view, should not have changed her feelings so much. Was she so fickle?

But it wasn't his words, or even his actions. It was the look in his eyes, the emotion beneath his voice, the way he'd visibly struggled to confess that he loved his teammates but had done it anyway, so he could make a point that she otherwise wouldn't have understood.

They'd somehow found a delicate balance, as if they were dancing and he held her in a dip. It would probably vanish in the next minute, when one of them said the wrong thing and the other lost their temper. But it was here now. And Raluca wanted to make it last as long as she could.

She dropped her hand to the bed between them. Nick grabbed it, his knuckles paling from the force of his grip.

"I'm scared to talk." His voice dropped, rough with desire and raw with honesty. "Everything I've said has come out wrong. But I can't just — I have to ask —"

Raluca tightened her hand around his. Their fingers locked together, their shifter strength creating a hold that no power on earth could break.

"Are you asking if I want you?" Raluca said.

"Yeah." Then his eyes blazed with wolfish intensity, brighter and brighter until she imagined them burning a brand right into her soul. "But if you say yes, you gotta take me as I am. I don't mean my temper. If I'm being an asshole, feel free to call me on it. Everyone else does. But I can't watch my mouth every time I open it. I'm not Prince Charming. I'm a fucking wolf from the streets. If you want me, you gotta want *me*."

When Raluca had taken her first leap off the balcony, she hadn't known if she'd be able to transform in time, or if the fall would kill her. But she hadn't cared. As she'd thrown herself into the air, her heart had lifted with the pure joy of freedom, of the chance to be something other than a princess cut to shape like a paper doll. To be Raluca, a woman and dragon questing for her true self, whatever that might be.

She had that same sense of freedom as she replied, "I want *you*, Nick. As you are, and everything that comes with you. Words included."

Nick swallowed. Raluca realized that he hadn't expected her to agree. She could hear him breathing, hard and fast, as if he too felt like he was in free-fall.

"Then take me," Nick said.

Inside Raluca, her dragon took flight.

"I had a fantasy…" she began.

Nick sucked in another harsh breath. "About me?"

Raluca had never told anyone about any of her sexual fantasies, not even the few men she'd had rather unsatisfying sex with. It hadn't even occurred to her to do so. But she could see the pulse beating at Nick's throat and see the bulge growing within his pressed pants, and knew that her words alone were driving him wild.

If he can be wild, you can be wild, hissed her dragon.

"I knew you would not be able to show tattoos at a ball," Raluca said. "So I imagined you in gloves. And I imagined pulling them off. With my teeth."

Wordlessly, Nick offered her his hand. Raluca delicately took the edge of kidskin between her teeth and pulled. The glove began to roll off, exposing his pale skin and the curling green of the vine. Her upper lip slid along his skin in a long, slow kiss, moving along the smooth back of his hand to his big knuckles, feeling the tiny raised scars scattered across them. He must have cut his knuckles over and over to make his shifter flesh accept those marks as part of his body.

Her lip slid over the hard slickness of his nails, and the glove came off. Raluca let it fall on the bed between them, then took his hand in hers and traced the vine, sliding her finger around his and then over the back of his hand, until she was stopped by his starched cuffs.

"How far does it go?" she asked.

"Take off my clothes and see," Nick replied, with a wolfish grin. "And by the way, that was about the fucking sexiest thing I've ever had anyone do to me, but I don't know if I can sit still long enough for you to do it all that slow."

"I don't know if I can, either," Raluca confessed. She was trembling with desire, her voice catching, her nipples hardening against the silk cups that contained them.

Nick peeled off his other glove and tossed it to the floor, then indicated the dragonmarks on her shoulder. "How far do *these* go?"

"Take off my gown and see," Raluca said immediately.

She stood up, turning to put the zipper tab within his reach.

"I remember that." Nick caught it and pulled. As he did, Raluca reached up stealthily and rolled off her damp panties. They came off as the gown slid down her body, falling into a heap of silk and gauze and jewels at her feet.

Raluca, once again clad in nothing but the black sheath undergown, indicated the silver zipper. "If you pull that, you'll get to see something you don't remember."

Nick took the tiny tab between his finger and thumb. His hands captivated her with their strength and startling dexterity. They were big and rough and looked like they should be clumsy, but their touch told her that he could juggle eggshells.

He undid the zipper in one quick tug. The dress fell at her feet, leaving her completely nude before him, clad only in her jewelry. She stood straight and still in the warm air, letting his hungry gaze roam over her naked body.

Raluca felt bare in more ways than one. He could see her chest move as her breathing quickened, see her nipples hardening and eyes burning silver, no doubt smell her arousal. With other men, she'd been reluctant to expose herself so completely, and had turned out the lights before undressing. But Nick had seen her spit wine all over a table, and he *still* wanted her. The only way she could change that was if she chose to push him away.

"Your dragonmarks," Nick said. His voice too caught; he too was breathing fast and hard, as he had when he'd swept her into his arms. "They *do* go around your breast. I kept wondering if they did."

"You can touch them, if you like."

Nick put a finger on the beginning of the dragonmark, at her shoulder. The intensity of the sensation made her gasp.

He froze. "Does it hurt? Or is it just sensitive?"

"Just sensitive," Raluca managed. "In a good way."

Nick grinned. "Gotcha."

He ran his finger down her dragonmark, following it as it swirled over her shoulder. Her entire body felt drawn into the path of his caress, so intimate and unexpectedly gentle. The pads of his fingers were smooth, and his touch moved easily from strong to feather-light.

Then he stepped up close, moved his hands to her waist, and began to trace the dragonmark with his mouth, kissing and licking his way from her shoulder to her chest to her breast. Raluca stood trembling as he worked his way around her breast, following the line of glittering silver as it spiraled around her breast and nipple. Electric shocks of pleasure went through her whole body, not just her breast.

It was just as it had been in the dressing room. Small touches from Nick were more powerful than the entirety of every sexual act she'd had before.

She bent down and kissed what she could reach of him, which was the tousled black hair on top of his head. She didn't have werewolf senses, but she enjoyed the scent of his hair. Like the rest of him, it smelled like leather and steel with an underlying warmth, masculine and enticing.

He tipped his head back, offering her his lips, and she kissed him there before he bent his head again. But Nick didn't stop at her breasts. He slid downward, kissing and nibbling past her dragonmarks, to her belly. Then he was down on his knees before her, still fully dressed. He glanced up at her, and she saw the same intensity of purpose blazing in his eyes that he'd had when he'd drunk the cocktail she'd offered him.

Then he bent to lick between her legs. Raluca jumped at the shock of pleasure. No man had ever done *that* before.

"Just sensitive?" Nick murmured.

He spoke from where he was, sending his warm breath over her wet folds. She jumped again, then grabbed on to his shoulders for support.

"Yes," Raluca managed. "Don't stop."

He didn't. His tongue flicked over her swollen bud, then moved to caress every tender inch of her. Raluca's control dissolved under his lips, leaving her shaking and crying out aloud. His strong hands held her safe and tight, and she clutched his shoulders with an abandon that she'd have never been able to do with a human man. But Nick didn't flinch. If anything, he seemed to enjoy the strength of her grip.

Raluca let herself be carried away on the tides of ecstasy until they peaked in a climax more intense than she'd ever be able to give herself. She drifted on its currents, warm and content, then came back to herself as Nick lifted her off her feet and laid her down on the bed.

She looked up at him and was startled into laughter. He was still in his suit, though it was crumpled and the handkerchief and carnation had come off.

"What?" he asked.

"You do look great in the suit," Raluca said, her words breaking up in fits of giggles. "But you don't have to keep wearing it!"

Even as she spoke, she worried that he'd take it the wrong way. But Nick laughed too, easily and without defensiveness, his eyes sparkling and his body taut with nothing more than arousal. "Take it off, then. I'm not sure I even know how."

Raluca rose, pulled him down to the bed so they were both sitting on it, and began to strip him. *She* knew her way around a white tie suit, if only from watching her cousins learn to put on theirs. Nick looked startled when she began with his feet, and she knew he hadn't expected a princess to touch his shoes.

"You knelt for me," she pointed out.

"Well, I wanted to do that," Nick replied. "And you liked it."

"I want to do this." Raluca slipped off his socks, discarding them beside the bed. She hadn't expected to be captivated by his bare feet, but she was. She'd never seen them before, and they were so nicely proportioned and strong-looking. She caressed them, and was rewarded with another surprised but pleased inhale. "And you like it too."

"A princess giving me a foot rub…" Nick cut himself off. "No. You're not a princess now. You're just Raluca, right?"

She nodded. Now that they'd found their balance, they understood each other so easily. "Just Raluca."

Rather than work her way up, she left his feet bare and started again from the top. It always looked so awkward when men took off their pants before their shirt. Besides, there were no tattoos on Nick's feet or ankles, and she was curious about those. She stripped him of his mother-of-pearl cufflinks and pearl studs (placing them respectfully by her own hoard pack), then bow tie, tailcoat, and waistcoat, as he sat laughing.

"There's just so much of it," Nick said at last.

"Not for long." Raluca unbuttoned his shirt, sliding a finger down his chest as she did so.

He sobered then, his thick black eyelashes fluttering as he briefly closed his eyes. His muscles tensed and he shivered once as she pulled off his shirt. She couldn't tell if it was from nerves or desire.

"Nick…" she began. Then she stopped, staring in fascination at his tattoos.

They *did* cover his entire chest. It was a single work of art, showing a pack of wolves hunting deer in a forest, all done in the same meticulous, exquisitely shaded and detailed style that she'd seen on his arms and hand.

The wolves had different colors of fur, some gray, some white, some black. But they clearly hunted as a unified pack, their eyes of yellow or green or blue fierce and intent. A herd of deer fled before them, and four deer lay dead on the fallen leaves, moss, and rich earth. Some of the wolves had either been injured in the hunt or spattered with blood from the deer; the scarlet drops on their fur stood out with stunning clarity. The gray wolf who led them all stood with his paws atop a fallen deer, his fangs showing white and his green eyes ablaze.

Raluca touched the lead wolf. The muscles on Nick's chest jumped, making the wolf seem to move.

"That's you, isn't it?" Raluca asked.

"Yeah." Nick swallowed, his breath coming faster. She could see the vein pulse at the fine skin along his throat, and feel his heart pounding. "It all has a meaning, it's not there to just look good. But don't ask me what it means just yet. I'll tell you after, okay? Not now."

She nodded. "It *is* beautiful, though. Whatever the meaning. And so are you."

He didn't laugh, though she belatedly recalled that in America, one didn't use that word to describe men. But he was. His shoulders and chest were much more muscular than she'd realized, but more wiry than burly. He wasn't as lean as a dragon, but he looked as agile and quick as she'd already seen him to be.

Raluca stroked his chest, then stopped as her fingers encountered something rough and pitted. It was invisible to the eye, hidden in the trunk and branches of a gnarled oak, but she could feel it. Scar tissue.

Nick flinched, and Raluca jerked her fingers away. But she couldn't pretend that she hadn't felt it. Shifters normally didn't scar at all. It would take either repeated injuries to the same place, or one bad enough to nearly kill…

"Later?" Raluca asked.

"Yeah. Should've warned you, sorry. One day I'll have a HANDS OFF sign tattooed on that oak." Nick took a deep breath, then managed a smile. "That's it for the landmines. Anywhere else is fine."

Even without knowing the story, Raluca felt a sympathetic twinge of her heart for him, both for the original wound and for the pain it obviously still caused him. But he didn't wish to speak of it now, and she trusted him to tell her later.

She continued her exploration of his body. He had little hair on his chest, and the black scattering he did have blended into the tree branches. Like his scars, the line of hair that ran straight down through his navel was invisible against a dark tree-trunk. Raluca only discovered it by touch.

"Keep going," Nick breathed, as she ran her finger down it.

He leaned back, levering himself up on his hands so she could pull off his pants. She took off his boxers with them, leaving him completely nude in one smooth motion.

His legs were as finely muscled as the rest of him, but it was his cock that caught her attention. It rose up hard and throbbing, exactly the right size for her hand.

When she closed her fingers around it, Nick made a sound halfway between a groan and a snarl, pulled from deep within his chest. "Raluca… I love how you touch me, but…"

It was exactly the right size for *her.* The lazy relaxation of her first climax vanished, replaced with an urgency that made her squeeze her hand tight. He groaned again, but not with pain.

"We can touch more later." Raluca lay back, tugging Nick down on top of her. "I too want you in me now."

His whole body moved into hers, his skin smooth, the muscles firm beneath it. He kissed her hard and stroked her face, and she felt not only desire but love in the touch of his fingers, the pressure of his lips, the heat of his mouth.

He pulled back, reaching down into the pocket of the pants that she'd tossed beside the bed, then frowned. "I picked up some condoms. Even though I was sure I'd never get to use them. Is that okay? Or do you not believe in any sort of birth control at all?"

Raluca stared at him blankly, then remembered their exchange in the dressing room. Now that she understood more about them both and the very different places they'd come from, she instantly knew how she'd misled him, and why. All that confusion and frustration seemed absurd now. All either of them had needed to do was ask.

"A misunderstanding, Nick," she said, trying not to laugh. "It's not that I don't believe in birth control. It's that I don't need it. Dragons conceive by will, not by accident. I won't get pregnant unless I choose to. When you mentioned it before, I too misunderstood. I thought you were insulting me by implying that I wasn't a true dragon."

Nick pulled his empty hand back up, put his head in his hands, and groaned. "Why the fuck didn't I ask? I could've had you then!"

"You can have me now."

"Yeah." His eyes glittered with an intensity that was both wolflike and very *Nick.* "Yeah, fuck what we didn't do before. Let's take what we've got right now."

She shivered with delicious anticipation as he moved against her, his steel-hard cock sliding against the wet heat between her legs. Then he thrust into her, drawing a cry of startled pleasure from her lips. From his, too.

"Raluca," he gasped. "You're so hot inside."

She didn't need to ask if he liked it. She could hear and see and feel how much he did. She did, too. She'd previously found penetration both disappointing and over far too fast. This was different. Nick positioned himself so he rubbed against her sensitive bud with every thrust, sending waves of ecstasy down her every nerve.

She moved to meet him, letting her body take over, not caring what she looked or sounded like. All that mattered was the moment, his pleasure and hers. His love and hers. She could feel the bond between them, a matter of heart and soul as much as body, vibrant and alive. They'd fought it as hard as they could, but they hadn't done so much as a crack of damage. It was as unbreakable as it was irresistible.

"I —" Nick was thrusting hard, panting. "I can't —"

She was on the brink of another climax, her entire body yearning toward it as much as his was about to be swept away by it.

"One more," Raluca gasped.

Nick's jaw clenched, and she knew that if she'd said "ten more" or "a hundred more," he'd have done it. But he gave one more hard thrust, and a burst of pleasure blossomed within her.

Her head fell back, her eyes fluttering shut as she let her climax wash over her. She heard and felt rather than saw Nick's own climax, his hot jet within her, his growl of satisfaction. Then he lay panting beside her. A moment later, they both reached out to hold each other close.

Raluca touched a lock of his black hair that had fallen across his forehead. It was damp with sweat, and very soft. "I like your hair. It's like silk."

Strands of her own hair lay draped across his chest, as if silver rain was falling on the forest. Nick gently tugged a strand. "I like yours, too. It's smooth, but like metal, too. It feels strong."

"It is." Raluca smiled. "I expect you and Lucas don't discuss hair care, but I can tell you that both he and I need special shears to cut ours. All dragons do."

"No, that's not really a guy topic. Not here, anyway."

"You think about it, but you don't speak of it," Raluca teased. "I am certain that Rafa takes great care with his."

Nick laughed. "I take that back. He does, and he is the one guy who is totally fine with admitting it. He claims it's a lion thing — you know, his mane shows his masculinity — but I think between being a Navy SEAL, a lion, and the size he is, he just doesn't worry about anyone thinking he's girly."

Raluca's dragon abruptly stirred within her. *Now is your chance! Ask Nick what jewelry he would consider manly.*

Raluca suppressed a snicker, then realized that she'd have to satisfy her dragon or never hear the end of it. Besides, she too wanted to adorn Nick with silver.

"I understand that jewelry is more commonly worn by women in America," Raluca said cautiously. "But I would very much like to give you some. It's important for dragons to bedeck their mates —" At Nick's look of alarm, she amended it to, "*Bedeck* could be only one piece. But I would wish you to wear it always. And it should be silver."

"Umm." Nick looked doubtful, then brightened. "Something punk?"

"Show me examples of 'punk,' and I will seek out something suitable."

"All right. Tomorrow, maybe."

They lay together in cozy, companionable silence, and then Nick's eyes flickered. Raluca looked at him curiously. He too seemed to be bracing himself to inquire about something important that he thought she might not like to hear.

"Ask," she said. "As we agreed. No guessing."

"Oh, it's nothing bad. I didn't want to make you feel self-conscious, but I was wondering..." Nick touched her throat. "Your voice is different. Ever since you said you wanted me, as I am. It was the other time we had sex, too. I like it — I mean, I like your regular voice, too — but..."

At first Raluca didn't know what he meant. Then she realized what had happened. For a panicky moment, she wasn't sure if she could do it again. But when she spoke again, it was not in her practiced chime, but in a deeper, more natural tone. "This *is* my regular voice. The other was vocal training, to make me sound like people imagine a princess should. I wasn't sure I even remembered how to not do it, until now. I suppose more of my true self is returning to me. I barely even know what that is, though. As far back as I can recall, I was trained to be 'the princess.' I was never allowed to be just Raluca."

"Fuck." Nick shook his head. "Being royalty is a lot more fucked up than I realized. I thought I got it from what Lucas told me, and how he was before he met Journey. And I know your story — some of it, anyway — but I didn't realize till now how it must have *felt*."

"You have everything you could want," Raluca said. "Every material thing, that is. But you can't leave, and you can't make choices, and you can't be yourself. Uncle Constantine controlled everything I did. *Everything*. I had a closet full of beautiful dresses, but he had selected them all, and every day he had my maid lay out the one he wished me to wear. He gave me tutors who taught me how to speak and how to move, and then he told me what to do and what to say. And every day of my life, a little bit more of what made me myself was taken away."

Raluca felt the shiver that went down Nick's spine.

"It sounds fucking horrible," he said. "Like a nightmare I had once, where I was a puppet. I couldn't move except when someone pulled my strings. I can't even imagine what that must have been like."

"You imagined it perfectly," Raluca replied. "That is exactly what it was like. I was a marionette, and Uncle Constantine moved my strings."

Nick pulled her closer into his arms. "Well, you're not a puppet any more. You're a real girl now."

Raluca smiled. Uncle Constantine had made sure she watched all the Disney movies with princesses, but he'd let her see the rest when she asked, so she knew *Pinocchio* too. "And I didn't even have to turn into a donkey first."

"Nah, you couldn't ever be anything but a dragon." Nick traced the dragonmark that curled around her shoulder. "That's nothing your asshole uncle made you into. That's the real you, one hundred percent. And he sure as hell didn't make you jump off that balcony."

"That seems to be a famous story," Raluca remarked. "How much did Lucas tell you about me?"

"Not that much, but he said he'd never known you very well, so he probably told us everything he knew," Nick said. "But he and Journey both gave us all the deets on the balcony jump. Guess it made a big impression on them. It sure would've made one on me."

Raluca settled herself into Nick's arms, resting her head on his shoulder. They fit against each other so easily, like pieces of a puzzle. "You know my story, but I still don't know yours. When I asked you to show me your America, I was attempting to find out more about you by seeing what you liked, but I must have phrased it in some offensive manner..."

Nick groaned. "Was that what you meant? I thought it was something like, 'Show me where low-lifes like you hang out, so I can go sneer at them.'"

It took Raluca a moment to mentally translate the first part into "Show me where the lowly peasants like you live," but she understood the second half instantly. "That was not my intent at all."

"Yeah, I get that now," Nick said. "I think we misunderstood each other a lot."

Raluca recalled their past interactions, and how they had changed once Nick had walked into this room. "Would you agree, in the future, that if either of us thinks that the other is saying or even thinking something unpleasant, that we explicitly inquire as to the truth of the matter, rather than jumping to the worst possible conclusion without ever speaking our conjectures?"

Nick blinked; she seemed to have spoken in a manner that required him to also mentally translate. Then he said, "Yeah, I think that's a good idea. So you think we have a future? You're not still planning to run back to Viorel?"

Once again, Raluca had the sense of falling and then soaring into unknown but lovely skies. "If you wish a future with me, then I wish one with you."

"I do," Nick said instantly. "You're my mate. I love you. I want to be with you forever, no matter how fucking many times we have to say, 'What did you mean?'"

"I love you, too." The words came easily to Raluca's lips, surprising her. It was as if she was now flying with the wind rather than fighting against it. "And I want to be with you, no matter how many times I have to hear that word."

"I could try to cut down," Nick said, a little doubtfully.

"Now that I am using my own voice, it seems wrong to stop you from using yours. I would prefer you to carry out what you vowed earlier." Raluca paused to remember his quaint phrasing. "I mean the removal of the shoulder chip. There is much in the world that is worthy of anger; why take it out on those who love you?"

"That's over," Nick said. His words were plain, but the determination behind them could move mountains. "There might be some slips, but…"

"I do not expect perfection. That was my uncle's mistake." Then, undeterred, she asked, "But why? That is not a rhetorical question."

Nick took a deep breath. "Because I'm a fucking hand grenade with the pin out. I'm still fucking furious about all this shit that happened to me years ago, but no one wants to hear about that, so —"

"I do."

Nick's bright eyes widened with surprise. "You do?"

"Yes," Raluca said. "I want to hear your story. I have tried to ask before, but…"

"But I took it the wrong way and blew you off." Nick moved restlessly, trying to resettle himself in bed without dislodging her from her position. All his muscles had tensed as soon as he'd mentioned his past, and were hard as rocks.

"Roll over," Raluca said, nudging him.

Obediently, Nick rolled on to his stomach. "Why —"

"Your muscles are very tight. If they are not massaged, your body will ache tomorrow." Raluca sat up and placed her hands on his bare shoulders. She had never given a massage before, but she'd received many after long, tiring days of dance and posture lessons.

"It's a sweet thought, but I don't think you can —" Nick began.

Raluca squeezed his shoulder muscles, first gently, then with more and more force. Finally, they released beneath her hands, softening and relaxing despite themselves.

Nick let out a long sigh. "Fuck, that feels good. I forgot. Shifter strength. Thanks, Raluca."

"Dragon strength," she murmured, and applied herself to the taut muscles of his back, slowly working her way downward until he lay sprawled on the bed, as relaxed as if he'd melted into it.

"So," Raluca said. "Your story. I still wish to hear it."

Nick sighed again. "I'll just get more tense if I talk about it. All that amazing massage work will go to hell."

"Then I will do it again." Raluca stroked his soft black hair, knowing she would never tire of touching it. "Nick. If you do not wish to speak of your past, then say so. And if you wish me to stop asking, then say that as well. We agreed not to guess at each other's meanings. You are making me guess."

Just as he'd warned her, Nick's shoulders began to tense. She dug in her fingers again until his muscles were forced to relax.

"You weren't kidding," Nick said. "Okay, here's the deal. I do want you to know my story. From what you told me, it's not like my life was any worse than yours, just differently awful. And I can tell you about it — I'm not all fucking traumatized like Shane or Fiona, it'll be a cold night in hell before you catch *them* talking about their pasts — but it's bloody and brutal and not the kind of story you tell to a fucking princess. Former princess," he amended.

"I have been the victim of two murder attempts," Raluca pointed out. "I consider that to be brutal."

"Yeah, I haven't forgotten that. But that's people trying to do shit to you. You've never done anything violent yourself."

"Nick," Raluca said. "Are you afraid that if you tell me what you've done, I'll be disgusted and horrified and run away screaming on my pretty, pretty princess shoes?"

Nick's brief, bright smile flashed, then vanished. Casting his gaze low, he muttered, "Yeah. Yeah, that is exactly what I'm —" He seemed to choke on the word *afraid*, finally substituting, "— worried about."

Raluca put two fingers under Nick's chin, tipping his head up and forcing him to look into her eyes. "Who got poisoned today? Who put a bulletproof vest on you? Who ate a Big Bacon?"

"Half a Big Bacon," Nick retorted instantly.

"Only because you told me I need not eat more. Had you not stopped the dare, I would have finished it."

"Yeah, I know. That's why I stopped you. I was afraid you'd make yourself sick. You are one fucking tough ex-princess."

"Tough enough for your story?" Raluca inquired.

"Of course you are. I'm not worried you'll be scared. I'm worried you won't want to be with a man who —" Nick broke off, then reached out and caught her hand, clutching it like a lifeline. "Don't let go of me, Raluca."

"Nick." Raluca closed her hand over his, holding him tight. "I never will."

Chapter Six

Nick

Nick's Story

Wolves need a pack. It doesn't have to be all wolves. I do fine with Protection, Inc., and I'm the only wolf in it. But we need to belong to a group. If we don't have one, it fucks us up.

My mother wasn't a wolf. Dad walked into a diner and asked for a cup of coffee, a waitress came over to pour it for him, he looked into her eyes, and boom. That was it. Mates for life.

Problem was, he was supposed to marry another wolf, or at least another shifter. He told Mom what he was, and once she got over the shock, she asked him to bite her and make her a shifter, too. It seemed like it would solve all their problems. Once she became a wolf, his pack would accept her, and she'd get healing powers and shifter strength and could turn into a wolf. Good deal, right?

Except it didn't work. Some people just can't shift, even if they're born into a wolf family. Or even if they're bitten. Mom turned out to be one of them. No shifting, no healing powers, no strength, no nothing.

Mom was disappointed, but the really big deal was that Dad's pack kicked him out. If you're a wolf, then your mate is automatically part of your pack, and his pack didn't want humans. Especially since they figured that not being able to shift was probably genetic, so if she couldn't shift even after she was bitten, her children wouldn't be able to either.

So Mom and Dad packed up and moved to Santa Martina. That was how much he loved her: he left his pack for her. And she was an orphan, so she didn't have anyone else. But they had each other, and pretty soon they had me, and then the three of us made a pack. I could shift almost as soon as I was born, so Mom homeschooled me until I was old enough to know not to turn into a wolf pup in public. Dad worked all day in a steel mill.

We didn't have much money, but we were happy. On weekends we used to drive out of town and go camping. Me and Dad would turn into wolves and run around, and Mom would chase us. I remember one time it was snowing, and Dad shook snow all over Mom, and she nailed him with a snowball. I turned back into a boy so I could throw snowballs too, only I forgot that I wouldn't have any clothes on. Next thing I knew, I was naked in snow up to my thighs. I couldn't shift back fast enough. Mom laughed so hard, she fell into a snowdrift. And then all three of us were covered in snow…

Anyway, we were a family and we were a pack, and we had nobody but each other. All three of us would have done anything for each other.

When I was fifteen, Mom got sick. At first she was just a little tired and under the weather, but it didn't go away. It didn't seem serious, so it was a while before she got around to seeing a doctor. Actually, Dad dragged her to one. They ran some tests, then asked her to come back in person to get the results. I was so young, I didn't realize what that meant. But when they came back home, I knew just from seeing their faces, even before they sat me down and told me she'd been given four months to live.

I couldn't believe it. I said there had to be some way to save her.

It turned out that there was. Mom and Dad went from doctor to doctor, until they found one who knew about a treatment that *maybe* could cure her. It wasn't guaranteed, but at least it would give her a chance. But it was experimental and ridiculously fucking expensive, and insurance wouldn't cover it. There was no way we could even begin to pay for it.

But the CEO of the steel mill was a billionaire. He could've saved Mom out of his pocket change. So Dad swallowed his pride, went to that asshole's office, and asked him if he'd give him a loan as an advance on future wages.

That fucker listened to his whole story, asking questions and pretending like he cared, and then he said, "Seems like you're going to be missing a lot of work, with a sick wife and a young son to care for. I'm not a charity, and I didn't get to be where I am by keeping on dead weight."

And then he fired Dad.

You think I have a temper — Dad had one too. He told me later it was all he could do to stop himself from turning into a wolf and ripping out that fucking rich asshole's throat, right there in the office. The only thing that stopped him was that he'd have gone to jail, and that would've left Mom and me alone.

So unless Dad could raise the money for her treatment himself, Mom was going to die. By then she was way too sick to do anything herself, and her friends didn't have any more money than we did. Dad had been exiled from his pack, and they sure as hell weren't going to help him save the woman who was the reason they'd thrown him out.

But there were other packs. There was one right in Santa Martina, but Dad had always kept away from it because it was a gang, and he was an honest working man. But he was desperate. So he went to the alpha and asked for help in the name of shifters' honor.

The alpha was a guy named Price. He was a mean bastard and he told Dad to fuck off.

That was Price's mistake. Like I said, I got my temper from my father.

Packs have laws about who gets to be alpha, but different packs have different ones. In Dad's old pack, they thought the person with the most life experience would make the best leader. So the alpha was the oldest wolf who was still strong. When that alpha died or got too frail, the next-oldest wolf who qualified took their place. There wasn't any fighting.

But Price's pack was a bunch of gangsters, with the strongest wolf as alpha. Their law was that anyone could challenge the alpha. Then the alpha had a choice. They could accept the challenge and fight, but it had to be to the death. Or they could step down without a duel and give up their position to the challenger.

Dad challenged Price. And then, so Price could see exactly what he'd be fighting, Dad shifted in front of him.

Price was a vicious fighter, but what he was best at was pickpocketing. He could steal the bullets out of your gun, then reload it and shoot you with it before you even realized he was there. A bit like a cut-rate Shane, though Shane takes not being noticed to a whole new level.

Dad's wolf was fucking huge. Strong, too. He'd never been in a real fight before, but he was furious and he scared Price — scared him so much that he stepped down instead of risking Dad tearing out his throat.

Next thing Dad knew, he was the alpha of a pack of gangster wolves. Price included. Dad could've kicked him out, but he didn't seem all that much worse than the rest of that crowd, and Dad knew what it felt like to be exiled from your pack. So Price stayed.

And that was Dad's mistake.

Dad sat down with the gang and worked out a plan to rob the CEO. It was pretty complicated and took a while to plan, then set up, then carry out. But they did it. Got away clean with a nice chunk of his money. Dad gave half of it to the pack and the other half to Mom's doctors. He'd gotten what he wanted, so he was planning on staying alpha just long enough to make sure he could pay for Mom's treatments. Once that was over, he meant to step down.

But it was too late. While Dad was going to the CEO, then to Price, then planning a heist, Mom was getting sicker and sicker. She got the treatment. But about a month into it, she died.

Her doctor said if they'd started earlier, like if that fucking CEO had given Dad that loan when he'd asked, maybe she would have made it.

The day after Mom died, the CEO was found in an alley. The news said he'd been mauled to death by an animal, maybe a runaway pit bull.

I asked Dad flat out if he'd done it. I told him I hoped he had and I was only sorry he hadn't told me, so I could've helped.

I'll never forget his expression. It was how he'd looked when we got the news about Mom. Like his whole world had collapsed under his feet. I wished I hadn't said a word, but I couldn't take it back.

Dad said, "It didn't bring your mother back. Don't ever kill anyone, Nick. You control your wolf. Your wolf shouldn't control you."

I didn't understand what he meant about my wolf, and I still thought he'd done the right thing. But he looked so sad that I told him I got it.

So Dad was left with no mate, no job, a gang he'd never wanted, and me. Like I said, wolves need a pack. Two is too small, and Mom was gone. The gangsters were all we had. Looking back, I think he kind of snapped after Mom died. I think we both did. We were halfway out of our minds with grief. So Dad stayed on as alpha, and I dropped out of school and joined the pack.

The pack got a lot less violent with Dad in charge. But it was still a gang. It just switched from mugging anyone they caught alone and beating them up if they didn't cooperate to stealing from rich people without hurting them physically.

Dad tried to keep me out of trouble and not let me help out with any crimes, but I wasn't that easy to control, I was around all the time, and I wanted to be in on the action. I liked hanging out with the other wolves and learning what they knew, like how to fight and hotwire cars and break into buildings. Eventually Dad started letting me do little things like carry messages, and from then on, it was a slippery slope. By the time I was seventeen, I was a full member of the gang.

Price looked like he'd eaten a lemon every time Dad gave him an order, but there was nothing he could do about it. Once I caught him trying to talk other wolves in the pack into challenging Dad. But no one was willing to do it.

I told Dad, but he just said, "Price can go if he wants. No one's keeping him here. Of course, if he leaves, he'll have to abide by his own pack laws."

Like I said, every pack has its laws. Whoever starts the pack makes them, and then they're kept forever, long after the pack founder dies, as long as the pack itself survives. A new alpha can't make new laws for the same pack.

It's a wolf thing, like the way dragons are all obsessed with gold and jewels. Wolves have to have packs, and they have to obey the laws of their pack. Maybe it's because wolves are wild at heart, and they need *something* to keep them in line, or they'd go totally out of control.

Dad's old pack allowed anyone to leave if the alpha gave them permission. The gang had a different law. It was that anyone could leave, but they had to run the gauntlet. The entire gang shifted into wolves, and stood in two lines. The person who wanted to leave had to walk between the lines in human form, and every wolf he passed bit him. Each wolf got to decide where and how hard. The bites couldn't be to places that would kill instantly or that would make it physically impossible to walk. Like, no biting through the Achilles tendon. But other than that, anything went. If you were still on your feet by the end, you could go. If you fell and couldn't get up, the pack tore you to shreds.

You have a fucked-up macho gangster pack, you get fucked-up macho gangster laws.

Nobody left while Dad was alpha, but some of the wolves had seen gauntlets. One was an old guy who wanted to retire and be with his family, so they just nipped him and let him through. The other was a guy Price didn't like. Price and his buddies bit him so badly that he passed out from blood loss two steps from the end, and that was it for him.

Price had made a lot of enemies as an alpha, so there was a good chance he wouldn't survive a gauntlet. And he didn't have the nerve to challenge Dad. So he stayed. He seethed every time Dad gave him an order, but he obeyed.

Dad ran the gang for a couple years. Then when I was eighteen, a new wolf came to town. I never did hear his story — whether he'd lost his pack or been run out of it or what. He just showed up one day and challenged Dad.

I don't know what Dad was thinking, either — maybe he figured he could beat that guy, maybe he was afraid he couldn't protect me if he wasn't the alpha, maybe he didn't care if he lived or died now that his mate was gone, maybe a little of everything.

He took the challenge. And the other wolf killed him.

I couldn't do anything but watch. Pack laws — no one can interfere in an alpha challenge. Those laws go down to our blood and bones. I don't know if it would've even been possible for me to jump in. But I just assumed Dad would beat him. It never even occurred to me that he might die.

It happened so fast. I never got to say good-bye. One second they were rolling around on the ground, and the next second Dad was dead and that guy was standing over his body.

He shifted and told us all, "I'm your alpha now."

I didn't think. I just said, "Not for long, you fucking aren't. I challenge you."

He laughed. That fucker *laughed* at me.

He said, "I'm not stepping down for you, kid. Take it back and beg for mercy, or come at me and die with your daddy."

I was barely eighteen. My wolf wasn't full-grown, either. There was no way I could win a fight with a big, strong, experienced, adult alpha. But I was so heartbroken and furious, I didn't care if he killed me, so long as I died with my teeth in his throat.

My wolf took over. I don't remember the fight. To this day, I don't even remember his *name*. All I remember is a red haze.

Then I was standing in that alley with blood in my mouth and two wolves dead at my feet. Dad was gone. And I was the alpha.

I buried Dad and had that fucker's body tossed into the town dump. And then I ran the gang pretty much like my father had, but not quite so non-violently. If a rich mark was a real asshole, I might rough him up a bit. Uh, or a lot, depending on how bad he was. Like, if he was the kind of person who'd fire a man for trying to save his mate's life. No murder, though. And no harming innocent working people.

I'm not saying I was Robin Hood. I was a fucking gangster. Okay, so sometimes I shoved an envelope of money under some single mom's door, but it was money I got from breaking and entering on the other side of town. I don't want you to think I was better than I was. I didn't hurt anyone who couldn't fight back and I didn't steal from the poor, and that was as good as it got.

I ran the gang for about five years. I got two challenges early on, both from outsiders who figured a teenage alpha was easy pickings. It was kill or be killed, and I killed them.

After that, word got around, and that was it for challenges for a couple years. Sometimes wolves came round who'd lost or been kicked out of their pack, and asked to join mine. If they seemed okay, I'd let them in. If they were an asshole, I told them to take off. One of the assholes challenged me, and, well, here I am.

A couple of the guys I let in couldn't hack it and ended up asking to leave. Thing was, they weren't criminals. They just needed a pack. If they kept looking long enough, they'd find one that suited them better. So I stood first in the gauntlet, which was the alpha's prerogative, and gave them a little nip, just enough to draw blood. The rest of the gang followed my lead, and both those guys walked away.

But Price stayed. He didn't like me any better then he liked my father, but he knew he couldn't beat me in a fair fight. And no matter how a wolf left that pack, whether the alpha throws them out or they go of their own accord, they still have to run the gauntlet. I kept hoping Price would choose to leave, but the alpha doesn't control the gauntlet. I could *suggest* how it goes, but every wolf gets to decide for himself. He knew and I knew that he wouldn't make it to the end of the line.

We fucking hated each other but I felt like I had enough blood on my hands. I didn't want his too. So he stayed.

And that was my mistake. My very fucking big mistake.

Then two things happened that changed everything.

The first was that Protection, Inc. moved their headquarters into this building. Before that, they'd been in another part of town. Hal didn't want a gang in his neighborhood, making people scared to come there and do business with him, so he arranged a meeting with me. He told me to go straight or move out. He said if we kept on committing crimes and weren't willing to go peacefully, he and his team would run us out.

I knew they were shifters, but that was all I knew. I had no idea what I was dealing with. I thought he was a condescending jackass and I told him to fuck off. I said if he and his buddies gave me any trouble, me and my pack would run *them* out.

At that point, Protection, Inc. was just Hal, Rafa, Fiona, and Destiny. I couldn't beat a grizzly bear or a lion myself, but I had a whole pack. I didn't think they'd be a problem.

Obviously, I'd way underestimated them. From then on, they were on my ass like white on rice. Every time we did fucking anything, either they tipped off the cops or one of them showed up to stop us in person. They were fucking hardcore. I think I fought every single one of them something like three times over. It always ended with both of us roughed up, but my pack or his team would always break it up before anyone could get seriously hurt. But they'd be back the next day. And, of course, so would we.

I had my hands full just holding my ground against them. So I missed something really fucking important going down inside my pack.

This kid Manuel joined right before Protection, Inc. moved in. He was just seventeen, and he came to us because his parents had been his pack, and they'd been killed in a car crash. He reminded me of myself at that age: pissed off at the world and ready to fight every last person in it. I'd meant to show him the ropes, but then Protection, Inc. showed up and I didn't get the chance.

I did notice that Price seemed to get along with him, but all I ever saw him do was chat and teach Manuel how to pick pockets. If I hadn't been so distracted, I'd have kept more of an eye on them.

What I found out later was that Price had taken that kid under his wing and treated him like a son. And Manuel was looking for a father. That asshole told Manuel that he had all the qualities of a true alpha, and the whole pack had just been waiting for someone like him to show up and save them from me. Everyone knew I'd become alpha when I was about Manuel's age, but Price spun that to convince him that he could challenge me and win. Every time I showed up beat to hell from some fight with Hal or Rafa — a wolf going head to head with a grizzly bear or a lion, and giving as good as he got — Price used that as proof that I was weak and not fit to run the pack.

Manuel was too young and inexperienced to know he was being used. And Price was fucking sneaky. I think a couple wolves knew what he was up to, but they were old buddies of Price from his alpha days. The wolves who were friends with me had no idea, or they would have tipped me off.

One night when we were all gathered to talk about what to do about fucking Protection, Inc, Manuel stood up. Out of the blue, he said, "Nick Mackenzie, I challenge you."

I couldn't believe it. That pup wouldn't last five seconds against me. Then I caught sight of Price. He wiped that fucking smirk off his face as quick as he could. But once I'd seen it, I knew what must have happened.

I said, "Manuel, Price is using you. He thinks I won't want to fight you —"

"Because you know you'll lose," Manuel said.

I lost my temper and snarled, "No, you fucking idiot! Because I know I'll win, and you're just a dumb fucking kid. He's hoping I'll step down so I don't have to kill you. But if I do, he'll challenge *you*. He's not strong enough to beat me, but he's plenty strong enough to beat you. So either you'll step down or he'll kill you. Either way, he gets to be alpha again."

Manuel had a temper too. Like I said, he was a lot like me at that age: more balls than brains. He said, "You're lying! Price is like a father to me. And I *can* beat you!"

Before I could get anything else out, he yelled, "Nick Mackenzie, I challenge you! Do you accept, or do you step down?"

Pack laws say once a challenge has been issued twice, that's the end of trying to talk them out of it. You have to act on it, one way or another.

I thought fast. I really didn't want to kill that fucking kid. But if I stepped down, Manuel would become alpha... for about thirty seconds before Price challenged *him*. And if Manuel felt so betrayed and angry that he took Price's challenge, which he probably would because I sure would if I was him, then Price would kill him. It looked like that dumb-ass teenager was going to be dead in the next ten minutes no matter what I did.

Manuel shouted, "Accept, or step down?"

Then I realized that there was a loophole. If an alpha steps down from a challenge but stays in the pack, the challenger becomes alpha. But if an alpha leaves the pack entirely, it throws the position open. Any wolf who likes can take a shot at it. And if more than two wolves want it, then it goes to a melee— a huge brawl, basically. It's not to the death, just to the last wolf standing.

Like I said, that gang had fucking macho laws, but whoever set them up wasn't an idiot. One wolf killed in a challenge, the pack survives. Five wolves killed, and you've just seriously weakened the pack. So there was a provision to make sure that wouldn't happen. I think it was meant to cover an alpha retiring without any challenger stepping up. But technically speaking, I hadn't answered Manuel's challenge yet. If I left right then, I'd be leaving as an alpha.

There were enough wolves who'd jump at the chance to take my place if it didn't mean dueling me that it would have to be decided by melee. I'd probably be handing the pack to Price, who was a fucking mean fighter when he wasn't worried that he might get killed. But he'd backed me into a corner where I either had to do that or kill a seventeen-year-old who didn't stand a chance against me.

I asked myself, *Am I willing to risk my life and throw away everything I've fought for just so one angry boy doesn't die today?*

My wolf growled, *Yes.*

I said, "I'm leaving the pack. Line up for the gauntlet."

Everyone stared at me. Nobody had expected that. They were

all so surprised, none of them moved.

"This is my last order as alpha of this pack," I said. "LINE THE FUCK UP!"

They all scrambled to obey. Next thing I knew, I was facing two lines of wolves.

You remember the rules. I stay human. They all bite me. If I make it to the end of the line, I get to leave. If I collapse and can't get up, they kill me.

It was supposed to be a test of willpower and toughness, but it was more of a test of what the gang thought of you. If they didn't want you to make it out alive, you wouldn't.

I looked down the lines. Some of the wolves were my buddies. Others were older wolves who hadn't been thrilled with taking orders from a teenager when I first took over. And then there were Price and Manuel. Price would try to kill me for sure. Manuel — who the fuck knew what he'd do.

I hoped to hell that most of the pack thought I'd been a good alpha. And I stepped between the lines.

The first bite was a nip, barely enough to draw blood. The second wasn't much harder. But those were from wolves who liked me. Next up was one of Price's buddies. He sank his teeth deep into my thigh. It hurt like fuck, and he tore the muscle. When I tried to take another step, my knee buckled. I nearly fell on my face.

It was just barely within the laws. He hadn't made it *impossible* to walk, just really fucking difficult. After that, I was concentrating so hard on balancing with one leg that couldn't bear much weight, I barely noticed the next two bites.

Then I got to Price. The line-up was in order of seniority, with older members first, so I had to face him three steps in. His yellow eyes were blazing with hate. Wolves can't break pack laws, but we can bend them. I thought he'd go for my other leg. If he did, I figured I'd crawl to the end and hope that was good enough.

Price lunged up, his mouth stretched wide open like the shark in fucking *Jaws*, and bit me in the chest.

A wolf can crush the thigh bone of a moose. And that's a regular wolf, not a shifter. Werewolves are much stronger than that.

Price didn't bite as hard as he could have, or he'd have killed me instantly and broken pack law. But he bit hard enough. A bunch of my ribs snapped like twigs.

I'd been injured before, but nothing remotely like that. One second my leg was a mess but I was basically okay, the next second I was dying. All the strength went out of me. My whole body felt like fucking dead weight. I could barely breathe.

I knew I'd die if I didn't get through the gauntlet and then to a doctor, fast. But my willpower was pouring out of me along with my blood. I was so tired, the thought of letting myself collapse was really tempting. I knew they'd kill me if I did, but at least I wouldn't have to keep walking.

My wolf howled, *Stay on your feet!*

So I did. I have no fucking idea how I managed it, when I was on the verge of passing out and one leg wouldn't take my weight. But I somehow managed to stumble forward. It was maybe ten steps, but it felt like ten miles. No idea what the other wolves did to me. Whatever it was, I didn't feel it. Everything started fading out, even my wolf.

I realized that I was blacking out. I slapped myself across the face. It worked. My head cleared a little, and my vision came back.

I was at the end of the line, facing the last wolf to join my pack. Manuel.

He could take me out if he wanted, easy. One more hard bite, and I'd go down.

Manuel closed his jaws over my hand and pressed his fangs into my skin, as if he was picking up something he didn't want to damage. He didn't even draw blood.

I thought, *He* is *like me. I wouldn't hurt anyone who couldn't fight back, either.*

Knowing I'd done the right thing, even if it had killed me, gave me enough strength to take one more step.

And then I was past the line. I would've kept going, because I was so fixated on *stay on your feet,* but that last step took everything I had. My knees buckled and I pitched forward. I thought I'd crack my head open — the whole thing went down in this nasty dark alley — but someone caught me. Then everything went black anyway.

I came to in a car. Manuel was burning rubber out of there. I was slumped down in the passenger seat. Blood was fucking everywhere — my clothes, his clothes, the seat, the floor, even the passenger window. If it hadn't been the middle of the night, we'd have been pulled over for sure.

I asked, "Where...?"

That was all I could get out, but he knew what I meant.

He said, "To the medic."

I knew what he meant, too. There was a sleazy underground shifter medic the gang used to go to for anything that wouldn't heal on its own. I'm not sure if he even had a license, let alone what it was, but he had medical supplies and more or less knew what he was doing.

It might be different where you come from, but in America, shifters don't go to hospitals if we can possibly avoid it. Human doctors notice that we're healing too fast. Shifters who go to hospitals and don't get out quick enough disappear sometimes. I always figured there was some creepy government agency grabbing shifters and doing who the fuck knows what horrible things to them.

Even apart from the "ratting me out to mad scientists" thing, I had about a hundred outstanding warrants and if the black ops didn't get me, I'd go to jail for the next thirty years. But I couldn't go to the medic either. If Price took over the pack, he'd be gunning for me, and that'd be the first place he'd look. And my injuries were way out of that guy's league anyway.

"No," I said.

"The ER?" Manuel asked. "I know it's risky, but if it's your only shot..."

I shook my head.

He looked at me like the whole fucking pack used to look at me. Like, *Give me an order, Nick.* And he said, "Okay, then where should I take you?"

I was having a hard enough time staying conscious, let alone talking. Let alone figuring out where the fuck I could go that knew about shifters, was safe, and would be willing to help a fucking gangster wolf.

My wolf said, *Protection, Inc.*

I thought he was out of his fucking mind. Those were the guys who'd been busting their asses trying to run me out of town.

But then I remembered my first meeting with Hal, when he'd thought he could make a deal with me. He'd made his offer, then said, "Shifters' honor."

Shifters never reveal other shifters. Ever. Even fucking Price wouldn't do that. So if I showed up on Hal's doorstep, he wouldn't dump me at an ER.

When my father went to Price for help, Dad had said, "Shifters' honor," too. Price refused him. So shifters' honor didn't mean you *had* to help another shifter. But it meant that if you were an honorable type of person, you *should*.

My wolf said, *Hal Brennan is honorable.*

I'd fucking had it with him and his team. But I was running out of time. And Manuel was still staring at me with those pleading pup eyes, like, *Please make this right, Nick. Please don't leave me with your blood on my hands.*

I said, "Protection, Inc."

Lucky for me, Hal was burning the midnight oil, because I sure didn't know where he lived. But we all knew where his office was. We'd graffitied the front, dumped rotting garbage on the doorstep to gross out his clients, and tried our best to break in. We'd never managed it and their windows were high up and unbreakable, but I did once use a window-washer's rig to spray-paint on them. I'm sure you can guess what sort of things I wrote.

Manuel pulled up at Protection, Inc., lifted me over his shoulder, and started ringing the bell and banging on the door. I could still see a little bit of graffiti they'd missed when they'd last painted it over.

Hal opened the door with a gun in his hand. We'd broken his closed circuit cameras the night before, so he wasn't sure if it was an ambush or someone who needed protection right then. He was surprised as hell to see us.

Manuel said, "Don't shoot! Nick's hurt really bad, he needs help —"

Hal interrupted him. "Why isn't his pack helping him?"

"He stepped down as alpha and ran the gauntlet." Manuel sounded like he was trying not to cry. "To save me."

Hal asked, "Which of you decided to come here?"

I said, "Me."

I'm sure Hal could see I really was hurt, but he must have wondered if it was a set-up by someone else. He was still holding a gun on us when he asked his last question. "What do you want me to do with the kid, Nick?"

"Protect him," I said. Then I started coughing, and I couldn't get enough breath to talk. But there was something else I had to say, so I forced it out. "Shifters' honor."

Hal's a big guy, but he moves fast. Makes decisions fast, too. Next thing I knew, he was carrying me upstairs himself, with Manuel trailing behind him. He laid me down on the sofa in the lobby. My jacket and shirt were in tatters. Hal ripped them both all the way off.

You'll probably never hear Hal curse, but he does if something really gets to him. He sure did when he saw what Price had done to me. Then he grabbed a pillow, put it over my chest, and told Manuel to hold it in place. I can't even imagine how much that would have hurt if he'd done it right after Price bit me, but by then I was in shock and didn't feel anything but pressure. The only reason I was still conscious was my wolf howling at me to stay awake.

Hal made a bunch of phone calls that I didn't really follow. While he was talking on the phone, he was moving fast to try to save me. He propped me up with some more pillows so I could breathe easier, got a first aid kit and switched out the other pillow for bandages, and put a bunch of blankets over me. Then he cranked up the heat. I didn't know anything about first aid then and I was really out of it, so I spent most of that time trying to figure out how he'd known I was cold when I hadn't told him.

Then his team started showing up, one by one. Fiona was first. I was starting to drift off, so I didn't see her come in. I just heard this hoity-toity voice saying, "My sofa!"

That woke me up a bit. I opened my eyes, and there was that blonde woman who could turn into a snow leopard, glaring daggers at me and the white sofa that I'd bled all over.

Hal said, "We'll get a new one. Just help me save his life, all right?"

Fiona stalked up to me, just like her leopard on the hunt. Halfway there, she said, "My carpet!"

I'd bled all over that, too. I found out later that she'd been in charge of decorating the new office.

Hal snapped his fingers. "Fiona. Get to it!"

Then Rafa burst through the door. He caught sight of me and *bristled*. "What's that fucking thug doing in our office?"

Hal had a phone in his hand; he hadn't stopped calling people since I showed up. He covered it and said, "Not dying here, if I can help it. Give Fiona a hand."

Rafa obeyed, but he sure didn't look happy about it.

Destiny showed up last. She must've been out clubbing when she got Hal's call, because she was in dance shoes and a sequined mini-dress. She stopped in the doorway, and her tiger glared at me out of her eyes. "So the gangster we've spent the last two months fighting gets hurt, and he comes running *here* for help?"

Manuel had been too worried about me or too intimidated to talk before, but that pissed him off. He said, "Nick called on shifters' honor. If you won't help him, what makes you any different from his gang?"

That got to everyone.

I don't remember what all they did, but I'm sure I would've died without them. Mostly I remember Hal kind of coaching me, telling me to listen to my wolf and let him help fight for my life. I don't know, it seemed to make sense at the time. Manuel sat on the floor and held my hand, which was about the only part of me that wasn't bleeding all over the place.

Between him and Hal and my wolf and Hal's team, who were trying hard to save me even though they didn't like me, I felt like I had something to hold on to and people who'd catch me if I fell. All I had to do was stay awake and keep breathing. It doesn't sound like much, but believe me, it was just as hard as walking the gauntlet. Only it went on for hours. There was no way I could've done it alone.

Finally a doctor showed up. Not that sleazy maybe-not-a-real-medic, an actual doctor. A black woman with cornrows and little wire-rimmed glasses. I found out later that her name was Dr. Bedford and she was a bear shifter from Hal's hometown, and that he'd arranged a helicopter pickup for her. It landed on the roof, just like you did.

Hal asked if I should be transported to her office, but she said I'd bleed out if I was moved and anyway there wasn't time. She gave me a shot to put me to sleep. Once I realized what she'd done, I said I was supposed to stay awake and she had to give me an antidote.

Hal put his hand on my shoulder and said, "It's all right. You can rest now, Nick."

My wolf agreed. *Go to sleep. Your battle's done.*

I tried to ask, *Did we win?*

But I was out before I heard the answer.

When I woke up, I was still on the sofa, but I was wrapped in bandages like a mummy and had tubes fucking everywhere. Fiona was watching over me, or maybe I should say glaring over me.

She said, "Don't shift. The doctor said it'll make you bleed out. Don't try to get up. Same thing. Just lie still. You should be fine with that. You're causing all the trouble you could possibly want just by being here."

There was obviously nothing worth staying up for, so I went back to sleep.

I found out later that Dr. Bedford couldn't do surgery on a sofa, so she had them lift me onto the nearest flat surface that could be disinfected. That was the lobby desk, which was an antique, and that was the end of it. After my gang and I spent months trying to trash the office without doing much more than annoy the team, I did thousands of dollars worth of damage just by bleeding on stuff. I had no idea carpeting was that expensive.

The team spent the next few days taking care of me. In their lobby, which meant they couldn't see any clients as long as I was there. Except for Hal, they were pissed as hell about the whole thing. Whenever Hal and Manuel were off getting some sleep or something, Rafa would lecture me on how crime is bad and gangs ruin everything for everybody, Fiona would pull out a ledger with a running total of the money I'd cost them and demand that I pay them back the instant I was on my feet again, and Destiny would give me inspirational speeches on how it's never too late to turn over a new leaf. It was exactly as annoying as it sounds, especially since I was on too many painkillers to make any comebacks.

But I'll give them this: that was the *only* way they got back at me. I was in such bad shape, I couldn't do anything for myself. If I wanted a drink of water, someone had to hold the glass and lift my head. Every single one of them did stuff like that for me, and they all did it like it was no big deal so I wouldn't be embarrassed. Much. The reason I was loopy on painkillers was that they made sure I was never in pain for longer than it took them to notice and give me a pill.

I wasn't crazy about being that dependent on people, especially my enemies, but my wolf didn't mind at all. The water, especially — that's a thing with wolves. If someone offers to let you drink from their hands, that's a really big deal. It's like becoming blood brothers. It made me feel weird, even though the team obviously had no clue about that. But my wolf thought it meant something whether the team knew it or not.

Wolves are pack animals. We're supposed to depend on each other. Protection, Inc. wasn't my pack, but my wolf was reacting like they were. So something about it felt all right to me.

Plus, they didn't scold me the entire time. Hal never did, and after a while the others either got bored or felt guilty, and started talking to me like I was just a guy who was hurt and could use some company. I couldn't talk back much — I mean, I physically couldn't — so I mostly listened. Rafa and Destiny and Hal had all been in the military, and the way they talked about it, it sounded a lot like being in a pack. I could relate. Fiona's traveled a lot, and she told me about parts of the world I'd never even heard of. It was a lot more interesting than I would've expected.

One day I woke up and found the entire team arguing with Manuel in the lobby. At first no one noticed I was awake, they were so focused on him. I didn't feel up to jumping in, so I just lay there and listened.

Hal had decided Manuel wouldn't be safe in Santa Martina as long as Price was around. All else aside, it turned out that the way Manuel had gotten me out of there was by hot-wiring Price's car. I'd thought it had looked familiar. So Hal had found Manuel a pack across the country that was happy to take him in. Not a gang, a family.

Manuel was fine with that. He was obviously done with being a gangster and hanging around all those criminals. There was just one snag. He hadn't officially left the pack yet. He'd been thinking of staying with Protection, Inc. as "laying low for a while," but once it came to moving to another state and joining a new pack, his wolf instincts kicked in big-time.

He was insisting that he had to go back and walk the gauntlet, and he couldn't leave until he did. He looked like he was having a nervous breakdown — sweat pouring off him, shaking, breathing a mile a minute — and he was yelling that he'd fight anyone who tried to stop him. That's what happens when you try to break pack laws, or someone else tries to make you break them. Your wolf fights you. Your *body* fights you.

The team wasn't getting it. Hal was trying to explain that Price would kill him, Fiona was saying basically the same thing only more sarcastically, and Destiny was coaxing him with how much better life would be with a pack of good people who actually wanted him. Then Rafa threatened to pick him up and drag him, like it or not.

Manuel yelled, "Just try it. I'll shift and rip your fucking throat out!"

Everyone shut up. They weren't scared, they were confused and frustrated. But it gave me a space to break in, because I sure couldn't speak loud enough to be heard over all that yelling.

I said, "Manuel!"

He ran up to the sofa, grabbed my hand, and said, "They're trying to make me break pack laws. Nick, you're my real alpha. Tell them I can't. I just can't!"

I looked up at them and said, "He can't. It's a wolf thing."

Hal came over too. He said, "Then what? Do we really all have to go stand over that pack while the kid runs the gauntlet?"

I thought about it. It did seem like the only way. Then I remembered Manuel saying, "You're my real alpha."

Pack laws are funny things. They work because wolves believe in them. Leave a pack the way it says you should, and that's the last time its laws have a hold over you. Join a new pack, and you're bound by new laws. Everything had gotten so fucked up and confusing by the time I left the pack, maybe I really was still Manuel's alpha. Or maybe all we needed was for him and me to believe it.

I spoke to him wolf to wolf, like those other guys weren't even there. "Do you accept me as your alpha?"

He nodded.

I said, "Then you only have to get past me."

Destiny shouted, "Nick, don't! It's too soon!"

She was too late. I shifted. Right away, I realized what she'd meant. All the needles and stuff pulled out, and my bandages came loose. Blood started soaking into my fur. And it wasn't just that. Shifting takes energy that I couldn't afford to lose. All of a sudden, breathing was back to being this enormous effort.

But Manuel's hand was right there in front of my muzzle. I bit him, just hard enough to draw blood. Then I gave him a little nudge, which was all I could manage. He stood up and took a step past me. And that was it. He was through the gauntlet.

The last thing I wanted was to shift again, but I had to. I was his alpha, so he was my responsibility. So I turned back into a man. It fucking hurt. All the bandages and stuff had slid around when I was a wolf, and when I shifted back, they broke or came off or tightened in the wrong places and made me bleed more.

I was covered in blankets, so Manuel couldn't see what shifting had done to me. I had to get him the fuck out of there before he found out.

I gathered the strength I had left, which wasn't much, and said, "Go to the other pack, right now. And don't join another fucking gang. That's my last order to you as your alpha."

"Sure," Manuel said. "I'm done with that anyway. Thanks, Nick. I'll write. Rafa will fly me there, to make sure I arrive safe."

Hal nodded at Rafa, and he grabbed Manuel and hustled him out.

I might have pulled the wool over the kid's eyes, but not over the team's. The second the door closed, Hal yanked off my blankets with one hand and pressed the other right down on my chest where Price had bitten me. It didn't hurt, which by then I knew was bad news.

Hal yelled, "Destiny, get the first aid kit! Fiona, call in a helo for Dr. Bedford! Nick, keep breathing!"

My body obeyed him automatically, just like his team ran to obey him and Manuel had obeyed me.

I thought, *Now that's a good alpha.* And before I could remind myself that he wasn't *my* alpha or that there were more important things to think about, like that I might be dying, I blacked out.

When I woke up again, I could tell that days had gone by. I felt way better, and the number of things hooked up to me was down by at least half. Also, I'd been moved. Finally. I was in a tiny bedroom. Hal was there too, perched on a chair that was way too small for him and reading a book.

He looked up almost as soon as I opened my eyes. "Good to have you back with us. Dr. Bedford thought you'd be waking up about now."

I said, "Did you bring me to your fucking *house?*"

Hal shook his head. "Nah, this is still the office. We had two spare rooms, so I put a bed in one. I'll probably put a bed in the other one too. We work around the clock often enough that we could use them."

It was weird to finally be able to have a conversation with him. Before, he'd just been talking *to* me. Now that I could talk back, I wasn't sure what to say. We obviously weren't still enemies, but we weren't friends, either. I didn't know what we were.

"Thanks for saving my life," I said. "And for finding a place for Manuel. He needed a pack, and he sure as hell couldn't go back to mine. Or whoever the fuck's it is by now."

"Price took over," Hal said.

"Fuck!" I banged my fist into the mattress. Bad move. My whole body hurt like hell now that I was out of shock and off the painkillers. But I was so furious, it steamrollered the pain. "I fucking knew it. I'm going to kill that motherfucker."

"Uh-huh." Hal leaned back. His chair nearly tipped over, and he sat back up in a hurry. "Are you thinking of taking over your pack again?"

"I can't. Pack law says once you go, there's no coming back. I'll just kill that asshole…"

Hal looked at me. He has a way about him. He thinks, and it makes you think, too. So I thought about it.

"Son of a bitch," I said at last. "I can't. If I can't be his alpha, I can't make an alpha challenge. I could just walk up and tell him to fight or die, but he doesn't do fair fights. He'd refuse. I'd have to jump him fast and murder him in cold blood, or he'd order his pack to rip me to shreds. I can't fight the entire pack. And some of them are my friends. If Price orders them to kill me, they'd have to try. I can't do that to them."

I couldn't do it to myself, either, but I didn't want to admit that.

"So, let me get this straight," Hal said. "You won't go after the man who plotted to kill you and nearly succeeded, because it would either hurt your friends or be flat-out murder. A lot of people talk about loyalty and fairness, but you're really walking the walk."

The way he was watching me made me twitchy. It was like he was reading… not my mind... like he was reading my *soul.* It pissed me off.

"The fuck I am," I said. "I'm a fucking gangster. But you're right, my pack and Price and I are done with each other. I guess I could move in on another pack..."

But even when I was saying it, I knew I was done with alpha challenges. "No. I don't know what I'll do, other than leave town. But I'll go as soon as I can walk, and then I'll be out of your lives forever. So thanks again for saving me and Manuel. And tell your team thank you. You all have shifters' honor — the real fucking deal. Anyone can save a friend, but it takes something fucking else to save an enemy."

Then I shut up, because Hal was giving me a weird look. I know what it means now, but I didn't then. It's his *I have plans for you* look. He said, "The same sort of something fucking else that makes you nearly get yourself killed saving the kid who'd just challenged you to a duel to the death?"

I had no idea why Hal was talking to me like that. It made me really suspicious. I just muttered, "Whatever," and hoped he'd shut up.

He didn't. Hal went on, "Twice. We nearly lost you when you shifted so Manuel could run the gauntlet. That took some quick thinking, at a time when it must have been hard to put any thoughts together at all. And courage. And sacrifice, again..."

I said, "What are you getting at?"

He said, "I'd like to offer you an alternative."

"What?" I asked.

"A job. Why don't you join Protection, Inc.?"

"You are fucking kidding," I said.

Hal shook his head. "I'm absolutely serious."

I could see that he was — Hal doesn't do sarcastic — but I couldn't believe it. "I fought every single one of you!"

Hal nodded. "Any wolf who can hold his own against a lion, a tiger, a leopard, and a grizzly is a wolf I want on my team."

The door flew open. Apparently the rest of the team had been eavesdropping and someone leaned too hard. They nearly fell into the room. It would have been funny if they hadn't looked so outraged. Actually, it *was* funny and the outrage made it even funnier. I guess having me in the office for a few days was one thing, but having me actually on their team crossed one hell of a line.

"Absolutely not," Rafa said. "I'm a Navy SEAL and a man

of honor, and I do not team up with criminals."

Destiny said, "He gave me a *permanent scar.*" She yanked down her sleeve to show this tiny little white mark on her shoulder. I guess I bit her pretty hard when she was a tiger.

Fiona pointed like she wanted to stab me with her finger. "You think we can trust *him* to guard our backs? Never!"

Do it, my wolf said.

I couldn't resist fucking with them. I turned to Hal and said, "I accept."

And then there was a whole lot of yelling. I'd meant to enjoy watching them all blow their tops while they thought I was serious, and then get to see it all over again when I told them I was just yanking their chains. But Hal sat there and calmly answered all their objections. The way he talked about me — I can't repeat it, it's too embarrassing. I'll blush or something. But he said more good things about me in an hour than I'd heard from anyone since I was fifteen.

Hal convinced them to give me a chance. And after that, I had to give *them* a chance.

Once I got my strength back, the first thing I did was help them boot my old gang out of the neighborhood. I talked to some of the wolves and convinced them to leave the pack of their own accord. I stood with Hal's team and watched while they ran the gauntlet, so we'd intimidate Price and his buddies out of killing anyone. The wolves who left got roughed up, but nothing that wouldn't heal overnight. They made their own pack. Nothing criminal, just a group of wolves in the city. Turned out that a lot of them had wanted out for a while, but they'd been scared of the gauntlet.

Price was fucking furious, but there was nothing he could do about it. He took what was left of his pack— the dregs, the guys who were criminals because they liked to hurt people— and that was the last we saw of them. He didn't just leave the neighborhood, he left the city. Last we heard of them, they were way out of our territory, wandering around picking pockets and mugging people and stealing cars. Really small-time stuff. Pathetic. Eventually we lost track of them.

The new wolf pack invited me to join, but my wolf said, *You have a pack.*

It was hard to believe, but once he said it, I realized he was right. I didn't have that empty, no-pack feeling gnawing away inside of me. I had a pack, and it was Protection, Inc.

Even so, for the first six months or so, I was half-convinced that at any second, Hal would take back his offer. Or I'd realize I could never hack it outside of a gang, and I'd have to drop out. But he didn't. And I didn't.

And here I am.

Chapter Seven

Nick

Before he started talking, Nick had intended to tell Raluca about the gang he'd run and the kills he'd made, and leave his feelings out of it. But she hadn't asked what crimes he'd committed. She'd asked him why he was so angry. So he had to begin with his father's first pack, and then go on to the CEO. His mother's death. His father's. Everything.

As he spoke, his rage poured out in a torrent. And not only that, but grief and guilt and all the other feelings he usually tried not to even think about, let alone talk about. By the end of it, he was completely wrung out, with the bedspread beneath him damp with sweat.

Raluca kept her word. She didn't let go of him. She didn't even flinch. Instead, she held him tight, stroking his hair and rubbing his shoulders, until he was done.

She didn't break the silence immediately, but she didn't need to. He could feel her love and support in the gentle but relentless strength of her hands, in the steadiness of her breathing, and in her presence. Raluca was his mate, and nothing he'd told her had damaged the bond between them. If anything, he'd strengthened it with his honesty.

"What happened to Manuel?" she asked. He hadn't gotten used to her real voice, and it once again startled him. It was no longer high and chiming, but resonant, deep for a woman. Less pretty, but more sexy. And far more real.

The unexpectedness of both her question and the sound of it distracted him from that fucking tidal wave of emotions. He rolled over, nudging her to move with him until neither of them were lying on any wet spots.

By the time they'd resettled themselves, his voice was steady. "He's in college now. Still with the pack in upstate New York. I've flown out to visit them a couple times. That's them in the photo in the lobby. Manuel's the skinny one with long legs. We were deer hunting, and I happened to be in the lead when an aunt shifted to take a picture. They're not my pack, but Hal wanted a photo of me that wasn't a team shot, and I didn't want to be on the wall as a lone wolf. I have a snapshot of me as a pup with my Dad and Mom, but I couldn't put that up either. I don't mind seeing Manuel, because he made it out. But if I had to look at my parents every day, I'd lose it for sure. It'd be about three days before I tracked down fucking Price and killed him."

Nick cut himself off. His heart was pounding with the force of his rage, his muscles taut and quivering as stretched wires.

"Your anger is justified." Raluca stroked his damp hair. "You and people you loved were terribly wronged. You were forced to commit acts you never would have freely chosen. You were manipulated by your own honor, and you nearly gave up your life for it. If I were you, I too would be filled with rage."

Nick let out a deep breath. He'd known by her body language that she must have thought something like that, but it was still good to hear. He hadn't cried when he'd told his story. He didn't cry, period. But hearing that from Raluca made his eyes prickle.

"Thanks." His voice shook a little, but this time he didn't try to stop it. Raluca wouldn't care.

She went on, calmly but with growing intensity, "And if I ever see Price, I am not sure that I could hold so tight to honor as you did. A wolf does not stand a chance against a dragon, no more than I would as a woman. There can be no fair fight between Price and I. But for what he did to you, I would be very tempted to seize him in my talons, soar upward until he begged in terror for his life, and then let him fall. Screaming all the way down."

"Whoa." Nick stared at her. He hadn't expected *that.* "Seriously?"

"Yes." Raluca's eyes burned silver. "In fact, if you wish it, perhaps Hal could discover where he lives now. *I* am not bound by pack laws."

Nick was tempted, but he shook his head. She had no blood on her hands, and she couldn't know what that felt like until it was too late for take-backs. "Nah, let's leave him to his sorry life. But if he ever comes after me again, feel free."

"I shall," Raluca said coolly.

Nick had no doubt that she meant it. He knew his teammates would protect him, but it was something new to have his mate swear it.

It was something new to have a mate at all. Once he'd stopped fighting his feelings, the depth of his love dizzied him. He'd never felt anything like it, protectiveness and sexual heat and camaraderie and adoration, all wrapped up in one astonishing package. Now that he'd given into it, he couldn't believe he'd managed to deny it for as long as he had.

More balls than brains, his wolf remarked. *Still.*

Shut the fuck up, Nick retorted silently, but he couldn't get any real anger into it.

Raluca's eyes cooled to stormy gray. She touched his chest. He didn't have to look down to see where she had her fingers. "The dead deer in the forest. Are those your kills as an alpha?"

"Yeah." Nick lifted her hand and laid it over the pitted scars on his chest. "And obviously, that's from Price. I don't know if it scarred like that because the original wound was so bad, or because I tore it open again shifting."

Raluca pulled her palm up so it hovered above the skin. But he could still feel her radiant heat, soothing as a hot compress. "Doesn't it hurt to be touched?"

"Not if you're gentle," Nick said.

She frowned. "Was I not?"

"You were." Then Nick admitted, "It just still burns me up. Not there. Here." He touched his heart, then his head. "Here. Not the gauntlet itself, but why it happened. How it happened. Price used Manuel like he was a tool, not a person. Fucking Price! All he ever fucking had to do was say, "Sure, shifters' honor, what can I do to help?" And then maybe Mom wouldn't have died and Dad wouldn't have killed anyone. Dad for sure wouldn't have stayed in a gang. He'd be alive today."

"Who else are you angry at, Nick?" Raluca asked softly.

"Who am I not?!" Fury burned through Nick as he spoke, as hot and frustrated now as when he'd been fifteen. "That fucking CEO — it wouldn't have cost him anything to help us, but he liked being able to sit back in his cushy office and pride himself on being a selfish fuck who valued money above people. Price's asshole buddies who helped him kill that poor son of a bitch who just wanted to leave. Dad's smug pack that thought they were better than humans. The whole fucking system that makes poor people beg for money just to stay alive. Those black ops guys who took Shane and came halfway to breaking him. Your Uncle Constantine—"

"What?" Raluca's hands stopped rubbing his shoulders, startled into immobility. "But you've never even met him."

"I don't have to meet him. He tried to kill Journey. He nearly killed Lucas. And you! I hate him for what he did to you!"

"Me?" Raluca sounded incredulous. "You're angry for *me?*"

Nick leaned on one elbow, his breath coming hard, his entire body burning. Raluca's confusion made him even more furious — not at her, but at the man who had molded her until she didn't understand why anyone, even her own mate, could feel rage on her behalf. "Yes, of course I fucking am! He manipulated you, just like Price manipulated me and Manuel. For all we know, he's trying to kill you right now. But I don't give a fuck if he isn't, I still fucking hate that bastard. You've never harmed a soul in your entire fucking life, and he tried to stop you from *having* a life. He took away your freedom, he took away your voice, he took away your *self!* You're surprised that I'm mad at him — that shouldn't be surprising. But it is to you, because he even took away your anger."

"No." Raluca's eyes were changing again, beginning to glow silver. Nick shut his mouth in a hurry. "He only tried."

"Were you secretly furious at him the whole time?"

Raluca shook her head, sending her cool hair slithering across his hot skin. "No. I felt unjustified. He was giving me everything I could possibly want, and doing nothing overtly wrong. And anger is considered an improper emotion for a princess. It was there nonetheless, but I smothered and ignored it. And after I was free, my uncle was locked up and out of my reach. I couldn't take revenge on him, so I turned my rage on someone else."

"Who?" Nick asked blankly.

Raluca's lips curved into an ironic smile. "You, Nick. I was furious at you. I have spent the last few days plotting vengeance against you. I knew you'd be humiliated at the white tie gala, and I looked forward to it. And when you played me that song in the car, I almost threw you out of it."

"Oh!" Nick had known Raluca was pissed at him, but not how deep it had run. "Well, don't worry about that. I deserved it. I was deliberately trying to piss you off. That chip on my shoulder —"

"Yes," Raluca said. Now her eyes reminded him of Hal's or Shane's: that piercing gaze that sees into your blind spot, coolly

evaluating everything you can't see — or don't want to see — in
yourself. "You and I are very much alike, are we not? Neither of us
can take vengeance against the people who harmed us most. And
both of us were told not to be angry when we had excellent reasons
to be, so we were forced to bottle it up until it exploded, like
champagne gone sour."

"But I wasn't..." Nick's voice trailed off as he thought about
what she'd said. "No, you're right. I was too. Dad told me to control
my wolf, and when I didn't, I killed someone. When I was in the
gang, I was always afraid that if I ever confronted Price, I'd kill him.
So I pretended I didn't care, until it was too late. I think Rafa and
Fiona and the rest of my team constantly telling me to chill out made
me feel like they're the only safe people to be mad at. If I ever got
pissed at anyone who actually deserved it, I might kill them. So I
kept on going ballistic on people I cared about and knew I'd never
hurt, and I drove them nuts without ever getting any less angry."

"A banked fire doesn't go out," Raluca said thoughtfully. "It
smolders and spreads. Every now and then, a spark goes up and sets
whatever it falls on aflame."

"That's me, all right. Setting things on fire every which
way." Nick sighed. "Now I feel bad for my team. And you. I'd
apologize, but I have a feeling I'd just fuck it up. I mean to them. I
could apologize to you. Again."

Raluca ruffled his hair. "No need. For myself, anyway. As
for your team, perhaps they would prefer your anger turned on their
behalf rather than on them. Have you ever told Lucas how you feel
about Uncle Constantine?"

Nick's face burned with embarrassment as he recalled
Lucas's return. "Uh, no. I just dropped a bunch of f-bombs on his
mate." At Raluca's expression, he added, "Not literal bombs. That's
American slang for that word you hate."

"Oh. That is convenient. Now I can refer to it more easily."
Raluca looked so pleased that Nick had to stifle a laugh.

"You gonna tell Lucas how *you* feel about Constantine?" he
asked.

"Yes, I shall. Lucas may try to turn it aside, out of pride, but I
think it will please him." She brushed her fingers over his lips, her
touch hot and feather-light. "It pleased me to hear it from you."

"Oh. I'm glad. I guess I'll tell him too, then. I might not stop there, even. Some stuff went down with Shane, too, a while back. I was scared that he'd die, and furious at the people who'd fucked him over. But I didn't say so. I yelled at him instead. It was when he was hurt, too. Like I don't know how much fun that is." Nick swallowed. "Fuck. There's gonna be a lot of changes. I feel turned inside-out."

"I too. But perhaps we can steady each other."

"Yeah." With Raluca at his side, Nick felt more secure than he had in years. She might look fragile, but he could lean on her without worrying that she wasn't strong enough to bear his weight or she'd look down on him for needing support. "You're a fucking pillar of steel. In high-heeled shoes."

"You as well," she said. "In boots."

They leaned in at the same moment to kiss. It sent a jolt of love and desire through him, as all her kisses did. As, he felt sure, all her kisses always would.

But between the party from hell and the murder attempt and all that emotion, Nick was too worn out to do more than kiss. Raluca obviously was too, though he could only tell by the intuition granted to him by their bond and from the faint shadows under her eyes. He'd been taught on the streets and she in a palace, but they'd both learned that showing any signs of weakness could be deadly. It would be a hard habit to give up.

"Ready for bed?" Nick asked.

She nodded gratefully. Nick held her close in one arm and reached up to turn out the light.

As she relaxed into him, his thoughts raced ahead to the next morning. He'd have to take back everything he'd said to Hal. No fucking way was Nick letting someone else protect his mate now. But what should he say?

When other team members had introduced their mates to Protection, Inc., the rest of the team — Nick included — had hazed their mates in various ways, to make sure they were strong and loving and loyal. Shane had used his power to inflict terror to test their courage, and when Shane had found his own mate, Lucas had used his dragon heritage to do the same thing to her. All the mates had passed their tests with flying colors, but it had been no fun for them, and Hal and Lucas and Shane had been furious when it was *their* mates getting hazed. Now that he had a mate himself, Nick knew exactly how they'd felt. Even the thought of anyone pulling that sort of crap on Raluca made him outraged.

On the other hand, maybe the team would skip it this time. Hal had personally saved the asses of everyone on the team, so of course they all loved him and wanted to make sure his mate was worthy of him. Lucas was the newest member, the rookie, so it was his teammates' job to look out for him. And anyone who knew Shane could see that he'd been through hell, so his friends wanted to make sure his mate wouldn't add a broken heart to his burdens. But Nick was just… Nick.

All the same, he didn't want Raluca to face the teasing and provoking and intimidating and weird impromptu tests of strength and loyalty and intelligence that the team had thrown at Ellie and Journey and Catalina. Maybe the best thing would be to hold off on revealing the mate thing for now. Later, when he had more time, he could tell his teammates one by one, alone with them, and make sure they didn't try anything.

Satisfied with that solution, Nick said softly, "Raluca?"

There was no response. Her breathing was deep and even. She was already asleep, just minutes after he'd turned out the light.

Nick couldn't help being a bit envious. Even after he'd gotten out of the gang, Nick had a hard time letting his guard down enough to sleep. It sometimes took him hours, and even then he often woke to his wolf's howled demands to check for dangers which existed only in nightmares that Nick himself couldn't recall. He'd resigned himself to never being able to convince his body or wolf that he was ever completely safe.

But tonight he lay relaxed, marveling at his good luck. To his werewolf senses, Raluca's hair and dragonmarks shone faintly in the darkness, like the paper stars he'd glued to his ceiling when he'd been a little boy. He breathed in her scent of steel and roses, and curled in even closer to the heat of her body. This was one night when he'd actually enjoy lying awake.

Go to sleep, his wolf said with a jaw-cracking yawn. *No one can hurt you or your mate here.*

"Will wonders never fucking cease," Nick muttered.

But neither Raluca nor his wolf responded; both were fast asleep. A moment later, Nick joined them.

Chapter Eight

Raluca

Raluca awoke to the sweetest sight that had ever greeted her in the morning.

Nick lay beside her, with one arm around her side and the other flung out, his nude body on magnificent display. The defined musculature of his back, its pale skin unmarked except for a few leafy branches dipping over his shoulders, would put even a dragon to shame.

I told you he had a very nice back, her dragon hissed.

And backside, Raluca answered, smiling. It was firm and compact, as fine a sight naked as it was in jeans.

She was tempted to pat it, but Nick was sleeping so soundly that she hated to wake him. His face was turned toward her, his thick black lashes easily visible against his cheeks, his chin roughened with stubble, his lips slightly parted. He looked boyish and, for the first time since Raluca had met him, at peace.

She wondered if that was how he'd have been if his parents hadn't died as they had, and none of the ensuing consequences had occurred. Maybe he'd have followed in his father's footsteps and worked in the steel mill. But Nick had too much fire in him for her to imagine him living a quiet life. If he'd grown up without adversity, might he have sought it out of his own accord?

Raluca hadn't moved, but no doubt her breathing had changed as she'd woken. Nick stirred, blinking his long lashes, then instantly pulled her in.

"Hey." Nick pressed a kiss against her shoulder, then her collarbone, and finally her lips. "You're really here."

"I have no intention of going anywhere without you."

He kissed her again. Then his bright eyes widened in sudden recall. "Oh, fuck. I have to talk to Hal. I told him last night you were going to get a new bodyguard. I need to head him off at the pass before he assigns someone."

He sprang out of bed, his lithe musculature flexing beautifully, then held out a hand. "Shower with me?"

Raluca accepted, feeling half in a dream. The bathroom off

the bedroom was plain and tiny, with barely enough room in the shower stall for two. But Nick's agility and Raluca's trained grace allowed them to move within it without colliding with each other or the walls. Water soaked his hair, turning it to shining sleekness, and streamed down his body, gleaming off his defined muscles and brightening his tattoos. They spent some time simply touching each other, enjoying the feeling of wet skin on skin and the intimacy of soaping each other's bodies.

But after a while, the warm water began to chill Raluca. She turned the heat up until Nick's skin flushed pink, then guiltily reached to turn it back down. "I'm sorry. It's too hot for you."

He caught her hand. "Don't. It's hot, you're hot. I like it."

"I like showering with you. I have never bathed with a man before."

Nick grinned. "So you just lost your shower virginity? If I'd known, I'd have held off till we had more time to enjoy it."

"We will have more time later, will we not?"

The same amazed delight that Raluca felt visibly radiated from Nick. "Yeah. We'll have all the time in the world."

But he kept darting glances away. Raluca knew he was impatient to speak with Hal, but unable to bring himself to end the time with her. She resolved his dilemma by turning off the water.

When they finished drying each other off, she reluctantly dressed in the black fatigues. They reminded her unpleasantly of how she and Nick had misunderstood and rejected each other the last time she'd worn them, but she could hardly wear a couture gown around an office. It needed to be dry-cleaned before she could wear it again at all, anyway.

"When will I be able to retrieve my clothes from the hotel?" Raluca asked. "Or will I need to purchase more?"

"Someone will fetch them," Nick said absently. He was staring down at his crumpled white tie outfit. With a groan, he said, "Hang on. I'll be right back."

He darted out with a towel around his waist, then bolted back inside with an armful of black cloth. As he began changing into his own fatigues, he said, "Team's already starting to arrive. This could get awkward."

"How so?"

Nick turned to the closed door, his entire body radiating

nervy tension. She could hear nothing, but no doubt he heard more. "We have to decide if we tell them that we're mates now, or later. My vote is for later."

"Would Hal disapprove of you guarding me if he knew I was your mate?" Raluca asked.

"I doubt it. He guarded his mate. No, there's this other thing…" Nick trailed off, cocking his head as he listened to more sounds that Raluca could not hear. "I don't *think* they'd do it, they already know you, sort of, and I — well, I'm just me."

"What are you talking about?" But even as she asked, Raluca's attention was elsewhere. She was rifling her hoard pack for jewelry that would go with the fatigues and dress them up, but which she hadn't already worn with them. It was a challenging task, especially as Nick was in a hurry and she meant to accompany him.

"It's a little hard to explain." Nick's eyes flickered as he listened to whatever was happening outside. "Do you mind if right now, we just tell Hal we made up and you still want me as a guard, and we save the mate talk for later?"

Raluca supposed that Nick expected his teammates to tease him over his newly mated state, as Destiny had when she'd thought he had a date. Though Raluca wouldn't be the target of any teasing herself, she sympathized with Nick's desire to postpone it.

"I am in no hurry. We can tell the others whenever you wish," Raluca said, and was rewarded with his relieved smile.

She finished finger-combing her hair and clipped it with a simple pin of gold and rubies. Nick also finger-combed his hair, but she suspected that was how he always did it. It fell easily around his face, and would no doubt dry into his usual appealingly tousled locks.

"Do you even own a hairbrush?" Raluca asked.

His blank look said it all.

They helped each other strap on their bulletproof vests, then button black cloth jackets over them.

"You look like a girl wearing her boyfriend's shirt," Nick said with a grin, then held up one hand. "Wait… Okay, coast is clear."

He opened the door to an empty corridor. They walked to the lobby, where Nick indicated the wolf photo. "There's Manuel."

"And you." Raluca examined the photo again. Nick's wolf

still looked so sad. "Perhaps you should take another photograph the next time you visit them."

Nick looked more closely at his shifted self. "Yeah, I probably should. Don't know if anyone but you would notice, but I sure don't look like I was having any fun." Lowering his voice, he added, "You come along next time. I'll clean up better, guaranteed."

He knocked on Hal's door. A deep voice rumbled, "Come in."

Only Raluca's princess training prevented her from giving a start at the sight of not only Hal, but Destiny, Rafa, and the blonde woman that Raluca had only ever seen in a photograph on Hal's desk. Nick didn't flinch, no doubt drawing upon his alpha cool, but Raluca felt him stiffen slightly beside her.

"Raluca, this is Fiona," Hal began. "She's done with her job, so either she or Destiny can —"

"Nope," Nick interrupted him. "Raluca's still with me. We made up. Everything's cool now."

Everyone stared at him.

"Hey, Fiona," Nick said before any of them could speak, in a less-than-subtle attempt at distraction. "How was the job?"

The blonde woman gave a shrug, her elegant eyebrows raised. "It was fine. Nick, after all the times I've offered to teach you how to go undercover in high society, why —"

Hal interrupted her. "Hold on, Fiona. Raluca, I want to hear it from you. Do you really want to stay with Nick?"

"Yes," Raluca said.

Everyone but Fiona instantly switched from staring at Nick to staring at her, all with identical looks of bafflement.

Irritated, Raluca thought, *Is it truly so shocking that he and I settled our disagreement?*

They are surprised at your voice, her dragon explained. *Only Fiona has never heard you speak before.*

Raluca didn't want to explain why she sounded so different. Hoping no one would inquire, she addressed Hal. "Nick is correct. We quarreled, but it was due to a misunderstanding. He saved my life last night. I do not wish to be guarded by anyone but him."

"Actually, if you still want to go to that nightclub tonight, I could use a little help," Nick put in. "Can I have two volunteers to guard the doors?"

Destiny, her eyes dancing with merriment, raised her hand like a schoolgirl.

At the same time, Rafa said, "I'm in."

"Oh, well. I'm tired anyway. I could use a night off." Fiona turned to Raluca and made a flawless curtsey with the skirt of her little black dress. "I'm very pleased to meet you, Princess Raluca."

Raluca, unable to curtsey in fatigues, bowed instead. It was incorrect for a woman, but it seemed like a better option than awkwardly offering her hand, as Hal had done when they'd met. "I am pleased to meet you as well. But I am no longer a princess. I am only Raluca."

Fiona smiled, but her green eyes stayed cool and watchful. They were as intense as Nick's, but a lighter shade: spring leaves, not emeralds. "In that case, *Raluca*, please make yourself free with my clothes."

Raluca gritted her teeth. She was certain that the woman was making a veiled insult, given that Raluca was already wearing her clothing with no invitation from their owner, but it was subtle enough to be worthy of Uncle Constantine. From Nick's lack of reaction, he'd completely missed the implications and taken the remark at face value.

What on earth had Raluca done to offend Fiona? They'd only just met. Was she really that annoyed over her clothes being worn without permission? Coolly, Raluca replied, "Thank you, I shall wear them whenever I feel like it."

"Oh, you don't need to," Destiny put in. "Rafa and I collected everything from the hotel. No signs of assassins, but we're keeping your belongings at Protection, Inc. for now. We stashed it all in the other bedroom first thing this morning. You know, the one you two weren't sleeping in."

Instantly, Nick said, "I slept on the floor."

Hal and Rafa again stared at him, Hal with a carefully straight face and Rafa with dawning realization. Raluca groaned inwardly. From their lack of reaction, Destiny and Fiona were still unaware of Nick and Raluca's actual relationship, but Nick had obviously just given it away to the men.

"Of course you did," Rafa said, his voice quivering. Raluca was certain he was trying not laugh. "Well. This should be an exciting evening."

"I fucking hope not," Nick said. "I'm counting on you and Destiny to stop any assassins before they get to the door. I'll pitch in if you need me, but I'm really hoping Raluca can get one fucking evening of goddamn fun without anyone trying to murder her."

"You make it sound so appealing," Rafa remarked.

Hal held up a huge hand, silencing them all. "Okay. Fiona, get some rest. Rafa and Destiny, scope out the nightclub. I want you both watching from the rooftops three hours before it opens. Maybe you can catch someone trying to set something up. If you don't, get down and blend in. Nick, you're in charge of this operation from the ground. Call me if you need me, of course."

Then a startlingly sweet smile altered the masculine planes of Hal's face as he looked from Nick to Raluca. "But I hope you do have just a fun night out. "

"Want me to teach you the latest moves before I go?" Destiny asked Raluca. "I saw your nightclub outfit. It'll look great on you."

"I saw it too," Fiona said to Raluca. "Wise of you to go to the cheap store. I'm sure you'd be very put out if Nick was injured protecting you and bled on an expensive dress."

An inferno of fury blazed up in Raluca. Her eyes felt like flames, and she knew they were glowing like molten silver. She took a step toward the blonde woman, intruding upon her personal space, daring her to back away. Fiona held her ground, but her eyes turned icy as her snow leopard readied itself for a fight.

Raluca's voice rang out with the power and depth of a great bell in a tower, echoing around the office. "As I'm sure you're aware, over-dressing is just as ill-mannered, improper, and insulting as under-dressing. And if Nick is ever injured on my behalf, I shall be too busy tending to his wounds and taking fiery vengeance on those who harmed him to pay any heed to my clothing."

A brief silence fell. Nick, who had opened his mouth, no doubt to defend her, closed it again.

"Also," Raluca added in a final knife-twist, "I can afford to replace any number of couture gowns. A spoiled one is of no importance to me. It's sad that the same is not true for you. But since you were so generous with your own clothing, in the future I will give you all my hand-me-downs. I have them often; I never wear last season's styles."

Raluca closed her mouth, satisfied with that devastating series of insults. She waited for her enemy to cringe in humiliation, or perhaps even flee.

But Fiona did not seem crushed in the slightest. Bizarrely, she looked *pleased.* Her eyes brightened with a golden sparkle, like summer sunlight falling warm on grass. She gave Raluca a smile that seemed absolutely sincere. "Good. That's all I needed to hear. You and Nick enjoy your evening. Call me if you need back-up."

With a graceful wave to her teammates and a wink at Nick, Fiona went out, shutting the door soundlessly behind her.

Raluca looked at Nick, but he seemed as baffled as she was. To the room at large, he asked, "What the fuck was up with Fiona?"

"Rough mission," Destiny said. "Sleep deprivation, stress, the works. Don't take everything so personally."

Emerald fire blazed in Nick's eyes. He opened his mouth, then caught himself and took three deep breaths. "Right. Right. Okay, me and Raluca are going to grab something to eat. We can be back before you leave if Raluca wants to get a dance lesson."

"I do," Raluca said. "Thank you, Destiny. Nick, let's go."

She opened the door and fled before anyone could say anything else. Nick followed her.

Once the door closed behind them, Nick grabbed her hand. "Let's get out of here. Unless you want to change first."

Raluca hesitated, then decided that she'd rather wear Fiona's fatigues than risk meeting Fiona again. "I'm fine. These are comfortable."

She was immensely relieved when they made it into Nick's car without running into anyone else. Now she understood why he hadn't wanted to reveal their mating. Hal and Rafa had obviously found it hilarious, and were undoubtedly just waiting for Nick to confess it so they could tease him. She wondered if Nick realized, but a glance at his face told her that he hadn't. She considered telling him, then decided not to. He seemed stressed enough already.

And no wonder, with the bizarre behavior of his teammate! Fiona's sudden switch from blistering hostility to apparently genuine friendliness, for no reason whatsoever, was even more unsettling than if the woman had been consistently unpleasant. If Fiona continued to be nice, Raluca would never know if she might be secretly plotting against her, or might turn around and insult her again for no reason.

"Does Fiona often change her opinions so quickly?" Raluca asked.

"Not at all. I have no idea what got into her."

"But the sofa…" Raluca began.

"The entire team had a grudge against me. Fiona was just a little bit more memorable about it. Anyway, she had a good reason to be pissed at me then. She had no reason to be mad at you. And the way she dropped it was really weird." Nick frowned. "Maybe I should go back up and make sure one of the paramedics checked her. She could've been drugged or something on the mission."

"Could anything like that escape Hal's notice?" Raluca asked. "If she returned acting strangely, surely he had her examined already. Or is having her checked now."

Nick relaxed. "Yeah, you're right. If it was a rough mission, he'd definitely have had Ellie or Catalina or Shane give her the once-over. I bet Destiny was right and Fiona was just really sleep-deprived. That can make you do weird things. Rafa and I were on a mission once where neither of us could sleep for three days, and by the end of it he was hallucinating pretty pink butterflies and it took me half an hour to figure out that the reason a door wouldn't unlock was that I was holding the key upside-down."

Raluca decided to give Nick's teammate the benefit of the doubt, for his sake if not for Fiona's. "In that case, I shall give Fiona a second chance. Perhaps she will not even recall this first meeting once she's slept."

"Speaking of sleep." Nick settled a casually possessive hand on her thigh. "We overslept big-time. Can I take you to lunch? To make up for Big Bacon?"

"Of course."

Nick still hadn't started the car. He took a breath, clearly edgy, as he said, "There's a place I'd like to take you. It really is my America. A neighborhood joint. Casual. American food. Good, but nothing fancy."

"That sounds lovely," Raluca said. "I did mean it when I said I wanted to see the real America."

"Okay." Nick started the car. As they began speeding with traffic, he added, "You don't have to like it. Don't pretend for my sake. If you hate it, we can leave."

Raluca now recognized the signs of Nick laying down his defenses against some impending hurt. "Is this a place that means something to you, Nick?"

"Yeah," he confessed. "Sorry. I should've told you up-front. It's owned by one of the wolves from my old pack. They all hang out there. Their mates, too. I've never brought anyone there before but my teammates."

"Ah-ha," Raluca said, smiling.

"Yeah, but the food really is good. If you don't like the burgers, it means you don't like burgers, period. There's a jukebox, too." At Raluca's baffled look, he explained, "An old-fashioned music player. The music's old-fashioned, too. But in a good way. Same as the food: if you don't like the music, you don't like country. That shit I played to piss you off was making my ears bleed, too."

Raluca laughed, looking at the wires dangling from the hole in his radio. "I shall be honest. But I would like to go."

Soon Nick pulled up in front of a building with a sign reading, "Dan and Kate's Diner." The neighborhood was clearly not wealthy, but it had the same vibrant quality as the mural of the woman with rainbow hair. Tall trees blooming with a profusion of purple flowers lined the cracked sidewalk, a man was selling ice cream out of a push-cart to a mob of eager children and adults, and the buildings looked small and cozy.

Nick scanned the interior, then escorted her inside the restaurant. He seemed edgy; despite his words, he clearly *wanted* her to like the place. Raluca too was nervous, wondering what she'd think and how he'd introduce her. Music, food, friends: she hoped she'd sincerely like at least one.

The interior was filled with the enticing smells of frying fat and grilling meat. A lively song was playing, but softly enough to not drown out voices. The tables were polished wood, the booths lined with soft red plastic. An odd machine stood at one corner.

There were only a few other customers, and they all looked up in surprise as Nick and Raluca walked in.

"Hey, Nick," a gray-haired man called as he walked in from the open kitchen. "Who's the pretty lady?"

Nick took a deep breath and addressed the room at large. "Her name's Raluca, and she's my mate."

The customers and waitress exclaimed in pleased surprise

and started calling out congratulations and questions, some teasing and some serious.

"How'd you meet?"

"You gonna make an honest man of him?"

"Are you a shifter?"

The gray-haired man held up his hand, and everyone fell silent. "Let Nick and his mate enjoy their lunch. You can quiz them and buy them drinks later. They'll be back."

"Thanks, Dan," Nick called.

"We will," Raluca said. She smiled at Dan. "I like the music."

Dan indicated the machine. "Jukebox is over there. It's mostly country. Not radio country, the real deal. Oldies, bluegrass, gospel, that sort of thing."

Raluca looked at the machine with new interest. "I do not think I have heard any of that."

"Let's fix that for you." Nick steered her to the jukebox. It had a panel of buttons and song titles and numbers listed in a book with plastic pages. "Do you know any of these?"

"No. You choose something." Lowering her voice, she added, "Your friends seem nice."

Nick looked immensely relieved. Then his bright smile flashed, and he said, "I'm sure they're glad you approve of them. They have wolf hearing."

Raluca almost blushed. She'd forgotten. But if anyone had eavesdropped, they were polite enough to give no sign of it. And at least they'd overheard something positive.

"This song makes me think of you." Nick hit a button, and a new song began to play.

Raluca shot Nick a menacing glance. "I hear twanging."

A woman's soulful voice rose above the guitars.

She don't need anybody to tell her she's pretty.
She's heard it every single day of her life.
He's got to wonder what she sees in him
When there's so many others standing in line.

Raluca took Nick's hand. Softly, she said, "I see everything I want in you."

Nick ducked his head, hiding his face from anyone who might be watching, but his fingers tightened around hers.

They stood still and listened. The singer had a beautiful voice, and the song, about a woman who chose freedom despite its cost, stole into Raluca's heart.

She's fragile like a string of pearls.
She's nobody's girl.

Raluca touched the strand of pearls around her throat, her eyes prickling with unshed tears. She'd had princes and dragons standing in line, but it had taken a wolf from the American streets to see her soul and show it to her in a song.

"Come on," he said, his voice catching a little. "Let's order."

They slid into a booth, with Nick sitting where he could watch the door.

The waitress was a plump middle-aged woman whose shirt bore a tag labeled "Kate." She smiled at Raluca. "I'm so glad to meet you. We've all been hoping for years that Nick would find his mate. I've never forgotten the moment I laid eyes on Dan. Your first meeting must have been so wonderful!"

Nick made an odd coughing sound, then another. He shot Raluca a desperate glance.

"Indeed," Raluca said smoothly, saving him from having to either confess or lie. "It was quite an experience for both of us. And I am very pleased to meet you as well. Some day you must tell me the story of how you and Dan met."

"I'd love to," Kate said with a sincerity that made Raluca certain that the story of Kate and Dan contained no misplaced rage, vengeance via giant hairballs and oyster forks, or assassination attempts. "But for now, would you like a menu?"

Raluca turned to Nick. "I would not know what to choose. Order for me, please."

"We'll both have the classic burger, fries, and cokes. Thanks," Nick said.

As Kate headed back to the kitchen, another song began. This one was by a man with a resounding deep voice, fierce and commanding.

Well, you wonder why I always dress in black.

Nick whipped around. Raluca followed his gaze, and saw Dan at the jukebox.

The gray-haired man tipped an imaginary hat to Nick. "Couldn't resist. She doesn't know country, so she couldn't pick one for you herself."

"What is this song?" asked Raluca.

"'Man in Black,'" Nick replied, much as he had said, "World's biggest lobster."

Nick was also dressed in black, but from the glances he and Dan had exchanged, Dan's choice of song was more pointed than a simple joke about Nick's clothing. But as Raluca listened to the song, she understood.

The man with the booming voice sang that he wore black as a reminder of the poor, of the unfairly imprisoned, of young lives lost in pointless wars and old people dying alone and forgotten, of everyone treated badly who deserved better and of all the injustices of the world. He sounded angry. Passionate. Challenging.

"Dan knows you very well," Raluca said.

Nick started to shrug, then caught himself. "Yeah. He does. And so do you. But just out of curiosity, what did you think about the songs as music?"

"I still don't care for twanging," Raluca admitted. "But the woman's voice was beautiful. The man's too, in a different way. And both singers sounded as if they truly felt the emotions they sang about. I like that. The 'Why I Am Drunk' songs did not sound sincere."

Nick laughed. "That's the perfect name for that crap. Congratulations, you do like some country. At least, you like classic stuff like Bonnie Raitt and Johnny Cash. I had a feeling you might."

Kate, who had stepped up with a platter of food, said, "Nobody is allowed in here if they hate Johnny Cash. Proves they have no soul. Enjoy."

Raluca had seen hamburgers in movies, but never eaten one before. She watched Nick pick his up in his hands and take a bite, then followed suit.

The meat patty was juicy and savory, the bun soft on one side and crisp on the other. Like her maid's sausage wrapped in ham, it was simple but tasty and satisfying. So were the crisp potato sticks.

Raluca picked up her glass of bubbling brown liquid and examined it with interest. So this was the famous Coke. It wasn't available in Viorel, and she'd never gotten around to trying it when she'd seen it in other European cities. It looked like dark beer, but she knew it was non-alcoholic and sweet. Other than that, she'd never heard it described, only seen it enthusiastically drunk in movies and TV shows.

She took a large sip, which she instantly regretted. It burned its way down her throat. Trying to pitch her voice below werewolf hearing, she murmured, "Is there a drink here that does not taste of chemicals dissolved in sugar?"

She failed miserably; a few stifled snickers rose from across the room. But they sounded amused rather than offended, as did Nick's open laugh.

"It's okay. You didn't insult the cook." Nick waved at Kate. "How about lemonade for my mate? And a glass of water as backup. And coffee. Second back-up."

"I do like the burger," Raluca said. "And the fries."

Nick grinned and flicked his fingers at her near-empty plate. "I can tell. They make the lemonade here, so you might like that better. No chemicals."

"Good." She pushed the revolting soda to Nick, who drank it with apparent enjoyment. "Is that very American?"

He laughed again, but not in mockery. It was good to see him so open and cheerful. "Coke is as American as it gets. It's okay. Lucas won't drink it either, or anything else that comes in a can. Might be a dragon thing. Tell you what, when I take you to a bar, I'll buy you a beer on tap. He likes those."

When I take you to a bar. Nick's words echoed in Raluca's ears as she finished her fries. She knew without asking that he would take her to his favorite bar, or would carefully select one he thought she'd like. There would be no more hairballs. Nick was showing her the best he thought his country had to offer. She wished she could do the same for him.

"Lemonade," Kate said. Her voice quavered, as if she was trying not to laugh. "Coffee. And water. Tell you what, if you hate everything but the water, just tell me what you do like to drink, and I'll have it for you for next time."

"Thank you," Raluca said as Kate hurried off, clearly not wanting to put her on the spot by watching her reaction.

Raluca tried the lemonade. It was overly sweet for her taste, though drinkable. The coffee, however, was excellent. Nick drank his Coke in pace with her, keeping her company. Though he never stopped keeping watch, and she was sure that should danger strike, he would instantly spring to action, he seemed relaxed and happy.

They sat drinking their coffee in companionable quiet, listening to the music. It was Nick's world, not Raluca's, but he'd invited her in and she'd been welcomed. She would have been even if she'd hated both burgers and Johnny Cash, she felt sure. If necessary, they'd have turned off the jukebox, or cooked something to her specifications. They'd all seemed so glad for Nick, they'd clearly have done anything to make his mate feel at home.

Her gaze traveled around the diner. Most of the people were older than Nick, some by twenty years or more. She pictured him at eighteen, alpha of a pack full of wolves his father's age, some friendly and some plotting against him. Even then, he'd had enough steel and fire in him to dominate them for years. If he'd been willing to sacrifice Manuel to save himself, he'd probably be ruling the pack now.

If she'd been willing to accept being nothing but a queen, she'd probably be ruling Viorel now.

"I am very glad we made the choices we did," Raluca said softly.

Nick's sharp gaze scanned the diner, then returned to her. He reached across the table to clasp her hand. "Me too."

Chapter Nine

Nick

Nick waited in the locker room for Raluca to emerge from the bedroom.

When they'd returned from the diner, Destiny had given Raluca her dance lesson while Nick had gone over their plans in more detail with Rafa. Then Rafa and Destiny left together to stake out the nightclub, and Raluca appeared in one of the business suits. He had no idea what she intended to wear to the nightclub, other than that Destiny had seen and approved it. When it got close to the time, Raluca had watched *him* change into black jeans and his black leather jacket with obvious enjoyment, then vanished into the room with the clothes rack and shut the door on him.

The door opened. Nick's jaw dropped.

"Surprise," Raluca said.

He didn't know what he'd expected, but it hadn't been this. Incredulously, he looked her over from head to toe, and then started over again at her feet.

She wore a pair of black leather shoes decorated with what looked like diamonds… Well, it was Raluca, so maybe they really were diamonds. They looked like she'd cut out pieces of the night sky to wear on her feet.

Above the shoes, her legs seemed to go up forever. Her skirt was made of multicolored sequins and was as short as a skirt could get. She spun in place, sending it flaring out around her until her thighs seemed surrounded by exploding fireworks.

Dazzled, Nick could barely tear his eyes from her lower body. But he did, because her upper body was encased in a black leather corset so closely molded to her body that he could see every breath she took. The heart-shaped top cupped and lifted her breasts, displaying the creamy globes almost down to her nipples. Her glittering dragonmarks stood out spectacularly against the black, as did her long, loose silver hair.

She had jewelry on too, but he barely registered it. He kept coming back to that barely-there glitter skirt, the fucking *black leather corset,* Raluca's daring in buying this outfit on her very first day in America, her legs, her breasts, her wine-red lips, and the joy radiating from every gorgeous bit of her.

"Well?" she said. "What do you think?"

"That is the fucking sexiest thing I've ever seen," Nick managed, then corrected himself. "*You're* the sexiest thing I've ever seen."

"Even though I was angry with you when I purchased it, I chose it so we'd match. I knew you'd wear that jacket again. It's hot, too." Her teasing smile sent a nearly unbearable wave of desire through his body. "*You're* hot."

Nick wished he could rush her back to the bedroom for a quickie. But Destiny and Rafa would worry if they were late. Maybe after the nightclub...

He grinned. "Let's go dancing."

Nick scoped out the nightclub as they pulled up. The sidewalk was crowded, but he spotted Rafa outside, apparently waiting to get in, and knew his teammate wouldn't have missed any danger.

They walked toward the club. A pounding hip-hop beat spilled out the door, along with flashing multicolored lights. He glanced at her to see if the music annoyed her, but she seemed unconcerned.

"Destiny play you some better hip-hop?" Nick asked.

Raluca gave him another bewitching smile. "Destiny showed me all sorts of things. You shall see."

As Nick passed Rafa, he moved as if he was pushing past, getting close enough to catch Rafa's barely-whispered, "All clear. Destiny's inside."

Nick nodded and escorted Raluca past the bouncer, who had been tipped in advance to let them in. The interior was hot and crowded, loud and perfumed with scents and sweat and alcohol. He scanned the room, looking for Destiny. She stood with the same seeming casualness as Rafa, leaning against the bar with a drink in hand. As he caught her eye, she nodded as if responding to something the bartender had said, sending him another "all clear" signal.

Nick led Raluca further in. She looked around with the same delight he'd seen light up her face when they'd passed the mural on the one good part of that fucking idiotic road trip, when she'd taken her first bite of a Kate and Dan's burger, when she'd listened to Bonnie Raitt, when she'd tried on shoes at that fancy shop. When she'd first touched him. *Every* time she touched him.

After every terrible thing that had happened to her, after an entire lifetime under the thumb of a man determined to crush her spirit and destroy her personality, Raluca had every reason to see the world through dark-tinted glasses. But instead, she sought out happiness wherever she went.

Nick tried to put himself in her shoes and see the nightclub as she saw it, as a place of beauty and wonder.

Bright lights flashed in a pattern, casting a kaleidoscope of moving colors onto the dancers on the floor. People were everywhere, laughing, drinking, dancing, kissing, all dressed to kill. The air seemed to vibrate with energy, and the beat of the music throbbed through his body.

The DJ, a punk Asian guy with a lot of piercings and spiked blue hair, snapped the fingers of one hand to the beat and scratched the record with the other.

A curvy black woman stood against the wall, kissing a muscular white guy with green eyes and black hair just brushing his shoulders. She was maybe 5'3" and he was at least 5'10", but she stood on her tip-toes and he bent down, caressing her back and sides.

A woman with brown eyes and olive skin set down her drink and moved to the dance floor. As she made a graceful spin, her rich dark purple hair flew out, giving Nick a glimpse of a butterfly tattoo behind her ear.

Everyone seemed to be having the time of their lives. Nick was too. Even though he couldn't kiss Raluca with Destiny watching, even though he was on duty and couldn't dance with her, even though the reason he was on duty was that his mate was in danger, none of that could cast a shadow over his joy. He had a pack, his mate loved him, he was confident that he could protect her, and he felt at peace with himself for the first time in at least ten years. How could he *not* be happy?

"Can I buy you a drink?" Nick asked.

"Certainly," Raluca said.

They didn't touch, but they didn't need to. Nick could feel the bond between them, unbreakable as steel and living as their own hearts. It told him that Raluca felt the same joy that he did, the same simple, unmatchable pleasure at being alive and in love.

He escorted her to the bar. Remembering the couture shop, he said, "A cocktail. Refreshing. Not too sweet. Rum and Coke for me."

When the bartender brought their drinks, Nick raised his glass. "Cheers."

Instead of clinking glasses, Raluca held up her other hand to halt him. Softly, so only he could hear, she said, "What *does* it mean to wolves, to drink from another's hands? When I did it in the dressing room, I only intended to tease and flirt. But when you drank, I could feel that it meant something more to you. When you told me your story, you said it was like becoming blood brothers. Is that the only meaning?"

Nick shook his head, then leaned in close and spoke quietly. "No. It depends on what sort of relationship you already have. If you're friends, then yeah, it'd be blood brothers. That's what my wolf thought Protection, Inc. was doing. And I guess he was right. But if you're in love, it's like getting engaged. The person who drinks is saying that they mean to give themself and hold nothing back. Usually, you'd both do it together. But even then in the dressing room, I did mean it."

"So you have already done your part," Raluca said thoughtfully. "Are there words?"

"Yeah."

"Tell them to me."

Nick saw where she was headed. He glanced at Destiny, who was scanning the crowd, then shrugged inwardly. If she saw, she saw. This was more important. "'I drink from your hands. I give you my heart.'"

"If you will, Nick." Raluca indicated his rum and Coke. Her hand trembled, but not from fear. Only love shone in her eyes. And that quiver showed him that she understood the importance of the ritual.

All the same, Nick couldn't help smiling as he switched their glasses. "The important part isn't the drink, it's the hands that hold it. This is a big moment, and you should enjoy every bit of it. So no American chemicals for you."

Raluca's smile answered his, then faded into solemnity. "Go

on. I have memorized the words."

Nick raised the glass to Raluca's red-rose lips. Looking into his eyes, she spoke with sincerity and passion. "I drink from your hands. I give you my heart."

Hearing the ancient lupine vows in his beloved dragon's voice struck him to the heart. He had to force his hand to be steady as he tipped the glass against her lips.

Raluca drank from his hands.

Our hearts are one, as are our lives, said his wolf. *Forever.*

Nick echoed his wolf's words. His voice came out gravelly, almost in a growl. "Did your dragon say anything?"

Raluca smiled. "Nothing so profound, I'm afraid. She said, 'What took you so long?'"

Nick chuckled as he returned her drink, but his amusement didn't break the spell. They sat together in silence, wrapped up in the awe of the bond and love of each other.

Raluca's words echoed and re-echoed in Nick's mind. He'd never thought much about mates until his teammates had started finding theirs, and even then, he'd never really believed that he too would find his. The few times he had imagined it, he'd vaguely pictured a completely different sort of woman, either a streetwise wolf shifter who was basically a female version of himself, or, on the theory that his teammates might be right that he needed to chill out and maybe his mate could help him with that, someone soft and submissive and sweet enough to make your teeth hurt. Neither of those imaginary women had seemed all that sexy, which was probably why he hadn't spent much time thinking about it.

He'd never imagined himself with anyone remotely like Raluca. If someone had tried to describe her to him — a foreign princess who'd never eaten a hamburger and didn't know how to drive because she'd always had chauffeurs, a woman who couldn't stand to hear the word 'fuck' — he'd have thought he'd hate her. And he sure as hell wouldn't have thought she'd be any sexier than the female Nick or that awful-sounding cross between a school counselor and a nurse.

But here was Raluca, the real person, in her diamond-studded dancing shoes. Raluca, who had wild sex in dressing rooms and risked her life to protect *him.* Raluca, the ex-princess who'd literally flown away from her entire life for a chance at freedom. Raluca, who understood his anger because she had a rage burning inside her to rival his own.

Raluca, his true love.

He'd never imagined her because she was so much more than he ever could have dreamed. He'd give his life to protect her without a second thought. But more than that, he wanted to live *with* her. When he'd been alpha of the gang, he hadn't thought he'd see twenty-five, and he hadn't much cared. Now he wanted to live to get old, just so he could spend all those years together with Raluca.

"I love you too," she said softly, as if she'd been reading his mind.

Then she slid off the bar stool and stood up, giving him an amazing view of that wild clubbing outfit of hers. "You cannot dance with me, can you?"

Nick shook his head. "Too distracting. I will some other time, though. After we catch those fuckers."

Raluca had obviously been expecting that, because she didn't look too disappointed. "In that case… Want to see my new moves?"

Nick grinned at the phrase; Destiny must have taught Raluca more than just the NaeNae. "You bet."

Raluca strode on to the dance floor. Several people watched her, curiously or with admiration. Nick bet a few women would catch her after she was done to ask her where she'd gotten those amazing tattoos.

She waited until a new song began. And then Raluca began to dance.

Her hips shimmied like they were made of water, making her glitter skirt flare out like a starburst. Her diamond heels clacked against the floor, drumming out a counterpoint to the hip-hop beat. Raluca moved with grace and beauty, lightness and precision, almost floating above the ground. Nick's heart lifted even more as he watched his mate dance. He'd guessed she'd be good, but he hadn't realized she'd be *that* good.

Nick laughed suddenly as he recognized the song: Pitbull's "International Love."

Raluca lifted her head and caught Nick's eyes. His appreciation seemed to give her even more confidence. She began to dance faster, her feet a sparkling blur, tearing up the dance floor with the wildest, fiercest moves he'd seen in his life. She was getting down like a street dancer, moving with passion and sensuality, fire and grace, and doing some dirty, dirty dancing. Her long silver hair flew out like dragon wings.

At long last, Raluca was cutting loose.

Nick was hypnotized. So was everyone else. The entire nightclub was watching, conversations falling silent as people stopped talking to stare, other dancers one by one coming to a halt just to watch her.

When the song finally ended, her feet slammed into the floor in perfect sync with the final beat. She stopped with her arms outstretched, going from top speed to statue-still in a heartbeat. Her hair kept moving for a moment after she stopped, then fell like silver rain. Nick leaped to his feet to cheer, and the crowd followed.

Raluca's eyes widened in startled pleasure. She started to lift a hand to beckon to him to join her, then dropped it, obviously remembering that he couldn't.

But maybe he could.

Nick gave her a "hang on" gesture, then cut through the crowd to where Destiny stood with her drink in hand.

"I didn't teach her any of that," Destiny remarked, her voice pitched so only Nick could hear. "That was one hundred percent Raluca."

He'd figured as much. "You must've given her the general idea. Listen, would you mind taking over? I want to dance with her."

The green depths of a tiger's eyes briefly shone out from under Destiny's usual soft brown. "I'm on it. Have fun with your mate."

Nick started. "You know?"

"Of course I know, you idiot," she replied cheerfully. "I've known all along. Why do you think I hazed her when we first met?"

"You hazed —" Nick broke off, remembering Destiny's arm-wrestling disguised as a handshake when she and Raluca first met. "How could you tell?"

"It was obvious. Idiot. You and she were looking at each other just like every other mated couple on our team. Only more pissed off about it." Destiny chuckled.

"Did you tell Fiona?" Nick demanded.

"Nope. She figured it out the same way I did."

Nick groaned aloud. Suddenly so many things made sense:

Destiny's test of strength, Shane's odd coldness, Fiona's insults that had turned on a dime into friendliness and approval once she'd provoked Raluca into announcing that she'd care for and protect Nick. "Does *everyone* know?"

"Probably. You two haven't exactly been subtle." With another laugh, Destiny gave him a shove toward the dance floor. "Go on, dance with your mate. Rafa and I have your backs."

Feeling slightly dazed, Nick pushed through the crowd to join Raluca on the dance floor. She was waiting for him on the edge, her skin flushed with exertion and her eyes glittering with excitement. Another song was playing, and the floor was filled with dancers.

Nick spoke in Raluca's ear. "Destiny and Rafa are taking over so I can dance with you. You were fucking spectacular. And by the way, apparently everyone figured out that we're mates, so don't worry about pretending any more."

Raluca drew in a startled breath, then smiled and turned her head to kiss him. Her lips were soft and hot, tasting of her cucumber-mint cocktail and the slightest salt tang of sweat. Her scent of metal and roses was dizzying. She'd bought perfume at the hotel, but she'd worn none. Nick was glad. Nothing could possibly be sexier than her natural scent.

She took his hand. "Come dance with me."

"I can't dance anywhere near as well as you," Nick warned her.

"I don't care if you can't dance at all. I just want to be with you tonight." She tugged him on to the floor.

Nick had told the truth about his dance skills, but he had a sense of rhythm and a werewolf's comfort with movement and his own body. He moved to the beat, following Raluca as best he could, enjoying being with her and not worrying about what he looked like. Once he began dancing, he found himself sensing her movements before he saw them and moving with her, reading her body language and echoing it with his own body.

Nick lost all sense of time as he danced with her, glorying in her beauty and their connection and the pure joy of moving with her, as if they were two wolves running in perfect sync. The beat of the music became the beat of his heart and hers, pounding in a single rhythm. He was tireless, for once using his shifter strength and endurance for nothing more than fun, and so was she.

They could have danced all night, but Nick was called back to earth when the nightclub closed down. He and Raluca came to a halt. The surprise and confusion he briefly felt was echoed in her expression; while they'd danced, apparently they'd both completely forgotten where they were, and lost themselves entirely in the movement and the music and each other.

Nick caught Raluca's hand and guided her so they walked out with Destiny, who gave him an all-clear nod as they reached the door.

They stepped outside into a quickly-dispersing crowd. Nick took Raluca's arm and guided her with seeming casualness until they stood alone with Destiny and Rafa in an alley beside the nightclub.

"Great dancing," Destiny remarked.

"Thank you," said Raluca. The night was chilly, but she seemed unconcerned. Nick edged closer, enjoying the heat of her body. With a laugh, she put her arm around him. "Warm yourself by my fire."

Rafa's eyebrows rose. "Guess we should leave the two of you to it."

"Hang on." Nick turned to Destiny and Rafa. "You didn't see anything, did you?"

"Nothing," Rafa said, and Destiny nodded. "Hal's still researching leads, but I'm wondering if whoever's behind this might've just given up."

Raluca turned to Nick's teammates. "I had a marvelous night. Rafa, Destiny, thank you for guarding me. Rafa, thank you for your kindness to me. And for dressing Nick for the ball."

"Any time." Rafa made a little bow, which somehow looked graceful and not weird, even though he was in club clothes.

Raluca seemed pleased with that, and curtseyed in return. She also did it gracefully, lifting her skirt about half an inch as anything more would have flashed them all. Then, surprising Nick, she gave Destiny a slightly awkward but sincere hug. "Destiny, thank you for the clothes you bought for me, and the shop recommendations, and playing me hip-hip that didn't make my ears bleed, and teaching me to dance, and telling me funny stories about Nick —"

"What?" Nick interrupted. Suspiciously, he turned on

Destiny. "What've you told her?"

Destiny gave him a sugar-wouldn't-melt-in-her-mouth smile. "Girl talk. Nothing you'd be interested in."

Nick doubted the hell out of that, but Raluca went on, earnestly clasping Destiny's dark hands in her pale ones. "You have been a true friend. I look forward to our girls' night out."

"Me too." Destiny grinned mischievously, giving Nick a vivid recollection of her joke — or had it been a joke? — about taking Raluca to a strip club. Though if she did, Nick was sure she'd pick a classy one and Raluca would actually like it.

"But if it's safe, may Nick and I be alone now?" Raluca went on. "I am not tired, and I would like to continue enjoying the fresh air and the night."

Nick wasn't so sure the assassins had given up for good, but they did at least seem to have given up for the night. Besides, they were out of the crowded, noisy nightclub now. Nick was perfectly capable of protecting Raluca if she just wanted to walk around the city at night.

"It's fine, guys," Nick said. "I can take it from here. Thanks. We'll see you tomorrow."

Rafa and Destiny took off, she with a chuckle and he with a suggestive wink.

Once they were gone, Raluca turned to Nick. "You've shown me your world. Would you like me to show you mine?"

Confused, Nick asked, "Viorel?"

"No, that's only where I came from." Raluca's eyes brightened until two stars seemed to shine from her face. "I'm a dragon, Nick. My world is the sky."

"You mean, you'd fly with me? You'd let me do that? Lucas never lets anyone ride him. Well, except Journey." Nick laughed, suddenly realizing why. "Oh. Is that something dragons only do with their mates?"

"Mates, or lovers. Sometimes best friends. Any others, only in case of utmost need. I have never allowed anyone to ride me. It seems very intimate." She brushed her heated fingers across his cheek, trailing them down to her lips. "But we are intimate. And I would like to show you the freedom of the sky. Is that something you might enjoy?"

Nick took a deep breath, his head spinning. Shane had taught the team to skydive, and Nick had loved it. But that was nothing compared to getting to ride a dragon! "Fuck, yeah."

He glanced around the alley, making sure no one was within sight or earshot. No one was. The streets of Santa Martina emptied out quickly once the nightclubs and bars closed for the night.

Following his glance, Raluca assured him, "Once you are riding me, I will become invisible to others. That is, other dragons would be able to see me. I am not sure about other shifters."

"I can't see Lucas once he goes invisible," Nick said. "None of us can. But Journey says she can see him if she's riding him."

"Good," Raluca said. "It might be disconcerting to seem to be flying unsupported through the air."

Nick grinned. "Yeah, it might."

Raluca backed away from Nick, until she stood in the middle of the alley with plenty of space on all sides. Her hair and eyes and dragonmarks and miniskirt glittered like the diamonds on her shoes.

The air around her began to sparkle silver. The specks of light gathered around her and began to spin, until Raluca vanished within a tornado of glinting silver. Then the glittering whirlwind vanished, and Nick saw a dragon.

Though all other colors were lost in the moonlight, Raluca's dragon shone with the pure silver of her hair. She was exquisite, slim and graceful, with translucent wings and talons like silver daggers. Her eyes were Raluca's eyes, gray as storm clouds and regarding him with excitement and love.

Nick's breath caught at the sight of her. "You're so beautiful."

A dragon couldn't smile, but her eyes brightened. She dipped one wing and bent her forearm, inviting him to mount.

Nick touched her back, marveling at the velvety softness of her hide. Moving carefully, he stepped on to her forearm and lifted his leg over her back. She was bigger than a horse, but slim. He easily settled into a hollow behind her neck, fitting into it as if it had been made to hold him.

She shook her head, sending her silver mane rippling. Nick realized what she was signaling him to do, and took hold of it. It felt more like feathers than hair, but he could feel that they were strong. He got a tight grip on it.

"I'm ready," Nick said. He'd spoken softly, but his voice echoed in the empty alley.

Raluca's flanks expanded between his legs as she took a deep breath. Then she spread her magnificent wings, their tips nearly touching the buildings on either side, and leaped upward.

Nick drew in his breath in amazement as Raluca soared up and up, out of the alley and above the buildings, into the sky. Santa Martina spread out beneath him, parts dark and others sparkling with multi-colored lights. The freeways flowed like rivers of rubies and diamonds. At first the sky was its usual orange-purple with reflected light, but as Raluca soared higher, it became darker and darker. Finally, it became black and then he could see the stars, pure and brilliant as Raluca's eyes.

The air was cold, burning his lungs, but her body warmed his. Even her mane was pleasantly hot in his hands. Skydiving was nothing compared to riding a dragon. This was like being a part of the night itself.

"Fucking awesome," Nick breathed.

Raluca flicked her tail, smacking him lightly across the back of his head with the tip. Nick laughed.

She soared and dove, becoming bolder and bolder with her aerial acrobatics as Nick cheered her on. He had a good hold on her mane and a grip with his thighs, and wasn't afraid of being unseated. He wasn't afraid of anything. It was amazing.

So this was Raluca's world. It was more beautiful and thrilling than anything Nick had ever experienced. And she had invited him into it, because he was her mate and she loved him and wanted him to share her joy.

He did.

Finally Raluca swooped downward, flying low over the tall office buildings that were now dark and empty for the night, until she found one with a nice flat roof. She landed light as feather. Nick slid off and stepped back.

Silver sparks gathered around her, spun in a whirlwind, and then winked out. The dragon was gone, leaving Raluca standing before him in her heels and corset and glitter skirt, her long hair whipping in the wind.

"That was amazing. It was…" Nick searched for words, but could find none that conveyed his feelings. Finally, he simply said, "Thank you."

Raluca gave him a smile that pierced him to the heart. "You do not need to explain. I understand. Has Lucas never told you of the three treasures of the dragon?"

Nick shook his head.

"Honor," said Raluca. "Gold. And the open sky."

"You're *my* treasure." Nick took a step toward her, then swayed. He felt slightly dizzy, not from the flight itself but from the sheer joy of it.

Raluca steadied him with one hand on his shoulder. Her touch seemed to sear through his entire body, setting him ablaze with desire. He caught her and pulled her to him, kissing her forehead, her throat, her soft lips. She opened her mouth to him and kissed him back with every ounce of the passion she'd had on the dance floor. Her mouth still tasted of the cocktail she'd drunk to pledge herself to him. But unlike that icy drink, it was hot inside. Her tongue was like a flame, if fire could burn with pleasure instead of pain.

Her dancing heels brought her to exactly his height. He didn't have bend to kiss her.

He wouldn't have to lift her to make love to her standing up.

Nick thrust his rock-hard erection against her mound. A bolt of intense pleasure rocketed through him at the touch, even through two layers of clothes. Raluca moaned and pushed back, rubbing herself against him with utter abandon. Her fingers clenched on his shoulders, tensing and releasing rhythmically with every thrust. She tossed her head, sending her hair slithering across his throat and down his back. It was cool where it touched his skin, almost shocking; he felt as hot as she was, and every touch of her silky hair was like a splash of water.

Her breasts heaved within the tight black corset, the pearly mounds lifting almost out of their leather cups. Nick bent to kiss her dragonmarks, sliding his tongue along them until he reached her breasts. Raluca gasped and trembled with every touch of his lips, every flick of his tongue, every thrust of his cock. Her scent filled the air, steel and roses and womanly musk. He didn't have to reach down to know she was getting wet. He could scent it, and it drove him wild. So did her eager responsiveness. The pleasure he was giving her excited him just as much as the pleasure she was giving him.

Her face was flushed pink and glowing with a light sweat. It made her seem lit from within.

"I love you," she gasped. "Make love to me here, under the sky."

"I love you too, babe," Nick said.

He was dizzy with love and desire, his hands shaking as he reached under her skirt. Her thighs were so smooth and hot. His fingers caught on lace. He tried to tug it down, but it caught on some kind of strap and buckle arrangement. Nick wished he could just tear it — he'd never be able to undo it in the state he was in — but Raluca cared about her clothes.

"Can you take off that strap thing?" he asked.

"My garter belt?" Her voice was shaky, her breathing fast and ragged. "Rip it off, Nick. I want you in me *now*."

Raluca's desperation was about the hottest thing Nick had ever experienced. He'd thought he was as hard as he could get, but his erection swelled even more at her words, tight and throbbing against his jeans. He ripped her panties in half. The straps snapped, and he dropped the whole thing to the ground. Hot liquid slicked his fingers. Her woman's scent grew even stronger, musky and intoxicating. He brushed his fingers against her soft folds, and she moaned at even that lightest of touches.

Nick was panting too, just as desperate as her. Together, they fumbled to get his jeans open, their fingers colliding, clumsy with eagerness. They finally managed to unzip his jeans and shove them and his boxers to his hips. He didn't bother to push them any farther down. Nor did Raluca take off her skirt. Neither of them could bear to wait even a second longer.

He lifted her skirt out of the way, and buried himself in her. Raluca cried out aloud with pleasure. Nick did too, unable to stop himself. She was so hot inside, it was a near-unbearable shock of sensation. Nick forced himself to hold still for a moment, biting his lip, so he wouldn't come there and then. Just being inside her, being gripped so tight by those impossibly hot walls, was such an incredible feeling, he was afraid to move. His whole body was shuddering involuntarily as electric jolts of pleasure thrilled his every nerve.

"Oh, Nick," Raluca whispered. She too was trembling, her head thrown back, her eyes closed. Her silver lashes fluttered against her flushed cheeks.

Nick took a deep breath, and began to thrust inside her. He slid in and out of her slick folds easily, despite her tightness. It was as if they were made for each other, inside and out. He heard himself mumble something like that. It sounded incoherent to him, but Raluca must have understood, because she said, "Yes. Yes, we are. I—"

She broke off into gasps, then cries. Nick had to hold her steady, clasping her tight to his chest as he thrust into her wet heat. Her black leather corset was cool against his skin, her bare arms and shoulders hot. He could feel in her heaving breasts and hear in her increasingly abandoned cries that she was close to coming. Nick felt like he was being pulled out to sea on a near-irresistible wave of bliss, but he made himself hold back. He didn't want to ruin her pleasure. He wanted to feel her come. And he didn't want it to end.

Raluca stiffened in his arms. Her heated walls clenched around his cock, and then she actually screamed. Her cry echoed across the sky. As her tightness pulsed around him, the current pulled him under. He came so hard, lights burst behind his eyes. For a brilliant moment, Nick forgot where he was. He forgot *who* he was. For an instant that felt like an eternity, he was lost to everything but ecstasy.

Then he slowly came back to himself, his senses returning along with his memory. He and Raluca were still standing up, clasped tight in each other's arms. Her scent was all over him, and the warm musk of their lovemaking hung in the cool night air. He pulled up his jeans, then settled back into her arms. She kissed him softly and leaned her head against his shoulder.

He turned to rub his cheek against her smooth hair, then looked up at the night sky. An enormous full moon glowed like a pearl amidst the blazing stars. That was Raluca's world. And now it was his world, too, just as everything that was his was now also hers.

"That was marvelous," Raluca said with dreamy satisfaction. "I would have been happy simply to dance and fly with you. But I do enjoy that you are such a skilled lover."

Nick grinned. "Tell me more. Every guy loves to hear that."

He'd been joking, but Raluca answered him seriously. "Well, to begin with, I have never climaxed with any man but you."

That surprised him. "Really?"

She nodded. "When I said in the dressing room that I had never done such a thing before, that was what I meant. Though I had also never had sex anywhere but in a bed. But yes, before I met you, I had found sex quite disappointing. I could climax by myself, and I expected that doing it with a man would be even more enjoyable. But in fact, it was better by myself, because at least then I *had* a climax. I had begun to think that I was simply bad at sex."

"No fucking way," Nick said, instantly pissed at every asshole who hadn't bothered to make sure she was having a good time and then let her blame herself. "Those guys were the problem, not you. You're the best lover I've ever had. You make love like you dance. You're fucking incredible. And if you ever think you're not, just ask me, and I'll tell you again. No. I'll *show* you again."

"I shall look forward to that," Raluca said. Then, curiously, she asked, "When you say I am the best lover, do you too mean…?"

"No. You're not the only woman who's ever made me come," Nick said, trying not to smile. He didn't want her to think he was laughing at her. "But you're the only woman I've ever loved."

"Oh." Raluca swallowed, her eyes brimming. "I am so glad we found each other."

She closed her eyes and let him kiss away her tears.

Nick could have happily held her all night. But a gust of frigid wind made him shiver. And if he was cold in his jeans and leather jacket, Raluca must be freezing.

"Let me give you my jacket," Nick said, reaching for the zipper. "And then I guess we should be getting home."

Raluca caught his hand. "I am not cold. I carry my own heat within. But I am a little tired."

"Me too. Think you can find the nightclub from here? If you can't, we could just fly back to Protection, Inc. and collect my car tomorrow."

"I'm not certain," Raluca said. "Let me look around."

They walked toward the edge of the roof. Raluca looked around, frowned, then stepped closer, peering down. Nick grabbed her elbow.

Raluca smiled. "Nick. I can fly."

"Oh, right." He released her, and stood watching as she paced along the edge of the roof, turning her head this way and that. "Collect the car tomorrow, huh?"

"Wait. I do not know your city well, but I can usually re-trace my flight path."

"I know the city. Not from above, but, if you give me a second, maybe I can spot it." Nick went in the opposite direction, keeping farther from the edge than her as he scanned the city below. He wasn't afraid of heights, but *he* couldn't fly and they were at least twenty stories up.

"Nick!" Raluca shouted.

He whipped around. She was pointing upward, into the empty sky.

Baffled, Nick said, "What?"

"A dragon!"

He took a step toward Raluca, but she flung out her hand to stop him. "Get back! He's landing!"

Nick jumped back, hoping it was far enough to avoid getting squashed.

A whirlwind of brilliant sparks lit the air between him and Raluca. For a moment, Nick thought it was Lucas. But they weren't quite the right color. Just as he realized that, the sparks vanished and a huge brass dragon crouched between them.

Three men rode the brass dragon. They had their backs to Nick, but even so, one's silhouette looked vaguely familiar. But before Nick could figure out why, they scrambled off, then vanished again in another whirlwind of sparks.

The brass glitter blocked his view of Raluca. Worse, it blocked *him* from Raluca. He wasn't sure they were enemies, but they were acting suspicious as hell. They'd landed right between him and Raluca, so Nick didn't reach for his gun; the bullet might go through one of them and hit her.

That had to be deliberate.

"Who are they?" Nick shouted.

"My cousin Grigor!" Raluca called back. "I don't know the others."

That didn't tell him much. "Is he a friend?"

"I don't know him very—" Raluca began.

The sparks vanished. Now Nick could see Raluca, on the

opposite side of the roof, with four men between them, all with guns already drawn. Two faced him, and two faced her.

One of the men facing Nick was a complete stranger, but the other looked vaguely familiar. After a puzzled moment, Nick recognized him as a waiter from the white tie ball, the one who had pushed his chair in. And presumably also picked his pocket and dropped poison in Raluca's wine. If it wasn't for the guns, Nick would have gone for him then and there.

But the weird thing was that the "waiter" wasn't the one with the familiar silhouette. Nick had only seen the guy once before; enough to recognize his face, but not a body seen from behind. Of the two men facing Raluca, one had glinting metallic hair and was presumably Grigor. The other, a big bruiser whose dark hair was flecked with gray, was the one who still looked hauntingly familiar, even from the back...

The big man turned around, leveling his gun at Nick's head. "Hands in the air."

Nick's blood went ice-cold with shock, then boiled with rage. Not because of the gun, but because of who held it.

"You motherfucker!" The words burst from Nick's lips without thought. "What the fuck are you doing here?"

"How dare you!" Raluca shouted. "I will —"

"Freeze!" Grigor yelled. "I can shoot faster than you can shift."

Nick's heart lurched. Lucas had said that dragonsbane could force a dragon to shift instantaneously, but it was very painful and dragons couldn't shift that fast of their own accord. Grigor's threat was real.

"Raluca!" Nick called out. "Don't do it!"

To his immense relief, she didn't attempt to shift. Instead, she folded her arms across her chest. Whatever emotions she felt vanished behind her chilly princess mask. "Who is the man who threatens my mate?"

Price smirked. "His alpha."

"The fuck you are! You were never my alpha, I was yours!" But as soon as the words left Nick's lips, he realized that he had to calm down. He could square off with Price later. Right now, he had to protect Raluca.

His thoughts spun in frantic circles. His gun was still in its concealed shoulder holster. Price would shoot him if he even reached for it. He might be able to shift faster than Price could fire. But not fast enough to get to Grigor before he could shoot Raluca.

But Nick had his phone in his jeans pocket. The emergency alert button was recessed to prevent accidental butt-dialing, but he should be able to hit it through his jeans. He let his hand drift toward his pocket, as if it was naturally going to rest on his hip…

"I see that!" Price yelled. "Hands in the air right now, or I shoot!"

Gritting his teeth, Nick put up his hands. He'd been so close!

"Grigor, I do not understand what is happening," Raluca said. "What are you doing here? Who are these men? And however did you find me?"

Her mask cracked as she spoke. She looked and sounded frightened and bewildered. Pain stabbed through Nick's heart. She was so helpless, so scared…

…Or was she?

Nick made sure his face didn't betray anything but his very real concern, fear, and anger. But behind his own mask, his mind raced. Raluca had gone back to her chiming princess voice. She'd been trained to conceal her emotions, her voice, her very self. Nick bet she was doing it right now.

"Ah. Allow me to enlighten you." The condescending smugness of Grigor's tone made Nick certain that Raluca *was* playing him to buy time. She knew him, so she must have known he was the kind of self-satisfied asshole who would jump at the chance to explain how smart he was.

Come to think of it, Price wasn't all that different. There was no way he'd kill Nick without gloating over his victory first. That had to be why neither Price nor Grigor had killed them yet. All Nick had to do was figure out how to get the better of them before they decided they'd had enough sadistic fun and it was time to dispose of him and Raluca.

He had no fucking idea how to do that.

Nick had been so busy thinking, he hadn't been paying attention to Grigor's speech beyond "Blah blah followed you here, blah blah tracked you there, blah blah hired surveillance experts and hackers and assassins because I'm so fucking rich." Nick made himself tune in, hoping something in it might give him an idea.

"As for how I found you in America to begin with, all I needed was logic," the pompous asshole was saying. "Who is the only person who you know and can trust to not want your throne? Lucas. Where does Lucas work? Protection, Inc."

"You want my *throne?*" Raluca interrupted, as if the idea had only now occurred to her. "But I gave it up. You don't need to kill me to take it."

"Yes, you simpering fool," Grigor snapped. "Of course I want your throne! And I do need to kill you. How could I ever trust that a pampered princess like you would give it up for good? Once you got tired of doing your own hair, you'd come running back home."

Grigor seemed easy to bait. Nick already knew Price was. Those two were obviously brothers under the skin: manipulative, murderous, smug assholes. Maybe Nick could use that.

"What I want to know is how *you* got involved," Nick said to Price. "Since when did you start hobnobbing with foreign fucking dragon princes?"

Price shot Nick a contemptuous look. "Since one offered me the chance to get some of my own back."

Grigor raised his voice, sounding annoyed at the interruption. "When I learned who was guarding the princess, I looked up his background and found a chance to kill two birds with one stone. I wanted the princess dead, Price wanted the bodyguard dead, and while both of us are recognizable to our respective targets, my hired men and the newer members of Price's pack were not."

"Cut to the fucking chase," Price snapped.

"Excuse me?" Grigor said icily.

Nick had bet those two were working together purely for convenience and didn't get along, and it looked like he was right. If he could get them pissed off enough at each other, it might distract them enough to drop their guards. He only needed a second...

With his free hand, Price indicated the fake waiter. "I taught Jim here everything I know about pickpocketing. He's not as good as me, but he's plenty good enough to dress up as a waiter, drop some poison in the princess's wine, and get something out of Nick's pocket."

"You motherfucker!" Nick clenched his raised hands. Price's gun hand didn't waver, but his gaze lifted for an instant, from Nick's face and body to just his fists.

Nick met Raluca's gaze from across the roof. He had only a split second, but it was the first time they'd made eye contact since Grigor had begun monologueing.

Be ready, Nick tried to convey.

He thought he saw understanding in her silver gaze. But he had to instantly look away from her and at Price, so he couldn't be sure. And just in time, too. Price's gaze moved down from Nick's fists to his face.

Smirking, Price added, "Not that getting one over on Nick was much of a challenge."

Grigor raised his voice. "As I was saying —"

So did Price. "Can you shut the fuck up for one —"

"JUMP!" Nick yelled, and flung himself backward off the roof.

He plummeted down, tumbling toward the distant streets below. The world spun around him.

Time seemed to slow. He could hear his own heartbeats thudding in his ears, with what felt like long pauses in between.

Boom. Had Raluca understood? He'd had to jump before he could see if she'd leaped too. If she'd hesitated for even a second, Grigor would've shot her before she could follow Nick. Had Nick gotten her killed?

Boom. Even if she had jumped fast enough, had she had enough time to transform?

Boom. The streets were so close. He'd be dead in another second. If he'd saved Raluca, it'd be worth it. It seemed so fucking unfair that he'd die without even knowing —

Something snatched at him, jerking him violently to the side and arresting his fall.

Nick gasped. With the rush of cold air into his lungs, the surreal sense of slowness came to an abrupt end. He was no longer hurtling toward the streets, but moving along and just above them. He craned his head, and saw that he was held in silver claws.

Silver *talons.*

Raluca's silver dragon had caught him in mid-air. She'd had to come so close to the ground to reach him, she must have almost crashed into it herself.

Nick tried to look past her, to see if anyone was shooting at them from the roof, but he couldn't tell which building they'd fallen from. They were in a maze of skyscrapers and streets, flying very low. Too low. Raluca was dangerously close to the streets and light posts and buildings, and moving far too fast to land.

"Look out!" Nick yelled.

As Raluca swerved to avoid one office tower, another loomed ahead. Her great wings beat hard, straining upward, trying to fly over it. She gained some height, but not enough.

"Left!" Nick shouted, his voice cracking with the force of it.

A wall of glass loomed before them. Raluca veered to the side, whipping one wing up.

They hurtled past the building, so close that Nick could have touched it. Then they were past it, and into open air. Raluca soared upward, her wings beating powerfully, heading for the sky.

Nick closed his eyes with relief. They'd made it. He'd saved his mate, and she'd saved him. They knew who was behind the plot. All they had to do now was go back to Protection, Inc. and tell the team. Everything would be all right.

The grip on him vanished.

Nick dropped like a stone.

A scream tore through the air. Raluca was a woman now. And she too was falling. Instinctively, Nick grabbed her, pulling her close as they both plummeted toward the ground.

He smelled dragonsbane. She must have been shot with a dart or spray gun or something, forcing her to shift in midair.

The streets seemed to rush up toward them.

Shane had told him what to do if his parachute failed to open. Nick twisted to direct his fall. But not as Shane had taught him, to save himself. Nick moved to take the full force of the impact, cushioning Raluca with his own body.

The ground struck him like a fist.

Chapter Ten

Raluca

Raluca had expected to die.

Once she'd caught Nick and soared into the sky, she'd been filled with the joy of flight and survival and love. She'd been so proud of herself for understanding Nick's plan and reacting fast enough for it to work, and of him for coming up with the idea and having the courage to carry it out. All she had to do was fly them both to safety, and everything would be all right.

Then a small, hard impact had hit her wing, like a thrown rock. It broke open against her hide, splashing her with a tiny amount of liquid. The unmistakable acid burn of dragonsbane seared her skin and wrenched her from dragon to woman in a shocking, agonizing instant.

As they'd fallen, Nick had clutched her tight. In the stretched-out moment before they hit, Raluca had hoped that holding her would give him some comfort in his last moments. But she felt nothing but a bitter rage at the universe.

Hasn't he been hurt enough? Raluca thought. *He deserves to live and be happy.*

And then, as the pavement rose up to meet them, she thought, *And so do I.*

At the last second, she closed her eyes.

The impact jolted her, but nowhere near as hard as she'd expected. She lay still and stunned for a moment. Then she realized that she'd hit the ground, and was still alive.

Impossible.

Dazed, she opened her eyes. She was lying on top of Nick. That must have protected her —

No. *He'd* protected her. Raluca abruptly recalled how he'd twisted around in midair. He must have deliberately moved so he'd hit the ground first and take the brunt of the fall.

"Nick?" Her voice came out in a hoarse whisper.

His head was turned aside, his face in shadow. He didn't move or answer. His body lay still, sprawled on hard concrete with his right arm and leg twisted beneath him.

The fear that she hadn't had time to feel when they'd been falling struck her like a blow, taking her breath away. She didn't know if he was dead or alive, and was terrified to find out.

Then she realized that she was still on top of him. If he was alive, her weight might be hurting him.

She scrambled off him, as gently as she could, and knelt beside him to peer at his face. His eyes were closed, his skin white as bone.

Raluca reached out a trembling hand to touch his cheek. It was cold. "Nick?"

He didn't stir.

She had to force herself not to grab and shake him, which might worsen his injuries. Instead, she bent over and put her ear to his chest. For a terrifying instant, she could hear nothing but her own pulse throbbing in her ears. Then she heard the steady thud of his heart, and felt his chest rise and fall.

Nick was alive.

Her mate had protected her, but not at the cost of his own life.

Tears welled up in Raluca's eyes, making burning tracks down her cheeks. But they were tears of relief. Nick was badly hurt, but he'd survived terrible wounds before. He was tough. She just needed to alert Protection, Inc., and they'd save him.

When she heard approaching footsteps, she thought with puzzled relief that the team had somehow arrived already.

Then she saw moonlight glint on metallic hair. Grigor was approaching, with Price right beside him. They were backed by not only the other two men from the rooftop, but eight or nine more with the same look: hard and mean. They had to be more of Grigor's hired assassins and Price's gangster wolves.

Raluca looked around wildly. She and Nick had fallen into a dark alley between two tall buildings. There was no one in sight but their enemies. The dragonsbane still burned on her arm, so she couldn't shift.

Grigor, Price, and their henchmen began to close in on her and Nick.

Those men meant to kill her mate. And her too, of course, but that seemed unimportant compared to the threat to Nick. He was wounded and unconscious, unable to protect himself. Even if he woke up, he couldn't fight with one leg and his dominant hand disabled.

If nothing else, Raluca could place her body between Nick and his enemies.

She leaped to her feet. Her dancing heels clattered against the concrete. Grigor laughed, reminding her of how absurd she must look in her corset and miniskirt. How helpless.

A blazing rage flamed up within her soul, searing away her fear. Raluca stood over her wounded mate, and her voice rang out to the rooftops with protective fury. "BEGONE, OR I WILL BURN YOU TO FUCKING ASHES!"

Several of the henchmen took an involuntary step back, and two flattened themselves against the walls. Price froze.

Grigor gave them all a scornful glance, then turned to Raluca with another contemptuous laugh. "With what? A cigarette lighter? You're nothing but a spoiled princess. You can't shift. You can't fight. Give it up. You have nothing."

A voice spoke from behind her. "She has a mate with a gun."

Raluca whirled around. Nick was sitting up, with his right leg twisted in front of him and his right arm hanging limp at his side. The right side of his face was scraped raw and bloody, and the left was white as paper. But he held a gun absolutely steady in his left hand.

"Raluca, get behind me and down!" Nick shouted.

She dove behind him, her heart singing with relief.

Gunshots rang out, making her flinch. But Nick's back stayed straight— he hadn't been hit. Raluca couldn't see anything. But she heard a lot of running feet and metal clattering, amidst a flurry of more shots.

"What's going on?" she whispered.

"I got two," Nick whispered back. She could hear the strain in his voice, and wondered, her heart lurching, how badly he was hurt. "The rest ducked behind dumpsters and stuff. Get my phone out of my right pants pocket and call Hal."

Relieved to have something to do, Raluca slid her hand into Nick's pocket. He flinched slightly when she touched his hip, making her wince in sympathy. But she gritted her teeth and reached deeper. Her fingers touched something sharp. She pulled out a handful of black fragments.

"Oh, fuck," Nick muttered. Then, louder, "Behind me!"

Raluca ducked back as Nick fired his gun several times, his shoulder moving as he swung his arm in a wide arc. She heard the ping of bullets hitting metal, along with more gunshots from farther away.

Nick rocked back suddenly, his breath going out in a sharp huff. But he didn't make any other sound. Raluca bit her tongue, forcing back her cry. If he'd been wounded, he surely wouldn't want to give it away.

"Are you hit?" she murmured, barely breathing the words, knowing his wolf hearing would catch the softest sounds.

"Yeah." He spoke so quietly that she strained to hear and understand. "Not bad, I think. But we can't stay here. We've got no cover. You're strong. Get me behind that dumpster. Move fast, on my go. I'll be shooting to cover us, so make sure my arm's free."

Raluca followed the jerk of Nick's head. The dumpster wasn't far, but with his injuries, she didn't like the idea of moving him at all. Especially when she wouldn't have time to be gentle. She tried to figure out the best way to lift him. She'd never carried anyone before.

"How —" she began.

"Go!" Nick began firing again.

Raluca had no time to think. She grabbed him under the arms and bolted for the dumpster, trying not to let his feet touch the ground. The gunfire was loud as explosions going off in her ears. As her heels clattered across the concrete, her heart pounded with fear that she'd be hit, that Nick would be hit, that the fall had broken his back and she was killing him by moving him so roughly —

And then she was behind the metal shield of the dumpster. She skidded to a stop, banging her shoulder against a brick wall. Nick flinched at the jarring impact. Raluca set him down as gently as she could, sitting up with his back against the wall, then peered at him anxiously.

"Where are you hit?" she whispered.

"My side."

Raluca lifted his jacket. The bullet had dug a furrow along his ribs, bloody but shallow. The relief in his expression when he saw it was echoed in her own heart.

"It's nothing," he said. "Forget it. We have bigger —"

A fusillade of bullets zinged off their metal shield. None penetrated it, but Raluca jumped at every one. The terror of the battle had caught up with her, and she was trembling all over. But she forced herself to calm down. She had to take care of Nick. Protect him, as he'd protected her. Only then, when she'd pushed down her panic, did she realized that maybe she could.

"Did you ever get another vial of heartsease?" Raluca whispered.

"Yeah." Nick gave a jerk of his chin toward his jacket pocket. "In there. If it's not smashed. But dragons aren't bulletproof. And even if you go invisible, Grigor will be able to see you. Just like you could see him and point so I could shoot him. I'm sure that's why he's still hiding, the coward."

Raluca was already unzipping his pocket. "I don't think he'll stay hiding for much longer. How many bullets do you have left?"

"Got you thinking like a bodyguard at last," Nick remarked. But the lightness left his tone as he admitted, "Not a lot. And you're right, he'll come out as soon as he thinks I've run out of ammo. Or else he'll send some of his mooks as a diversion, and force me to use it up on them. But you were fast enough to catch me! If you can shift, you can get us out of here."

Raluca's heart sank as she again touched a pocketful of sharp fragments. Like the phone, the vial had smashed in the fall. Looking up at Nick's hopeful face, she was forced to shake her head.

The disappointment she saw struck her like a blow. That had been his last hope, she realized.

"Won't the police have been called?" she asked. "All these gunshots…"

"This is a business area. No one's around to hear. If anyone was, the cops would've been here by now." Nick's eyes narrowed, his long lashes flickering as he thought. Finally, he said, "I'll hold them off for as long as I can. If we wait long enough, who knows, maybe someone will come by. But when Grigor and Price make their move, listen for my go. When you hear it, run. I'll cover you. Go get help."

As more bullets ricocheted against their shield, Raluca knew it for a hopeless plan. Nick meant to sacrifice himself for even the slightest possibility of her escape, but it was barely a chance at all. And it was one she would not take.

"Nick," Raluca said, gently but in a tone that could not be denied. "I will not leave you to die alone."

"But —"

She put her finger over his lips. "I will not. Do not waste our last moments arguing. You would not leave me. I will not leave you. Your plan would only have us die apart. I prefer to stay with you."

Nick opened his mouth, but she pressed harder until he closed it and nodded. Then she took her hand away. She couldn't hold him for fear of hurting him more, so she leaned in and kissed his lips. He responded with a desperate passion, but only for a few seconds. Then he pulled away, keeping watch.

He couldn't touch her with his hands, with one arm injured and one holding his gun. But he leaned his head against hers, so their cheeks pressed together and his damp hair mingled with hers.

"I love you," he said. "We got to dance together tonight. You flew with me. You met my friends. We made love under your sky. I don't regret a fucking thing."

Raluca's eyes burned with tears, but her heart was strangely light. The fear and bitterness had left her, and she no longer raged against the unfairness of the universe. "Neither do I. These last few days have made my entire life worthwhile. I love you. I would rather be here with you now then safe in a palace, alone."

Grigor's voice rose in a shout. "He's out of ammunition! Go get him!"

Raluca didn't move. Nor did Nick. His gun hand was steady as they sat together, ready for the end.

A burst of flame lit the alley. Hot air buffeted Raluca and blew Nick's hair back.

A golden dragon swooped down. Three people rode him, but he was moving too fast for Raluca to recognize them. More enemies? Raluca had another cousin who was gold...

The dragon breathed another billow of flame. Yells arose from farther down the alley.

"Can you see the dragon?" Raluca asked.

But Nick obviously could. Despite his pain, his face cracked into the biggest grin she'd ever seen. "It's Lucas! And he's brought the cavalry!"

The golden dragon landed. Now Raluca could recognize his riders: Hal, Rafa, and Destiny. They were armed and wore bulletproof vests, but they'd obviously come in haste; Hal's vest was strapped over pajamas, and Rafa's over his bare chest. Destiny still wore her pretty club dress but, Raluca noticed with a touch of envy, had switched out her dancing heels for sturdy boots.

Hal, Destiny, and Rafa scattered to do battle with their hidden enemies. Lucas launched into the air, then arrowed along the alley. Bright sparks whirled above a dumpster, and then a brass dragon flew up to meet Lucas in mid-air.

The crack of gunshots made Raluca jump.

"Don't be scared," Nick said. "The team will protect us."

The absolute confidence in his voice made Raluca relax as well. More in fascination than fear, she watched as the two dragons soared upward, out of the narrow alley, and began to battle in the sky, high overhead. They darted in and out, flashes of brass and gold, lighting the darkness with bursts of orange flame.

A blur of motion caught Raluca's eye. Before she could open her mouth to shout, something big and heavy slammed into her and Nick, knocking them both down. Raluca's shoulder and elbow banged against the ground, and Nick's gun flew from his hand and skidded across the cement.

Raluca had only a confused glimpse of black fur and white fangs before Nick shoved her out of the way. Hard. She went flying, and again landed painfully. Dazed, she lay still for a moment. Then she realized that Nick would only have done that if she was in deadly danger. Which meant that *he* must be in deadly danger.

She scrambled up, and saw two wolves where Nick had been. It was the first time she'd seen Nick's wolf, apart from the photo, but she recognized him immediately: the wiry body, the soft gray fur, and the green eyes, now blazing with battle rage. The wolf attacking him was big and black, with yellow eyes.

Nick's wolf lay sprawled on the pavement with two legs limp and useless, his fur stained everywhere with blood. But he was fighting anyway, propping himself on his good legs and snapping ferociously. Incredibly, Nick was keeping the black wolf at bay. The black wolf darted in and out, forcing Nick to turn quickly back and forth. With his injuries, that had to be excruciatingly painful. He was holding his own out of sheer determination. But any moment now, he'd move a fraction too slowly, and the black wolf would kill him.

The black wolf had to be Price, Raluca realized suddenly. Who else could hold such hatred in his yellow eyes? Who else would be so honorless and cowardly as to attack Nick when he was wounded and barely able to defend himself?

She looked around for help, but nobody was in sight. Raluca shouted anyway. "Hal! Destiny! Rafa! Nick needs you!"

But from the yelling and gunshots, and the roars and growls and howls, the team was busy fighting their own battles. She doubted they'd even heard her.

Then Raluca remembered Nick's gun and ran to pick it up. She pointed it at Price, then hesitated. She'd never fired a gun before, and the two wolves were practically on top of each other. If she shot at Price, she'd probably either miss entirely, or hit Nick.

Price snarled, feinted, then rushed in, biting at Nick's throat. A scream burst from Raluca's lips. Nick whipped his head around, protecting his throat, but the black wolf sank his fangs into Nick's shoulder.

Raluca bolted forward and swung the gun like a club. Price didn't have time to release his grip. She connected solidly with his head.

Price let go of Nick with a snarl of pain, then his yellow eyes fixed on her. His lips writhed away from his shining fangs as he gathered himself to leap for her throat.

A hand closed over hers, twisting her wrist. The gun fired.

Price fell dead at her feet.

Stunned, Raluca looked down. Nick sat naked and bleeding among the shredded ruins of his clothing, his hand still wrapped around hers with his finger on the trigger.

"Thanks." Nick's voice was barely audible. His skin had gone from white to ashen, his features taut with pain. Sweat beaded his face, but he was shivering. "I... I think I'm..."

She dropped to her knees, letting go of the gun, and caught him just as his eyes slid shut. He collapsed against her chest, his head falling to the side to rest against her shoulder.

Raluca could feel him breathing, shallow and fast. He was very cold. She held him close, hoping to warm him with her own body. Then she reached out for the remains of his shirt. Maybe she could use it for bandages.

A man stepped out of the shadows. For an instant, Raluca thought it was Shane; he was about the same height and had the same leanly muscled build, the same predatory grace, and even the same way of emerging from darkness. Then she saw his sharp features and eyes black as a midnight sky. The man was a stranger.

She snatched up the gun and pointed it in his general direction. "Get away from my mate!"

The stranger put his hands in the air. He didn't smile, but something about his body language suggested that he was only doing it to humor her. "Easy. I'm a friend."

Raluca wasn't taking any chances. "Back off."

Patiently, the dark-eyed man said, "I have medical training. I can help him. Feel free to hold me at gunpoint while I'm doing it, if you like."

Raluca hesitated. The offer to help Nick was tempting, but she had no idea who the man was or if he could be trusted. And once he got close, he could easily disarm her.

Nick moved in her arms, then caught himself with a groan. His eyes fluttered open, his gaze drifting from her to the man before them.

"What're you doing here?" Nick mumbled.

"Well, I'm *trying* to help you," the stranger replied. Gesturing at Raluca, he said, "But I've hit a bit of a roadblock."

"Let him," Nick said to Raluca.

"You know him?" Raluca asked. She'd normally trust Nick's judgment, but he sounded dazed.

"Sort of. He's a…" Nick looked uncertain, then settled on, "Well, Shane knows him."

"Should I stand guard?" Raluca asked doubtfully. She could still hear fighting in the distance. Overhead, Lucas and Grigor were a pair of bright sparks in the sky, darting and flashing like shooting stars.

The man shook his head. "I'll do that too. Anything comes close, I'll be on it. You just keep holding him."

Raluca glanced at Nick. He nodded his agreement, looking more clear-headed. "Shane *trusts* him."

She laid down the gun.

The dark-eyed man came forward and began examining Nick in a way that made it obvious that he did, in fact, have medical training. She could feel Nick trying not to flinch, though the man's touch seemed gentle. Since Nick was done with the gun, she took his left hand in hers. He gripped it hard every time the man touched an especially painful spot. The stranger's dark gaze flicked to their hands every time; nothing seemed to escape him.

Hoping to distract Nick, she asked, "That was Price, wasn't it?"

"Yeah. Fucking coward. He nearly got me, though." Nick managed the faintest flicker of a smile. "But you wreaked vengeance on him, just like you said you would. Not fiery, but you can't have everything."

"Who's Price?" the stranger asked.

"The black wolf," Nick said. When the stranger continued to look puzzled, Nick added, "An old enemy."

"He did all that to you?" the man asked incredulously.

"No, Price just bit me," Nick said. "Before that, I jumped off a building. And then I got shot."

"Oh. Well, that explains everything." The stranger spoke in the same gently sardonic tone as when he'd offered to let Raluca hold him at gunpoint. "You really ought to go to the nearest ER —"

"No!" Nick exclaimed.

The man went on as if Nick hadn't said a thing, "But since you can't, have someone take you to Dr. Bedford. It's a long haul, but you need a doctor, not just a paramedic. Your leg's broken in at least three places. I can splint it, but you need to get it set by someone with more training than me. And soon, before it starts healing crooked."

"I know. My shoulder too, right?"

The dark-eyed man shook his head. "That's just dislocated. I can fix that for you right now."

Nick flinched. "Oh, fuck. Yeah, go ahead. Get it over with."

The man's eyebrows rose. "What do you think I'm going to do? Pull on it?"

"Aren't you? That's how I've seen it done."

"Who have you seen do that?" The man seemed appalled at the idea.

"This sleazy guy who treated gangsters out of his apartment."

"Oh. Well, let's see if I can improve on that standard."

The man lifted Nick's right arm. Raluca braced herself for him to do something painful, and she could feel Nick doing the same. But though the man began moving and rotating Nick's arm and hand, he did it slowly and carefully. Finally, he folded Nick's arm across his chest, then turned his palm over. There was a sharp pop, and Nick yelped in pain. But an instant later, he heaved a sigh of relief, and some of his tension eased.

"Nice job," came a voice from beside them.

Raluca almost jumped out of her skin. Nick tried to, but the man put a hand against his chest, holding him in place. Shane had somehow appeared without either of them noticing him, and was standing next to them with a gun in one hand and a first-aid kit in the other, and several blankets draped over his arm.

"About time," said the dark-eyed man. "I thought I'd have to use what's left of his clothes."

"Nah. *I* came prepared." Shane knelt beside Nick and opened the kit.

"Wait." Urgently, Nick asked him, "Do you have heartsease? Raluca needs it."

Shane's hard face creased in concern. He instantly reached into his pocket and handed Raluca a vial. She gulped it down. The pain in her arm vanished, and the chill that had invaded her body eased. She wished Nick could be healed so easily.

Her dragon, whom she'd been unable to reach since her fall, stirred within her, wings rustling. *We must fly to protect our mate!*

He needs us right here, Raluca sent back.

Her dragon subsided, but Raluca felt her simmering frustration.

Now that her pain was gone and her worry for Nick had eased, she began to notice things that she'd missed earlier. Shane wore jeans and a T-shirt, with a bulletproof vest and a holster strapped over his clothes. But when Raluca took a closer look, she noticed that he'd put his shirt on backwards. The entire team had obviously come in great haste.

The stranger also wore jeans and a T-shirt, but no armor. If he had any weapons, they weren't visible. His clothes didn't fit well; either they were too big for him, or he'd recently lost weight. He wasn't just lean, like Shane, but too thin for his frame; when he leaned over, his collarbones stood out sharply. His eyes really were black, not dark brown; she couldn't tell the irises from the pupils. Beneath his eyes, his pale skin was smudged with shadows dark as bruises.

Something about the man reminded her of Lucas when he'd walked into the throne room after he'd been poisoned with dragonsbane, or of Nick when he'd taken her hand to pull the trigger: as if he was performing a task with sheer willpower, and would collapse the instant he was done. But she wasn't sure what had given her that idea. Shane's friend was too thin and looked tired, but nothing in his movements or expression betrayed illness or injury.

Who *was* he, anyway? Nick obviously didn't know anything about him other than that Shane trusted him.

Shane filled a syringe. Nick eyed it with alarm. "I can't —"

"It won't put you to sleep," Shane said. "Believe me, you don't want us to splint your leg without something for the pain."

"Yeah, okay." Nick let Shane give him the injection.

Shane and the dark-eyed man set to work bandaging Nick, then put a sling on his arm. By then the injection had taken effect. The lines of pain in Nick's face had smoothed out, and he didn't even wince as the men gently straightened his leg, then bound on a splint. Finally, they wrapped him in the blankets. The way Shane and his friend worked together, passing each other instruments without having to be asked, reminded Raluca of how Ellie and Catalina had examined her after the ball.

"Hal and the team are mopping up," Shane said to his friend. "They'll be here in a minute. Come back to the office with us, and you can meet everyone."

The man hurriedly stood up. "No. No. I have to get going."

Shane got up as well. "What do you mean? You're here. I thought you'd come to stay."

"No, I came because a couple days ago, I had a sense that you were in danger," his friend replied. "There were some problems, it's not important, but I couldn't get here right away. By the time I arrived, the sense of danger was gone. But I tracked you here to make sure. You seemed to be doing just fine on your own, but your buddy was hurt. So I went to him."

"You can sense if I'm in danger?" Shane sounded surprised.

His friend shrugged. "Got me. This was the first time. Actually, I wasn't sure it was you. I could just feel that someone in this direction was in trouble, and I figured it had to be you or Catalina. You're the only people here who I can track. It wasn't her, was it?"

Shane shook his head. "She's fine. She's still in training."

"Then it *was* you. What was going on three days ago?"

"Nothing." Shane's face was hard to read, but he seemed troubled. "I wasn't in any danger. I wasn't even on a job."

His friend's skin had always been pale, but at that, it went white. "Oh, that is just what I need. If my power's misfiring —"

"Then you should stay!" Shane caught his friend's arm. "I'll help you. We'll all help you!"

The dark-eyed man extracted his arm from Shane's grip. "I'm fine. But your teammate needs you. Stay with him."

With that, he vanished into the shadows. Shane took a step after him, then visibly forced himself to stop. Speaking more to himself than to anyone else, he muttered, "He's *not* fine. He looks like he hasn't slept or eaten in weeks."

"So did you, when you joined the team," Nick said. "You got better."

"That's *because* I joined the team." Shane's whole body was tense with frustration. "He won't take my help. And he's got nobody else."

"Who is he, Shane?" Raluca asked.

"I can't say. It's his secret. I hope some day he'll come in from the cold and tell you all himself." Shane shook his head, as if forcing himself to focus, and settled back down beside Nick. "Never mind. Hang in there, Nick. We'll get you out of here once the fighting's over. It shouldn't be long. I think everyone's done but Lucas."

He was right. All had gone quiet except for the sound of approaching footsteps. Hal and Rafa and Destiny came running up. Destiny's arm was bitten, Rafa was limping, and Hal's face was bruised, but none of them seemed seriously hurt. They crouched down around Nick.

"Nick!" Destiny exclaimed. "I'm so sorry! We were trying to protect you. I have no idea how Price got past us."

"Price is good at that," Nick said, then corrected himself. "Was."

Rafa looked worried, but tried to put on a joking tone. "I let you out of my sight for one minute…"

Hal said, "Ellie and Catalina are waiting out of the danger zone in an ambulance they… uh… borrowed." Before Nick could protest, Hal added, "Just to take you to Protection, Inc. I'll call them in as soon as it's safe."

"Isn't it safe now?" Nick asked, frowning.

"I don't know. Lucas is still up there… I think." Hal shaded his eyes, peering up at the sky. Raluca followed his gaze. Lucas and Grigor still appeared to be fighting, but they were so far up that Raluca couldn't see any details. Hal didn't seem able to see them at all. "Wish we had someone else who could fly."

He does, hissed Raluca's dragon.

"You do," she said.

Nick stiffened in her arms. "Raluca —"

Hal shook his head. "No. You're not a fighter. It's too risky."

"Nick needs help." Raluca had spoken impulsively before, but as she went on, she knew the truth of her words. "Lucas may also. And if Grigor escapes him and dives to attack you, none of you will even be able to see him coming. Nick saved me, and all of you helped me. I wish to help you now."

Hal frowned. Raluca could see that he agreed with her reasoning, but was reluctant to let her risk herself.

"I am a free woman now. My choices are my own." Then Raluca turned to Nick. "But if you wish me to stay with you, I will."

Nick took a deep breath, then squeezed her hand. "I'll be fine. Kick his sorry ass right out of the sky. You know you want to."

"You really are two of a kind," Hal said. "All right. Go for it."

Shane took Raluca's place, both moving carefully so they didn't jar Nick. Raluca bent to give him a light kiss, then stepped away from them all.

She let her heart fill with the pure desires of a dragon.

Honor.

Gold.

The open sky.

And vengeance, her dragon hissed.

The dark alley dissolved into silver sparks. Raluca's blood burned within her, but with a painless heat rather than the agony of dragonsbane. Her wings stretched out, her talons emerged, and a furnace roared inside her. With a sudden leap, she was aloft, her wings beating hard as she arrowed straight upward, toward the distant fighters overhead.

Raluca had always been a very fast flyer; it was only that which had allowed her to catch Nick before he could hit the ground. Few dragons could have done the same. Her speed enabled her to quickly reach the heights where the gold and brass dragons fought.

Once she was close enough to see them, she understood why they were still in the air. Grigor wasn't fighting Lucas, but trying to evade him and fly down to the alley. Lucas was flying below him, blocking him at every turn with slashing claws and bursts of flame. But while Lucas was bigger and able to prevent him from flying down to attack his friends, he wasn't fast enough to catch Grigor. Neither dragon was injured, but both were obviously weary.

Raluca, however, had been flying for mere minutes. She was still fresh. And she was faster than Grigor. Both dragons, intent on their fight, didn't see her until she was almost upon them. Raluca caught Lucas's eye, then darted upward.

Grigor, his attention divided, hesitated for a fatal moment, allowing himself to get trapped between Lucas below and Raluca above. In that instant of indecision, both dragons struck.

Lucas lunged up as Raluca dropped down, folding her wings and landing with her full weight on Grigor's back. She dug her talons into his wings, pinning them to his sides. Before Grigor could twist to flame either of them, she bit down on his neck, not piercing his skin but holding his head in place with the threat of it.

Lucas's golden wings beat hard, his muscles straining as he bore the weight of them both. Raluca felt Grigor tensing his legs, no doubt to claw Lucas's back. She bit down harder. He retracted his talons, and let Lucas lower them both to the ground.

They landed with a jarring thud. Raluca spread her wings, lifting off, and dragged Grigor off Lucas's back. She stayed on top of Grigor, pinning his wings and keeping her teeth locked on his neck, as Lucas became a man in a whirlwind of brilliant sparks.

He wore a plain button-down shirt and black slacks, neither tailored nor expensive, and no jewelry at all. His golden hair, chiseled features, and perfect posture were the only elegant things about him. Raluca was puzzled, then remembered that he had been undercover. Like the rest of his team members, he obviously hadn't had time to change.

Lucas got in a huddle with his teammates while Raluca waited, uncertain what to do. Then Destiny handed Lucas an odd-looking gun.

Lucas aimed the gun at Grigor and said, "You can let go of him now."

Raluca sprang off him. The instant she did, Grigor leaped into the air. Lucas fired the gun. It made a soft popping noise rather than a bang. In mid-air, Grigor became a man with a yell of pain, and fell about ten feet down. He hit the ground with another yelp.

Hal pounced on him and handcuffed him, then yanked him to his feet. "Rafa, call Ellie in."

As Rafa pulled out his phone, Raluca thought of human things — her concern and love for Nick, her pleasure and relief at Grigor's very literal downfall, and her plan to buy shoes without high heels, immediately — and became a woman.

Her first glance was to Nick, who was still sitting up with his back against Shane's chest. He managed a smile as she ran to his side. "You were amazing. I knew you could beat that asshole."

Hal hauled Grigor closer. Her cousin was bruised, scraped, and limping, and looked furious. "How dare you use my own dragonsbane gun on me!"

Destiny laughed. "Finders keepers."

But Lucas glared at him. "How dare you try to murder my friends and usurp the throne of Viorel!"

Hal gave Grigor a shake. "You're done with murder. And you're not getting the throne. Price is dead. Fiona is delivering the rest of your crew to the nearest police station. The cops know us here, and they'll believe us when we tell them what happened — minus the shifting, of course. Especially when we're turning over wanted gangsters and international assassins. They'll all be in jail for a long, long time. As for you, I've got just one question. Did Constantine have anything to do with this?"

Grigor's indignant expression seemed completely sincere. "No! I loathe the man. And I want to be a real king, not a puppet. He's the last person I'd ever conspire with. Or even speak to!"

"Excellent," Lucas said. "In that case, the two of you can share a cell for the rest of your lives."

Nick looked at Raluca. "Is that enough vengeance for you?"

Raluca imagined Grigor and Uncle Constantine, locked up forever in a dark, dank dungeon, with a drop of burning dragonsbane always on their skin to prevent their escape. Worse yet, with no company but each other. She smiled. "It is. In fact, this will give me revenge on my uncle as well. Their loathing is mutual."

Nick started to chuckle, then cut himself off, wincing. "Good. They deserve each other."

Lucas gave Hal a plaintive glance. "I may lock him in Protection, Inc. for the night, may I not?"

"Lucas, of course I'm not asking you to fly to Europe tonight," Hal replied. "You just got back! Lock that asshole in a bedroom for as long as you like."

"Take Raluca's clothes out first," Destiny said.

"Nick…" Lucas gracefully knelt down, then paused, as if uncertain what to say. It was odd to see him caught in an awkward moment, when he had been so assured when Raluca had seen him last. Finally, he said, "I am sorry I came too late to protect you."

Nick seemed taken aback. "You came just in time."

"In the *nick* of time," Rafa suggested. Destiny punched his arm.

"In that case, I'm glad," Lucas said, ignoring the others. "I only wish it had been sooner. I hope your wounds heal quickly."

"They will," Nick said. Then he too paused, making Raluca realize that the awkwardness was mutual. Then, determinedly pushing past it, he added, "I'm glad things are about to get even worse for fucking Constantine. He deserves it for what he did to you."

"Thank you, Nick," Lucas said, with surprise but no more self-consciousness. Then he turned to Raluca. "You were magnificent. And I'm very happy to see you again."

"Thank you. I'm happy to see you as well." She'd never loved Lucas as a mate, but she looked forward to having him as a friend. He'd always been kind to her, even when she'd taken her helpless anger at their unwanted engagement out on him. "I hope we can fly together soon under more peaceful circumstances."

"I look forward to it," Lucas said, smiling. "Please don't think America is always like this. That was the first time I've ever fought in the sky."

Raluca smiled, then stood up and turned to Grigor. "I have something I wish to tell you. Before you are conveyed to your wretched dungeon, I wish you to repeat it to everyone you see."

"I will ensure that he does," Lucas said. "And I can also repeat it, if you wish."

"I do." Raluca drew in a deep breath, speaking loudly enough for everyone to hear. "Renouncing the crown was not a girl's whim, but a woman's true desire. I *do not* want to be queen. I will *never* want to be queen. Look at me now. Truly look at me."

Raluca followed Grigor's appalled gaze from her sequined miniskirt to her black leather corset. Both were torn and blood-stained, not that she cared. But her disreputable state probably helped to drive her point home.

"*This* is what I want." Raluca made a wide gesture, encompassing Nick, his team, and all of Santa Martina. "This is my home. These people are my family. And this man is my mate."

She knelt by Nick and kissed him gently on the lips. He responded with surprising enthusiasm. She hadn't expected him to have that much energy, but either he was feeling better or he really wanted to help her with her demonstration. Raluca was drawn into the kiss, returning his passion with her own until she momentarily forgot why she was kissing him and where she was. They only broke off when Nick ran out of breath. When Raluca looked up, she was satisfied by Grigor's incoherent sputterings of horror, outrage, and disgust.

"That is all," Raluca said.

Nick added, "And tell them that if anyone wants to mess with my girl, they'll have to go through me and my team first." He indicated the body of the black wolf. "Ask Price how that worked out for him."

Grigor was still spluttering with impotent outrage as Lucas transformed into a dragon, unceremoniously grabbed him in his talons, and flew off with him.

An ambulance pulled into the alley, sirens wailing and lights flashing. Catalina and Ellie jumped out, carrying a stretcher. Hal ruffled Ellie's blonde hair as she passed him, and she glanced up with a quick smile.

"There you go, Nick," Hal said. "They've come to take you home."

Nick's eyes glistened at Hal's words. He blinked hard and didn't reply.

Hal briefly rested his hand on Nick's shoulder. Then he and Shane helped Ellie and Catalina lift Nick on to the stretcher. Nick reached out, catching Raluca's hand.

"Shane, go in the ambulance," Hal said. "Raluca too, of course. The rest of us will meet you there. If any more of us get in, you won't have room to turn round."

Raluca climbed into the back of the ambulance with Nick, trying to keep out of the paramedics' way without letting go of his hand. Hal hadn't been joking; it was a tight squeeze.

Catalina took the driver's seat while Shane and Ellie tended to Nick in the back, driving fast yet smoothly as the siren wailed.

"How did you find us?" Nick asked.

"We got an alarm when your phone broke," Shane said. When Nick looked puzzled, Shane went on, "Fiona put it in the last time she fixed up our phones. If one breaks, it sends an alarm to the others, along with the last location it was in."

"I thought that didn't work," Nick said. "Hal stomped on a phone to test it, and nothing happened."

Shane shrugged. "It didn't work *reliably*. She installed it anyway, just in case. Lucky for you, it worked this time. Lucas had just come in, so he took Hal and Destiny and Rafa, because they were closest. Hal called Fiona and me. We drove in, then snuck up from behind."

The ambulance slowed, blocked by an enormous truck. Catalina flicked a switch, and her voice boomed out over a bullhorn. "MOVE TO THE SIDE. THIS IS AN EMERGENCY VEHICLE. GET OUT OF OUR WAY!"

The truck swung aside as if it was embarrassed, and Catalina resumed darting in and out of traffic.

"Catalina drives like you," Raluca said to Nick, partly because it was true and partly to distract him from all the needles Shane and Ellie were sticking in him. "Don't you wish you had a siren and flashing lights, too?"

Nick seemed to welcome the distraction. "What I'm really jealous of is her bullhorn."

"Oh, God, don't give him any ideas," Ellie remarked.

"F-bombs would resound up to the very clouds," Raluca said.

Nick grinned up at her. He was very pale, but clearly feeling better. "Speaking of f-bombs, I heard the one you dropped on those assholes in the alley."

"No way!" Ellie exclaimed. "Did you really?"

Shane's ice-blue gaze fixed on Nick in mock disapproval. "You're a bad influence."

Raluca tried not to blush. She had thought Nick had been unconscious when she'd screamed at the gang. "I was very angry."

Nick squeezed her hand. Mischief glinted in his eyes, but it was outshone by the radiance of his love and pride. "Don't be embarrassed. It was the most fucking awesome thing I've seen in my entire fucking life."

"What did you say, Raluca?" Catalina called out. "This is sounding good."

Raluca's face burned. She was glad she'd done it, and glad that Nick had appreciated it, but there was no way she could bring herself to repeat it.

"I'd just come to," Nick said. "I opened my eyes a crack, and saw the whole fucking gang descending on us. Price and his guys. That asshole dragon dude and his assassins. As far as they and Raluca knew, I was still unconscious. And she couldn't shift. But she stood up and put her own body between them and me, in high heels and a mini-skirt and a black leather corset, and yelled louder than Catalina's bull-horn, 'Get lost, or I'll burn you all to fucking ashes!'"

Everyone stared at Raluca. Even, to her slight alarm, Catalina.

Hastily, Raluca said, "I believe my actual word was 'begone,' but otherwise, yes. As Nick says."

To her relief, Catalina returned her attention to the road.

With immense satisfaction, Nick said, "My mate is fucking badass. I never thought I'd have one of the greatest moments of my life when I was lying in an alley with my leg broken and my worst enemy coming to kill me, but that seriously was one of them."

Raluca loved his pride and delight in her, but she had to say, "Treasure the memory, because I will never speak that word again."

"Oh, believe me, I will," Nick replied. Then, with another boyish grin, he added, "But I wouldn't make any vows like that. Remember, I'm a bad influence. And we're mates. We're gonna have a long time together."

"Goes both ways," Shane remarked. "Maybe you'll get a vocabulary upgrade."

"Not fucking likely," Nick said, then grew more serious. "Shane, I wanted to tell you… I'm sorry I yelled at you when you'd been shot. I wasn't really mad at you. It was that you looked so bad, I was scared you were going to die, and I was so fucking furious at those guys who hurt you, I — " He broke off, his chest heaving as he tried to catch his breath.

"Stop talking. You're making more work for us." Shane turned a dial on one of the machines hooked up to Nick. To Raluca's relief, that seemed to help Nick's breathing. Then Shane said quietly, "I know, Nick. I've always known. Don't worry about it."

Nick relaxed. His eyelids fluttered, then closed, and his hand went slack in hers.

"Is he all right?" Raluca asked.

Shane nodded, his fingers on Nick's pulse. "His vital signs are good. He's just dozing."

"It's normal," Ellie added. "He'll need to sleep a lot for the next few days."

"You might too, Raluca," Catalina called from the front. "This sort of thing can be exhausting if you're not used to it."

"This sort of thing?" Raluca repeated. "Being attacked? Having to fight for my mate's life and my own? Seeing my mate almost get killed? I certainly hope I never get used to it!"

Shane leaned over to flick Catalina's arm. "Not everyone in this bus is an adrenaline junkie superhero."

But for once, his blue eyes were warm. Shane had the same fond look that Hal had worn when he'd ruffled Ellie's hair, and Ellie had given Hal before she'd turned back to her work. It was the same way Nick looked at Raluca. No wonder the team had figured out that they were mates.

The ambulance pulled into Protection, Inc.'s underground parking lot. Shane and Catalina carried Nick's stretcher out. Like

Shane and his mysterious friend, he and his mate moved in perfect sync, easily keeping the stretcher level despite their different heights.

Once they were all crammed into the elevator, Ellie reached for the button for the lower floor, but Shane shook his head. "Better take him to the lobby. The doctor's coming by helo. It'll save time if he has to be medevaced."

When they reached the lobby and Nick was lifted on to the pristine white sofa, Raluca remembered his story. At least this time he'd already been bandaged and wouldn't bleed on anything. Shane and Ellie had cleaned but not bandaged the scrapes on his face, but Ellie covered his pillow with a blanket before she slid it beneath his head. Once he was settled in, Raluca sat on the edge of the sofa and held his hand.

Lucas came in a few minutes later, and was quickly followed by Hal, Rafa, and Destiny. They all clustered around Nick. Hal and Lucas pulled up chairs, Destiny perched on the sofa arm, and Rafa sprawled on the thick carpet. Shane stood with his arm around Catalina's shoulders, and Ellie settled into Hal's lap. Everyone spoke softly, so they wouldn't wake him.

"How is he?" Destiny asked.

"He'll be fine," Ellie assured everyone. "He's not in any danger."

"Do we have an ETA on Dr. Bedford?" Hal inquired.

Rafa replied, "Two more hours."

"And Grigor?" Hal asked.

"Locked up downstairs. I'll fly him to his dungeon tomorrow." Lucas stifled a yawn. "Or the day after."

The door opened, and Fiona came in. She wore an elegant business suit, but her long white-blonde hair had been pulled into a hasty ponytail rather than braided.

"Everything's squared away with the police," she began, her normal tone sounding loud after everyone else's whispers. Then she caught sight of the sofa. "Nick!"

Nick woke with a start.

Fiona ran to his side and dropped to her knees, her eyes wide with concern. "Nick, don't try to talk. Shane, how bad is it? Have you called the doctor?"

Before Shane could reply, Nick looked around, first in confusion, then dismay. "Oh, fuck. Fiona, I'm sorry."

"Sorry about what?" Fiona asked.

"The sofa," he said. "And the carpet. Again."

Raluca followed his gaze. She'd been so focused on Nick that she hadn't noticed before, but the carpet was now marred by a trail of reddish footprints, and the white sofa had somehow gotten stained with blood.

"To hell with the sofa," Fiona said. "You're what matters, Nick. Are you in pain? Would you like a drink of water?"

Nick was silent for a moment, staring at her, then ducked his head and muttered, "Got something in my eyes."

Fiona patted his face with the sleeve of her expensive silk jacket, blotting up sweat and blood. "Is that better?"

Nick cleared his throat. "Yeah. Thanks, Fiona."

"He'll be fine," Shane said reassuringly. "He broke his leg and some ribs, and his shoulder's bitten. He's got some other injuries too, but that's the worst of it. The doctor's on her way."

Raluca was still puzzling over the footprints. They led straight to where she was sitting. And that was also where the sofa was stained. Then she remembered how much blood had gotten on her.

"The sofa and carpet are my fault," she confessed.

"Having anything white in a bodyguard agency is just asking for it," Catalina said cheerfully. "Whose idea was that, anyway?"

Regaining her composure, Fiona said, "Mine," in a tone designed to shut down any further discussion.

"Guys," Hal said firmly. "Nobody cares about the sofa."

"Except Nick," Rafa put in.

Catalina and Ellie burst into a fit of giggles, quickly followed by Destiny and Rafa himself. Then Hal too began to chuckle. So did Lucas. Even Shane, whose face wasn't made for humor, started to laugh. At that, Nick gave up his attempt at glaring at Rafa and joined them.

From Fiona's expression, she and Raluca were united in disbelief that anyone could laugh at a time like this. But only for a second, and then Fiona gave in and laughed until tears ran down her face. Raluca felt as if she was surrounded by lunatics.

Then a tickle rose within her chest. She tried to resist it. But a moment later, a most unladylike snort emerged from her lips. Then another. And then Raluca gave in. She laughed at Rafa's wisecrack, at Nick's complete failure at being annoyed by it, at the doom Nick had once again brought to Fiona's décor, and at her own actual responsibility for it. She laughed out of relief that she was alive and safe, and that Nick would be all right. And she laughed in camaraderie with the people who cared so much about him. His team, his pack, his family. *Her* family.

Like Nick, Raluca had come home.

Epilogue

Raluca

Nick took Raluca's elbow as they walked up to the roof of their new home, but not because he needed her support. After a week in bed and another week alternating resting with working out at the Protection, Inc. gym, Nick's limp was gone and his strength was back. He held her arm because he liked to touch her as much as he could, just as she loved to touch him.

Dr. Bedford had set Nick's leg and examined him, but hadn't thought he needed her hospital. So once Lucas had flown Grigor to join Constantine in the dungeon, Nick and Raluca had moved into the bedroom at Protection, Inc. It had been easier on Nick than returning to either the hotel or his own apartment, and Raluca's clothes were already there.

Lucas's mate, Journey, came to visit Nick there once she returned to the US. She'd been traveling in Madagascar while Lucas had been working undercover. Journey had lived in Brandusa and visited Viorel, and loved both countries. Raluca enjoyed meeting her. Though she'd made America her home, it was good to have friends she could talk to about Viorel without having to explain everything.

Once Nick recovered enough to start driving again, he took her back to the diner and introduced her to the rest of the wolf pack and their mates. Kate and Dan thoughtfully provided her with a selection of fresh-squeezed, unsweetened juices. And Destiny made good on her promise of a girls' night out, and gathered Fiona, Catalina, Ellie, and Journey for a wild night that started at a bar, continued at a club featuring men in varying states of undress, and concluded with a picnic beneath the stars.

Once Nick was ready to move out of the bedroom, they set out in search of a home to share. He refused to even show Raluca his apartment, which dated back to his gang days, saying it was so crappy that he was embarrassed to let her see it.

"I didn't even let the team in," Nick said. "You help me pick something better. I'm not poor any more, so don't worry about the price."

"I can pay as well," Raluca replied.

But Nick shook his head. "I'm going to let you bedeck me. Let me pay the rent."

They chose a spacious top-floor apartment with a roof where Nick could barbecue and lift weights, Raluca could take off and land, and both of them could relax and look at the stars.

On Nick's suggestion, they decided to throw a housewarming party on the day they moved in. Before the guests arrived, Raluca and Nick turned to each other and said, "I have something—"

They both broke off in confusion, then smiled. She had an idea of what Nick might have; he'd vanished for a long stretch of the day before, and kept patting his pocket after he returned.

"Come up to the roof," Raluca said. "There is something I wish to give you, under the open sky."

Once they reached the roof, she opened her purse and removed a velvet bag. "Take off your jacket."

When Nick carefully laid his jacket on a chair rather than tossing it over the back, she knew for sure. Her heart warmed even more as she opened the bag. "It is your mating gift. I know it isn't exactly a surprise, but I wanted to be sure you would like it."

With a grin, Nick offered her his left arm. "Go on. Bedeck me."

She'd had it custom-made after a consult with Destiny on the meaning of "punk" and with Nick on the meaning of "manly." Then she'd taken him to the jeweler to have his arm measured, so he knew it would be an armband of some kind. But the details would be a surprise. Nervously, Raluca hoped he'd like it.

He will love it, her dragon hissed. *It is stunning. And punk.*

Raluca snapped it on. Nick lifted his arm, turning it this way and that in fascination. A heavy silver dragon wrapped around his left arm, as if it had coiled itself around his tree branch tattoo. Its edges were cut with deliberate roughness, and it had no fine detail or inlay. But its deceptive plainness conveyed a stark beauty and a sense of power. The dragon was clearly not resting or sleeping, but lying in wait.

"I love it." Nick's voice was husky. "I was going to wear whatever you gave me, and like it because it came from you. But this is really… me. It's like my tats. I want it on my body forever."

Raluca gave a sigh of pleasure. It satisfied her to the depths of her heart to have finally bedecked her mate, to see him wear her silver, and to hear his sincere happiness at receiving it.

I told you, hissed her dragon.

"Now let me bedeck you." Nick reached into his pocket and held up a velvet case. He opened it to show her an elegant band of silver set with a single, perfect diamond.

Delighted, Raluca held out her hand and let him slide it on to her finger. "It will be the greatest treasure of my hoard."

They kissed until they heard the doorbell ring. Then Nick put his jacket back on, and they went to greet their guests.

The entire team showed up, along with Nick's wolf pack friends and their mates. Everyone trooped up the stairs after Nick and Raluca; it was to be a rooftop barbecue. Raluca, who knew nothing of barbecuing, had left that part to Nick.

Once everyone reached the roof, Nick threw out his arm in a wide gesture. "Check out our view!"

Rafa's sharp eyes caught the glint of silver that had shown from beneath Nick's cuff.

"What's that you're wearing?" Rafa demanded, his lips quivering with mischief. "Come on. Show off your pretty, pretty bracelet."

Nick took off his new black leather jacket and displayed Raluca's mating gift without a trace of embarrassment. Instead, he looked proud.

As everyone crowded around to admire it, Rafa made another try at getting a rise out of Nick. "Now all you need is a nice gold chain and rings on every finger, like Lucas."

Nick didn't take the bait. "Nope. I've got one fucking awesome piece, and that's enough for me."

Raluca knew differently, but didn't comment. The armband was the gift he'd wear in public; the other was only for her and him, in the privacy of their bedroom.

"Also, it doubles as armor," Nick went on.

Shane's strike was blurringly fast, and out of nowhere; Raluca hadn't even realized he was standing nearby. But Nick whipped up his arm and blocked it. Shane stopped his blow just before it would have bounced off the silver dragon.

"Nice," Shane said.

"Armor was Nick's idea," Raluca said.

Hal laughed. "Yeah, I didn't think it was yours."

"I was kidding her about that," Nick said. "But she took me seriously, and I'm glad she did. It's badass."

Fiona examined it with interest. "It's quite a beautiful piece. And you could strike with it, as well."

Shane, Fiona, and Nick began exploring the fighting possibilities of his mating gift, striking and blocking at nerve-wracking speeds. Raluca watched until she was convinced they weren't going to kill each other by accident, then went to greet the rest of the guests.

The only housewarming guest Raluca didn't know was the man who had come with Hal and Ellie. He had almost as many tattoos as Nick, and the same sandy-blonde hair, blue-green eyes, and snub nose as Ellie.

Ellie introduced him to Raluca. "This is Ethan, my twin brother."

Ethan shook Raluca's hand, then turned to Nick. "I don't have a real housewarming gift. I drove straight up from the Marine base. But I did get this on the way."

He produced a cooler full of American beer. Raluca politely thanked him, repressing her true feelings about liquids in cans. But Nick grabbed it with genuine enthusiasm and immediately cracked one open. "Hey, thanks, man."

That set off a flurry of gift-giving. Nick and Raluca were deluged with presents, from the practical (a promise from Fiona to personally set up their home security system) to the precious (a bottle of the rare liqueur dragonfire from Lucas and Journey, which Raluca happened to know was worth its weight in gold.)

Once the thank-yous were done, Dan, Kate, and Hal went to help Nick barbecue (which turned into them taking over the cooking), and everyone settled down to chat and drink and admire the view. Once Journey noticed Raluca's new ring, they all admired that too.

"When's the wedding?" Kate asked.

Raluca looked at Nick, who shrugged. "Feels like we're already married. Up to Raluca, I guess."

Destiny punched his shoulder. "Nick! Did you give her an engagement ring, and forget to actually propose?"

Raluca rescued Nick, who was starting to turn red. "We made our vows earlier, and shall discuss the wedding at our leisure."

"Yeah, that's right," Nick said, recovering.

He sprawled in a chair with his arm around Raluca's shoulder. He looked relaxed and happy, content to be with his mate and his friends. Raluca was happy too, but the more everyone spoke, the less content she felt. The wolves all had jobs or children or both. Journey didn't work, but that was by choice: she traveled instead. Ethan was a Marine. Ellie was a paramedic. Catalina was a paramedic and was about to become a bodyguard as well. Raluca had Nick, of course. But soon he would be back at work. And then what would she do with her days?

Nick seemed to sense her thoughts. Quietly, he asked, "What's the matter, babe?"

Raluca was about to say she'd tell him later, then reconsidered. She had no reason to keep secrets from his friends, many of whom had become her friends too, nor would they make her embarrassed about her lack of purpose. In fact, they might have some ideas.

"I have a question," Raluca said. "Is there anything Americans traditionally do when they're not sure what to do with their lives?"

"Road trip," Nick said instantly. "I'll take you. No World's Biggest, I promise."

"I meant something like a job," Raluca said. "Not a vacation."

Nick laughed. "I know. The idea is that while you're on the road trip, you figure out what you want to do."

Journey nodded. "Nick's right. The traditional American way to find yourself is to go somewhere else, to get a new perspective. But it doesn't have to be a road trip. You could travel the world."

"I already did that," Raluca said.

"Join the Marines," Ethan suggested.

Rafa snorted. "Navy SEALs beat Marines."

"PJs beat SEALs," said Shane.

Destiny rapped her teammates on the head. "PJs and SEALs don't take women. Anyway, if you want a military career, the Army is obviously the best."

"She doesn't want a military career," Nick said, saving Raluca from having to find a polite way to say so. "Get a grip."

"It *is* an American tradition," Hal pointed out, flipping a steak.

Fiona set down her cocktail. "You're all missing the obvious. Go to college. Take different courses. See what appeals to you. Once you get a sense of that, if it's something that needs a degree, you're already on your way. If not, you drop out and do whatever it is that you want. It's traditional, and unlike everything else that's been suggested, it's something Raluca might actually enjoy."

"I would enjoy the road trip," Raluca said, unable to resist coming to Nick's defense. Then she added, "But college is an interesting idea. Thank you, Fiona. I will think about it."

***

After the party ended, Nick and Raluca were left alone in their new home. They'd walked the guests out, so they were in the living room. The apartment seemed very quiet after the noise and chatter of the party. And after being with so many people, being alone together felt very intimate.

"Sorry about the non-proposal," Nick said.

Raluca smiled. "I truly do not care. As I said, we had already made our vows. The wedding is a formality. However, I should like a proper one. It will take some time to plan…"

"Yeah, you do that part. Have fun with it. I'm fine with anything, so long as you're there. Just like our new apartment." He gave her a wolfish grin. "Want to try out our new bed?"

"I would. And I have something else I would like to try out, as well."

Nick's breath caught at her words. "A new position?"

"You shall see," she teased.

Raluca gave a startled gasp as Nick pounced. He swept her up in his arms and carried her into the bedroom. She lay back, enjoying his strength and grace, especially after all the days he'd spent in bed with his leg in a cast. But he walked without a hint of weakness, and carried her as if she weighed nothing.

He pivoted as they came to the doorway, making sure he didn't knock her feet into the frame, and his black hair fell in tousled locks across his forehead. She raised a hand to toy with it, tugging lightly. It was so soft. Raluca never tired of touching it.

"I love how you play with my hair." Nick bent his head, and she obligingly ran her fingers through it.

Then he laid her down on the bed. It was king-sized and luxurious, with four polished wooden posts and a canopy. It had been Raluca's choice, but she hadn't had to do much persuasion once she pointed out that since they both had shifter strength, a smaller or less sturdy bed might break beneath them.

Nick stood at the end, waiting, his green eyes gleaming with curiosity. But when Raluca did nothing but lie where he had placed her, teasing him with her silence, he took off his boots, then sat on the bed and began to undress her. She shivered with excitement as he removed her shoes, briefly cupped her feet in his strong hands, then unzipped her dress. She wriggled out of it and draped it over a nearby chair, then lay back again and let him take off her bra and panties.

The air was cool on her bare skin. Her nipples hardened as Nick reached out toward them, before he even touched them. But she made herself put her palm against his chest, holding him away. "Not yet."

Raluca took a moment to savor the sight of him fully dressed in black jeans and black leather jacket, leaning over her naked body, before she said, "For what I want to do, you must be nude."

His grin was more hungry than playful. "I'm going to like this, aren't I?"

"We shall see."

Nick undressed quickly. He was breathing deeply, making the tattooed leaves on his muscular chest seem to stir in a breeze. His old scars were still there, but he had no new ones; all his wounds had healed without leaving a trace behind. When he pulled off his jeans and boxers, his cock rose up hard and throbbing.

Then he knelt naked on the bed before her, wearing only the silver dragon coiled around his left arm. Its winding shape emphasized the strength of his forearms, and its sharp angles highlighted the curves of his muscles. Because it was silver, the metal of Raluca's dragon, she could sense it when she was close. And with the heightened bond of their mating, she could feel the warmth of Nick's arm, the softness of his skin, and the hard swell of his muscles through the silver, as if she was touching him herself.

"This is the dragon mating ritual," Raluca said. She trailed her fingers along his arm, tracing the edge where skin met silver.

Nick sucked in a deep breath. "I wear this to bed?"

She smiled. "Yes. But I would like to bedeck you a little more."

"A ring?"

Raluca glanced at his big-knuckled hands, his deft fingers. Rings *would* look good on him. Perhaps she could bedeck him that way later. But for now... "No. Something more versatile."

She rolled over, reaching for the safe behind the bed where she kept her hoard. As she unlocked it, she could almost feel Nick's hungry gaze on her back, her backside, the nape of her neck...

"Don't touch," she warned.

She'd guessed right; the bed rocked slightly as he settled back.

"You're making me crazy, Raluca," he muttered.

"So impatient," she teased. But she was impatient too. She could feel the warmth coming off his body, and smell his natural masculine scent. Heat gathered between her thighs, and she shivered with excitement. It made the safe hard to unlock; she fumbled several times before she managed to get it open. Then she drew out her surprise.

Nick's eyes widened as she dangled it before him. "Is that...?"

"It is another mating gift. But this one is only for us to use in private." She handed him the long, thin length of silver chain.

His fingers closed convulsively around it. The delicate skin of his throat bobbed as he swallowed. "What do I do with it?"

Raluca smiled. "Have you truly no idea, Nick?"

"Oh, I have ideas!" He tugged it between his hands, testing its strength. "But you said it's a dragon ritual. Is there something specific I'm supposed to do?"

The sight of him naked with the silver dragon on his arm and the silver chain in his hands was almost too much for her to bear.

Abandoning teasing, she said, "No. The ritual is only to wear your mating gifts in bed. You are already wearing the dragon, and I am wearing your ring. The chain was simply an… an idea of mine."

"A fucking hot idea." Nick's voice was hoarse, almost a growl.

"You could wind it around your other arm," Raluca said, savoring the image. "You could bind my wrists to the bedposts, or I could bind yours. Or —"

"I know what I want." Nick caught her hand in his. Then he wound the chain around their wrists, sliding cool silver around and around her heated skin and his, until his right hand and her left were bound together.

She tugged experimentally. They were caught tight. She clasped his hand, locking their fingers together. And then they fell to the bed, unable to hold out for one second longer. They kissed with passionate abandon. Nick's stubble was rough against her lips, his mouth hot and eager. His body pressed against hers, moving urgently as the desire she felt.

The silver chain and armband were cool, a thrilling contrast with the warmth of his skin and heat of hers. Every time he moved, her arm was tugged by the chain that bound them, and every time she moved, he was tugged as well. Not only did she love the touch of silver and the sensation of their wrists being tied together, but every single movement was a reminder of their closeness. Whatever she did affected him, and vice versa. It was a metaphor of their love made real.

Raluca wanted to tell him how clever he was, but before she could, he reared up above her. Their bound wrists were already pressed into the mattress above their heads, but Nick moved her other hand there as well, and pinned it with his own.

"Love you," he whispered. "My dragon."

Raluca's heart was too full to reply. After all those terrible moments when she'd thought he was dead or they were both about to die, she finally felt in her heart and soul and body that they had triumphed over death, and were reclaiming their lives and love.

Nick bent to kiss her, his mouth hot and hungry. She surged up against him, needy and desperate with desire. He slid into her like a key into a lock. She gasped into his mouth, shuddering with the intensity of the sensation. Each thrust rubbed against her sensitive pearl, and each movement of his body pushed their silver-bound wrists against the sheets.

Nick was panting and flushed, his eyes brilliant and intent, his black hair disheveled. He'd never looked so handsome. The silver dragon glittered on his strong left arm, the one he'd used to save her with. He'd used his entire body to save her. She was as overwhelmed with love as she was with pleasure.

"I love you, Nick," she gasped.

He gripped her hands tight as he came inside of her. Then her own climax broke over her, shaking her body with burst after burst of pleasure. But even more than the physical delight, Raluca felt deep in her soul that she and Nick were one, bound heart to heart. Forever.

They held each other close, enjoying the afterglow. The silver had warmed against their bodies to the temperature of their skin. Raluca gave her wrist a little tug, smiling to feel his arm move as well.

Nick tugged back. "That was a fucking amazing idea of yours. You're just as wild as me, you know that?"

"I do now," Raluca said. "You set that part of me free."

Nick slowly unwound the chain, taking his time and kissing her fingers, until their wrists were freed. He let it dangle from his hand and twist in the air currents. "Next time it's yours. Surprise me."

Raluca smiled. "I will."

Nick got up and put it back in the safe that held her hoard. Then he stretched, interlacing his fingers above his head, displaying his fine musculature. "Want to go flying?"

Raluca too felt more energized than sleepy. "You are full of good ideas tonight."

They showered quickly, then dressed and went to the roof. Night had fallen, and the sky was spangled with silver stars. For all the times that Raluca had taken Nick flying, it never stopped feeling special, intimate, and precious.

She became a dragon and waited for him to mount her. Once his strong legs gripped her sides, she became invisible and soared aloft.

Raluca now knew the city better. She flew here and there, with no particular destination in mind, simply enjoying the sky and Nick's presence.

Then he nudged her. "Look down."

She saw a bunch of buildings amidst an expanse of grass. It was brightly lit, with people walking around with books or backpacks, alone or in pairs or groups. Many but not all were young, and all seemed busy and purposeful.

"Santa Martina University," Nick explained. "It's not far from Protection, Inc. Or our apartment. You could even fly there, if you could find a place to land."

Raluca dove downward, making Nick hold tight to her mane, and circled until she found a space between buildings with no windows facing it. She could land there easily, and no one would see. Then she circled the university again, swooping low to inspect the classrooms, the fields where sports were played, the picnic benches, the library. It seemed a pleasant place.

She imagined herself there, carrying her books in a fashionable designer bag. The image was unexpectedly appealing. So was the idea of studying, of learning new things, of making some friends of her own, and of starting anew in a place made for people to discover themselves and their heart's desires.

"You like it, huh?" Nick asked.

Raluca dipped her head in a dragon's nod.

"I go to work, you go to class. Then we meet up and go flying. Go dancing. Make love. Sounds good to me." Nick laughed suddenly. "It sounds better than good. It sounds fucking awesome!"

Luckily for Raluca, her dragon's form prevented her from replying aloud. If she'd been a woman, she'd have blurted out that it sounded fucking awesome to her, too.

She had her mate, she had her friends, she had a home, and she was on the path to finding her purpose. Her heart light as a cloud, Raluca arrowed upward, into the open sky.

A note from Zoe Chant

Thank you for reading *Warrior Wolf!* I hope you enjoyed it. If you're starting the series here and would like to know more about Protection, Inc. the first book is *Bodyguard Bear*, the second is *Defender Dragon*, and the third is *Protector Panther*. All of those books, along with my others, are available at Amazon.com. You can find a complete list of my books at zoechant.com.

The songs on the diner jukebox are real. They're Bonnie Raitt's "Nobody's Girl" and Johnny Cash's "Man in Black." So is the song at the nightclub, Pitbull's "International Love." I made up the songs Nick plays Raluca on the radio, but they were inspired by being trapped in cars with similar ones playing.

If you enjoy *Protection, Inc.,* I highly recommend Lia Silver's *Werewolf Marines (Laura's Wolf, Prisoner,* and *Partner)* and Lauren Esker's *Shifter Agents (Handcuffed to the Bear, Guard Wolf,* and *Dragon's Luck)*. All three series have hot romances, exciting action, brave heroines who stand up for their men, hunky heroes who protect their mates with their lives, and teams of shifters who are as close as families. They are all available on Amazon.

The cover of *Warrior Wolf* was designed by Augusta Scarlett.

Printed in Great Britain
by Amazon

37814780R00128